the homeplace

Morie Smith

For Steven, Olivia, and Henry

You three are my whole heart, and I couldn't be more thankful you're mine.

prologue

"MOLLY JONES, what in the world do you think you are doin'? You have no business being out here on this county road in the middle of all this. You're a housewife and a mama, not the newest member of the Texas Rangers." His burly salt and pepper handlebar mustache wiggles maniacally as he scolds me through the open window of my Ford Expedition. The golden six-point star pinned to his chest gleams in the spring early morning sun and blinds me for a split second as dust from the gravel road blows past us in a gush of west Texas wind. I pull my sunglasses down from their nest of my messy top-knot and smile widely and sweetly as I twirl them around by the ear stem before placing them over my grass green eyes.

"Why, Sheriff Cooper, I have no idea what you're talking about. I'm merely trying to get home as quickly as I can. I have brownies in the oven for the potluck after church and they are on the verge of burning. I told Shep I would check those yearling bulls in the southwest traps quick before church and I took too long, so I was just cutting through this stretch of county road to get back to the house as fast as I could. As you've just said, my place is in the kitchen, especially now as my brownies will be well done if I don't get there soon." I finish off with a tight, but firm smile. The elderly grump squints his eyes at me with a look that says he doesn't really believe my words, but he can't really disagree with them, either. He adjusts his tan-grey Stetson hat on his sweaty head and yanks his state issued flak jacket down over his generous belly. He has no grounds to keep me and he knows it, and I can tell this is what really irritates him.

He hesitates briefly like he wants to give a rebuttal, and I take his slightly long pause to beat him to the punch. "It looks like you have more than enough to deal with right now, so I'd better be letting you get to it! Tell Mrs. Tammy I said hi and we'll see y'all later!" I quickly yank the button to automatically roll my window back up as I throw it in drive and head down the road, probably a little faster than I should have, dodging police barricades weakly blocking the road. I'll probably get an earful later tonight or tomorrow from my husband as this will absolutely be public knowledge by lunch, but for now, I've escaped, and that was my goal.

I don't have brownies in the oven. My husband is a major germaphobe and it is pretty common knowledge we don't participate in church potlucks for that reason. Plus, brownies give me major heartburn; I love them, but they don't love me anymore, so I've just given up making them, although I do have a killer recipe. Actually, I probably shouldn't joke about that though because that's exactly what I am doing out here.

We have the absolute worst human for a neighbor. He wouldn't spit on you if you were on fire, and his only relation-ship with anyone around here is hurling insults and berate-ments for petty to non-existent disagreements and grievances. He is in his late seventies and has been a widower for more than thirty years. He is the constant example I use with my children about being kind and merciful to others and extending grace. We have dealt with him for ten years since we bought and built up our ranch across the skinny gravel county road from his, lined all the way up and down with large acreage century ranching families.

I say dealt, because yesterday evening, the most hateful man in Crawford County, Richard MacDougal, was found face down in his dinner never to gripe at anyone again. Not a soul in this county is sad, and every soul in this county has their own reason they're glad he's gone.

chapter
one

"Mia! Are you in here? I picked up your recital costume from Ms. Phoebe!" Arms overflowing with a sequined pastel tutu in a garment bag, a large water tumbler, a travel coffee cup, dry cleaning, my purse, and a take-out bag full of Chick-fil-A trash, I stumble through our side door into the kitchen. Remnants of a lunch prepared by a twelve-year-old and a ten-year-old litter the butcher block countertop and I sigh as I dump as much as I can in the empty space. I walk around the corner to our laundry room to hang the recital costume and dry cleaning as I casually glance around for signs of our daughter and son, who are supposed to be cleaning their rooms, but are likely doing anything but. It's spring break this week, so we are supposed to be having a quiet, relaxing week at home together, but I think we're all ready to get back to our regularly scheduled program as no one does well with down time around here. Next door to the laundry room, my husband Shep is in the office staring intently at his double computer screens filled with numbers in grids: cattle expected progeny differences, or EPDs, as they are known around here. Cody Johnson is playing softly from a Bose speaker in the corner, and the shutters on the floor to ceiling windows overlooking our front pasture are wide open letting in spring sunshine.

I met Shep twenty years ago as he started medical school and I started graduate school. We finished school and his postgraduate training, and he worked as a physician for about ten years before diving off into ranching and cattle seed stock operations full time. He was a fantastic physician, but from the purchase of his first cow/calf pair, he was hooked, and there was no going back. He worked for a local hospital system long enough to build up capital to get the ranch running, while working cattle at night and on the weekends. There are jobs you are trained to do, and jobs you are called to do. While he is trained to be a physician, he is called to be a rancher, and I get to see it through the love, care, time, and energy he pours into our cattle every day. It's a sweet blessing in this life to see your spouse living their calling.

"Hey, what are you up to?" I hear him quietly call as he maintains eye contact with his screens. I walk through the open barn door of the office and sit across the room from him in my own desk chair. He refers to his left screen in front of him, and then types a series of numbers on the right screen.

"Just came in from errands in town. Where are the kids?"

"Lexie and Lacie came down so Mia took the Gator with them to the south tank. Hayes is still cleaning his room. That boy is slower than the speed of smell at his chores," He makes a few notations on a yellow legal pad in front of him. "What's going on in town?"

"Not much. I went to Pilates and then by the ballet studio to pick up Mia's recital costume and your dry cleaning. What are you up to?"

"Just checking the numbers on the calves out of the north-west pasture before I submit them to AAA. Hank's coming by this afternoon to help me push the cows up to the traps near the pens so we can start weaning next week." He leans back in his chair and flips his Red Rock Cattle Company hat backwards before turning to face me. He opens his mouth to say something right as the Cattle Company land line rings loudly. We play a silent round of rock-paper-scissors in which my scissors beat his paper, so he rolls to the phone and presses the speakerphone button.

"Red Rock Cattle Company, this is Shep."

"Shepherd Jones, do you think I run a charity grazing operation?" We both roll our eyes as a shaky, hateful voice rasps through the speaker.

"Mr. MacDougal, good to hear from you. What can I do for you?" Shep seems to have patience for days, and I'm incredibly thankful it was his call to answer. Granted, as a millennial who hates talking on the phone, I'm always glad when it's his turn.

"You got cotton in your ears, boy? I just said, do you think I run a charity grazing operation?"

"I heard you, sir. What exactly are you getting at?"

"Your cattle are on my land. Get 'em off before I call the sheriff."

"Sir, all our herds are in pastures on the north side of our property with at least one pasture in between you and us. With all due respect, if you have stray cattle on your land, I don't believe they are ours."

"I've watched your sale barn trash jump fences, boy. I know yours when I see 'em, and I'm seeing 'em. I'm calling the sheriff now, so if you want 'em, you better get over here before they do." A loud dial tone abruptly fills the office and I roll over in my desk chair to hit the button on the receiver to silence it. Shep sighs loudly and flips his hat forward.

"Are you going over there? You know those can't be ours,"

I reason as he saves his work on the computer screens and stands to head out the door.

"I know they aren't, but they're somebody's. I'm gonna go check tags and brands and see if I can save someone a headache."

"You're a ranching saint, Shep Jones." I kiss him on the cheek as he walks past my chair out of the office and follow him out into the kitchen. "You want me to go with you?"

He grabs the keys to the ranch truck from the row of hooks next to the garage door and slips into his work boots. "Yeah, if you don't mind. Hank won't be here for a few hours and it never hurts to have help. Doesn't sound like Dick MacDougal wants to wait."

Ten minutes later, we bump down the gravel county road in the red ranch truck with the Red Rock Cattle Co logo slicked across the sides and trailer in tow. We turn off the road about a half mile down from our place and cross an open gate and cattle guard. Three Hereford cows with bright orange tags in both ears are lazily skimming overgrown grass next to the fence on either side of the road. Shep pulls a little up the road from the girls and stops. After opening the back of the trailer, he quietly and calmly walks behind the group and starts confidently pushing them toward the open trailer, using the driveway like a lane to move them. I shake a feed bucket near the open door to the trailer and watch as they calmly walk up to the trailer and climb in fairly uneventfully. We close them up and drive up the driveway to head back out. As Shep is turning around in Mr. MacDougal's circle drive, the old man comes hobbling out of his run-down house with arms waving.

"That's right, you get those mangy excuses for ground beef out of here! And keep your cattle on your land! I'm not gonna tell you again! You are never gonna get my land no matter how hard you try!"

Shep abruptly stops and throws the truck in park. He jumps out of the truck as I roll my window down, shocked that he managed to get Shep's goat and convince him to argue with him.

"Mr. MacDougal, I've told you countless times that we run registered black Angus cattle. They all carry our double R brand on the left hip, and have red ear tags. These are three Hereford cows with the lazy S brand on the right shoulder and orange tags. You've lived on a ranch your whole life, sir, I know you know the difference. Why do you insist on giving us a hard time? We've been nothing but neighborly to you since we've moved here. I've got better things to do with my time than coming running at your beck and call that isn't even right 99% of the time."

"You city slicks are all the same! You think you can roll in here with your big doctor money and buy up a family's land and call yourself a rancher? How dare you steal this land from good, hardworking folks like us! My great- great granddaddy settled on this land in the 1800s, and I'll die before I let any of you vultures take it!"

Richard MacDougal has typically one major grievance with anyone he comes in contact with that he continually harps on, and ours is the fact that we bought our property in the recent past and haven't been here for generations. We are basically akin to developers and other groups who take advantage of people by scamming them out of family heirlooms and buy them for pennies on the dollar, sometimes flipping them for obscene profits and subdividing to move in as many people as possible. Rumor has it that MacDougal has been approached by a developer or two, and has been even meaner to them than us, if that's even humanly possible. The joke's on him because our property was actually owned by a development company, and we kept it as ranch land instead of proposed plans to make it a subdivided neighborhood. As we well know, but developers don't, mesquite trees are harder to get rid of than you think, and they're not exactly desirable to build hundreds of houses on. This is a years-long grievance of Mr. MacDougal's, but he seems particularly passionate about it today, despite the fact that it doesn't seem relevant. I make a mental note to ask Shep later if he thinks MacDougal is starting to show a touch of dementia or something.

"Sir, we're not trying to take your land. We love this land and this lifestyle as much as anyone else out here, and frankly, it's insulting for you to treat us like we're trying to take anything from anyone. We bought our ranch fair and square, and have built our cattle business from the ground up with blood, sweat, and tears. We'd appreciate it if you'd treat us with the same respect that we try to treat you with." Shep extends a hand toward the old man and gets a cane waved back at him.

"I told you, I'm not going anywhere! You will not steal this land from our family!"

Just as he starts a rant with obscenities, a tan Crawford County Sheriff's truck pulls up into the drive, and a pot-bellied Sheriff Cooper plops out.

"Gentlemen, did we get this stray cattle issue resolved?" He asks as he waddles up to Shep and Mr. MacDougal, smoothing down his bushy handlebar mustache. Cooper has been sheriff of this county for as long as anyone can remember, and while he's a little rough around the edges, his wife Tammy is as good as gold. She runs our church women's Bunco group and is the first to show up with a pan of poppy-seed chicken if someone in your family has so much as a sniffle. I've interacted with Cooper more than I would like to over the years with my slight lead foot and a tendency to cut it close to the school tardy bell, but overall, he is a kind man with a deep-rooted need for justice and order.

"This sorry no-good thief has been trying for months to get me to sell my land and leave and I won't, so he dumps his problem cows on my place to tear up my fences and eat all my grass. If he or his cattle set foot on my place again, I'm pressing charges for trespassing!" Mr. MacDougal raves, shaking a cane toward Shep and Sheriff Cooper with spittle flying everywhere.

Sheriff Cooper looks at Mr. MacDougal, and then at Shep, and then into the back of our trailer. He quietly mutters to Shep, "Those ain't yours, are they?"

"They're Shoemaker's on the west side over there. I'll take them back and make sure they don't have a hole somewhere," Shep mutters back. Sheriff Cooper nods and then moves closer to Mr. MacDougal.

"Richard, Shep is going to take care of these cows, don't worry. Can I help you get back inside?"

"I'm not going inside until they are off my property! Get these dirty thieves out of here!" MacDougal stumbles a little as his cane comes up off the ground. Both men rush forward and catch him, setting him back up on his feet and trying to walk him up to the sagging front porch. "I told you clowns I'm not going in until they're off my property!"

MacDougal tries to wriggle away from the two younger men like a small petulant child as they guide him up the three rickety steps. Once they are on the porch, Shep drops his side abruptly and heads back to the truck. He jumps in the driver's seat, throws the truck in drive and all but speeds off the property. I lean over to check the side mirror as we fly down the driveway and see little old man arms waving on the porch and what looks like the sheriff trying to calm him down. I'm not usually one to mouth off, but I was one more accusation away from getting out of the truck myself and giving him a "listen here, old man" kind of "come to Jesus" chat.

Shep turns left out of the gate and heads about a quarter mile down to the Shoemaker ranch. As we pull in, Asa Shoemaker's ranch manager True meets us at their gate and directs us down to a set of pens to unload the cows.

"Sorry you had to deal with that asshole, Shep. These three had calves weaned about a week ago and have been getting into trouble since. Cooper called us because MacDougal called the emergency line saying he had five gray bulls fighting on his land. That man needs his eyes checked. And his head checked while he's at it." True closes the gate to the inner pen once the cows are out of the trailer, shaking his head in disbelief. True and MacDougal have never gotten along because MacDougal thinks True has no respect for authority. The reality is True didn't load cows in the order MacDougal wanted once when he was a teenager, and it's been adversarial ever since. But in all honesty, the club of people who don't get along with Dick MacDougal is basically all of humankind. The cows move down the lane from the pen into the adjoining pasture, searching for grass. I notice then that they have a few ribs more visible than usual, but they are probably just trying to recover body condition from having calves recently.

"Not a problem, we had the trailer hooked up anyway. He could have zebras in his front yard and accuse me of dumping them on his place, so it doesn't really matter whose they are or where they belong. Just glad we could get them moved pretty easily," Shep replies, closing up the trailer. He leans on the edge of the trailer as True comes to stand next to him in the shade. I hop out and join them, handing out bottles of water from the cooler Shep keeps in the backseat of the truck.

"He was ranting about us trying to take his land like a developer tried to come make him an offer or something. Have y'all had anything like that recently?" I ask, always interested in picking up a little piece of gossip here and there.

"Yeah, a group sent a letter to Shoemaker and then called to follow up. They want to clear a thousand-acre square to build luxury 50-acre ranch estates. Something about the extremely desirable nature of our school district and a lack of "adequate" housing options for people moving in. I think winning state year before last is pushing people here. Lowballed 1500 an acre. Shoemaker told 'em to go to hell, and I'm sure MacDougal said the same. Probably said he'd meet them there when he's finished here," True replied, rolling his eyes. "They hit you up yet?"

"Nah, not yet. We bought ours from a group out of Houston that decided it wasn't right to develop into something like that back then, so they may be looking for something else and not bother us. We'll see. Molls, you ready to go? Probably need to check on the kids and make sure the house is still standing," Shep nods toward the truck and I nod back.

"Good to see you, True. Hopefully it will be for a better reason next time," I laugh as I give him a quick hug and walk around to the passenger side. True was only thirteen when we moved here and met him at church when we started teaching the junior high Sunday school class. His mom and I have been friends for years, and it's been sweet to see him grow up and do so well running a big operation. I always worried about him a little because his dad wasn't really in the picture, but he seems to have figured it out on his own, and has overcome that adversity.

Shep jumps in and we head back to our place. As we pull up, our daughter Mia and her best friends, twins Lexie and Lacie, are out on the driveway playing basketball. Our son Hayes is just beyond the driveway tossing a baseball against a rebound net. I'm unreasonably pleased to find both of our little angels outside soaking up vitamin D, but know in my heart this means they are avoiding chores and hope I'll excuse it since they aren't glued to a screen or bickering with one another. Shep parks the truck and trailer near the pens closest to the house and jumps out. In a few swift moves, he sweeps the ball from the girls and makes an easy layup.

"Keep practicing, girls. One day you'll be as good as your old man," He chuckles, heading in the side door of the house. I distribute hugs to the girls as I pass through and have a brief stare down with Hayes that inspires him to toss the baseball in the bucket on the driveway and head back in, presumably to work on his room. I let myself in the side door behind Shep and head to my side of the office. He is already perched back in his spot in front of the EPD spreadsheets and I smile to myself knowing he probably works more cumulative hours now than he did when he was a practicing physician, but is infinitely happier.

I sit down in front of my iMac and start sorting through the gold wire letter tray I have for the kids to put notes from school, schedules, and all other information I need to know so it doesn't all get lost. Sitting at the top of the box is a hot pink half sheet of paper from the junior high cheerleading sponsor.

Good morning, cheer parents! I've attached a QR code for a Sign-Up Genius for time slots to work the bake sale fundraiser in one week, as well as slots for what baked goods you will bring to sell. Please sign up for at least two hours to work, and for at least 4-5 dozen or large items to sell. All items to sell must be home-made and individually wrapped. This is our biggest fundraiser of the year and pays the majority of our camp costs. If you have questions, please contact me at blane@buffalocreekcisd.edu.

Becki Lane

Cheer Sponsor, Buffalo Creek Junior High School

· · ·

I heave a sigh, and pull out my planner from my desk drawer to flip to the dates of the fundraiser before opening the link to the sign-up. Becki Lane has been a thorn in the collective side of the class of 2029 since our kids were in kindergarten by being the most obnoxious over-the-top competitive mom in the state of Texas (and that's saying something because Texas likes to win). At some point in the last few years, she managed to get herself a job as the cheer sponsor at the junior high most likely to secure a spot for her daughter Hainslee on the squad. What's sad is that Hainslee is actually pretty good and more than likely would have made it anyway. Now we all get to endure her mother, which is like the ultimate real-life example of misery loving company. The girls had tryouts several weeks ago, and Mia made the squad, along with the twins and another one of their friends, Emily, with Hainslee rounding it out at five. I would have considered trying to talk Mia out of this endeavor, but she's been dreaming of this since she started kindergarten and I wouldn't take it away from her just because I can't stand Becki Lane. But that doesn't mean I can't work as hard as possible to limit my time around that hag.

"What are you working on all huffy and puffy over there?" Shep asks, turning to grab a sip of coffee from the cup on his desk. I turn to face him with my planner in my lap, drumming a felt tip pen on the pages.

"Trying to figure out when Becki Lane is working the cheer fundraiser bake sale so I can not work at that time. Is that coffee from this morning?"

"Yeti, ol' son. Still hot and fresh," He answers, raising a small stainless steel Yeti mug with the Red Rock logo etched on the side like he is making a toast. He nods in satisfaction, and flips open the lid to take another sip. "I thought she was your new best friend. I saw her trying to talk to you at the basketball game."

"Ugh, she was trying to tell me that I was going to be the

mom in charge of equipment transportation. Aka, lugging around all their pom poms and megaphones to all the things. I told her I'm pretty sure that's what the school district pays her to do with our tax dollars, thank you very much."

"You didn't say that to her, did you?"

"No, not technically out loud. But I thought it."

"You're going to haul all that crap for them, aren't you?"

"Probably so."

Shep laughs and turns back to his computer. "Good luck with that." He lives in a space between laughing at the misery we all feel being around this insufferable woman and gently pushing to just ignore her and take the mature route. Obviously, the mature route is more desirable, but the only perfect person is Jesus, and even though I try on the daily, I'm not as much like Him as I'd like to be.

"I know, the things you'll do for your kids, man. Speaking of... Hey! Did you finish your room? What are you up to?" Just then, Hayes walks by bouncing a basketball absently on the hardwood floor. He's not my overly social kid, but he's also not a homebody. Fourth grade has been an interesting transition for him in feeling like he's too big for little kid things but not as big as he wants to be for bigger kid things. My biggest mom win with him right now is that I've not heard him utter the words "I want a mullet" ever, so I'd say I'm on the side of victory with him for the most part.

"Not much, thinking about playing some PlayStation. I finished my room," He replies, letting the basketball roll into the back of the brown leather couch next to him in the living room. Shep saves his spreadsheets on his computer and gets up.

"Get your boots, Hayes. We need to meet Hank to move some cows up closer to the pens. You can go with me. You look like you could use some time out of the house," he says as he kisses me on the cheek and goes to head out the door. "Be nice to Becki Lane. She's not worth your time."

"Yeah, yeah. Hey, I need to make you a dentist appointment, too. When you do want to go?"

Shep stops short in the doorway and shakes his head. "Uh, nope. No, thank you."

"Hey, yes, thank you! You can't just not go," I reply, giving him a bit of a nagging look.

"We'll see ya later!" He and Hayes skip out to the garage to grab boots and head to the pens. Out the window a few minutes later, I see the Gator flying down the gravel road toward the horse barn with Hayes at the wheel with a giant grin on his face, a face that's too cute for his own stinking good. I roll my eyes and turn back to my computer.

After consulting our schedule over the next few weeks, I sign up to work my total requirement of two hours and to make five Bundt cakes. At this point, I'm wondering what the cost of this stupid camp is and if we can just pay for it and be done. It's good for the girls to earn this money instead of be given it, I remind myself, even though it still seems to require me to mainly earn it, but at least we can pretend like they contributed. I move from my digital mailbox to the stack of unopened mail sitting in front of my iMac screen. Under a few invoices for cattle feed that need to be entered into our business accounting program, there is a sparsely marked envelope addressed just to the business PO box.

Red Rock Cattle Company-

Greetings! We hope this message finds you doing well! We are LT4 Holdings, a development corporation based in Dallas, TX. We have roots in ranching and farming, and know how precious your land and operations are to you. There are thousands of Texans just like you that are interested in having a similar lifestyle, if they could only have the space. Here is where you come in: for a generous price per acre, and a percentage of sales once the development is finished, you can be part of this historic opportunity. We'll have representatives in your area in the coming weeks to meet with you and explain more about this mutually beneficial relationship and opportunity. The sooner you act, the more return you will see from your investment, so don't wait! If you have any questions, please don't hesitate to reach out to our home office at 214-559-3687.

I frown, and wonder how I didn't see this before. I typically open suspicious looking mail, or mail that looks like good news immediately from the PO box. This has to be the same group reaching out to MacDougal and Shoemaker. Obviously, our answer is the same as theirs, but at this rate, with this type of shotgun approach, odds are going up that someone in the near vicinity says yes, especially for the offer of proceeds on the back end. Someone will think this is some golden investment opportunity and fall for it. Fewer children are wanting to come back and run their parents' operations, and even fewer people are able to buy into it and start from scratch like we did. MacDougal isn't completely crazy; heirloom ranch operations are slipping away every day. People are free to do whatever they think is best for their family, but in all honesty, we didn't exactly plan or want to have a hundred neighbors when we moved out here.

chapter
two

"THE STEADFAST LOVE of the Lord never ceases... His mercies never come to an end; they are new every morning! Great is thy faithfulness!" Two days later, our little family of four is sitting side by side in our regular pew, four from the back on the left side, at the Buffalo Creek Church of Christ for Sunday morning services. We are one row back and a few seats over from Ms. Gertrude Simms, the sweetest older lady in the entire world, who also happens to sing like a goat. Some songs are more noticeable than others, and this morning the music minister seems to have chosen a rather goat-y line up and my wonderful kids and husband cannot lock it down. I mean, I can't say I'm 100% locked down, but I've got a lot more chill than those three jokers and their stifled laughs. When the Psalmist said to make a joyful noise to the Lord, I don't think Ms. Simms's vibrato is necessarily what he had in mind, but she's never noticed all the stares and snickers she gets every week and keeps up the joy. Thankfully, we are down to our last hymn and I can herd my people on out before everyone completely breaks down.

"That concludes our services here today. Thank you all for coming, and we hope to see you all this evening for small group fellowship. Have a blessed day," the music minister dismisses the congregation following our final song, and I turn back to my seat to gather my purse and Bible as Mia and Hayes disappear to find their friends and Shep turns around to work out some details for cattle work with the owner of the ranch to our west, and Shep's good friend, Hank, who sits in the row behind us with his family.

"Mol-ly! How are you!? I haven't seen you at all this week! Did you have a good spring break at home with the kids?" A nasally voice at one octave higher than it should be hits my ears and causes my eyes to momentarily cross as I gather my things.

"Hey, Jolene. We had a great week at home, what about y'all?" I push on a smile as I turn around to face the mountain of fire-red ringlets and large grin of Jolene Casey. Jolene raised six boys that are all grown and flown at this point, so she's made it her business to make everyone else's business her business. I've had a lot of practice over the years in watching what I say around her because every word has potential to become town gossip or be twisted into some sort of backhanded, passive-aggressive comment. When we first moved here and I learned her ways (after being burned more times than I wanted or could count), I sounded like I had some sort of aphasia in how slowly I spoke to her, carefully thinking and choosing every word to combat her negativity. She still gets me about half the time but I have a better tolerance in letting it roll off these days. I see Shep cautiously cut his eyes to me from his conversation and back to Hank, trying to gauge how far away to be. Shep is one of those guys that can get along with anyone, but he definitely has people he avoids if at all possible. Jolene Casey is at the top of that list for him.

"Oh, we had a great week! Seven of the fifteen grands got to visit and we had a really fun time at the new water park resort up in Lubbock. Have you taken the kids there? I know y'all don't leave the ranch much, but you should really go!"

My eyes narrow in on a small fleck of black pepper sitting on her incisor and I focus on it instead of the insinuation that we are agoraphobic and rarely go anywhere.

"No, we haven't been yet. But, you know, there's no place like home, especially during calving season!"

"Oh, but you did get out! I heard about your little run-in with Richard! That poor man just has the saddest life, don't you think? I always just feel so sorry for him! You'd think more people would understand and be kinder to him, you know?"

"He's something, alright. He could really benefit from a caretaker of some sort to help him make phone calls to the correct people, and improve his general demeanor. But, yes, I do agree he has a very sad life."

"Well, one of these days he's not going to be around anymore, and I think we'll all miss him more than we think," she chirps, looking past me to make eye contact with someone else and wave them down.

"Highly doubt it," I mutter under my breath as she bustles away to her next conversation and I take the opportunity to escape.

"You ready for lunch? Where are the kids?" Shep asks as he finishes up with Hank and turns back to me.

"Mia ran off with the twins, and I think Hayes is over with Carlisle. We're still going over to your parents', right?"

"Yeah, I told Mom we'd be there about 12:30 so we need to get going." Shep waves an arm to get Hayes's attention and nods toward the door to let him know it's time to leave. We walk to the foyer where Mia and the twins are clustered on a bench looking at something on someone's iPhone that I probably wouldn't love.

"Mia, let's go. Lunch at Gramps and Nana's." Shep rolls past the girls with Hayes and I stop to make sure she actually extrapolates herself instead of lollygagging with the twins. She heaves a sigh and gives hugs all around the group before scowling and following me out. I give in to the temptation of wanting to be a cool, fun mom for the most part, but there is a little something fun about embarrassing your pre-teen every now and then, too.

———

"If I've said it once, I've said it a thousand times: there is nothing better than a Red Rock Cattle Company pot roast!" Forty-five minutes later, we are seated around the large farmhouse table at Frank and Billie's, Shep's parents. Billie has made one of her signature meals: Mississippi pot roast, mashed potatoes and gravy, and other assorted vegetables from her raised bed gardens with big fluffy hot rolls. We have lunch after church with them about once a month since they live about forty-five minutes from us, and this is our Sunday for March. Frank and Billie have a small ranchette property with a classic white farmhouse they bought fifty years ago, but is at least a hundred years old. Over the years they've updated parts of the house, but mostly everything is historical and vintage, and being in the house is like stepping into an old western movie.

"I don't think so, I think the ground beef is the best," Frank disagrees with Billie, shaking his head disapprovingly as he scoops himself a large helping of green beans dripping with butter. You might think that the best or most popular cuts of meat are a ribeye, or a filet, but if you ask Frank and Billie Jones, they will judge you based off, and rave about, a pot roast or ground beef every time. We only process a very small portion of our herd, but we've kept them supplied with beef for several years now, and I still giggle when they talk about how tender a roast is, or how juicy a pound of ground beef is.

"Do y'all ever eat ribeyes?" Shep asks, seeming genuinely curious. He has worked tirelessly for years on the genetics of our herd, with marbling being one trait he's significantly improved over time, and it gets his goat every time that they rave over two cuts that don't showcase marbling much at all. "Just wondering, because if you don't, we'll take them off your hands."

"Sure we do, I fried one up a few days ago, thank you very much," Billie retorts, and I watch Shep let out a small, almost imperceptible, shudder, and try not to laugh to myself. Shep is a grill master, and has been for years, so he of course feels like it's a bit sacrilegious to cook a steak indoors, especially frying. But we'll chalk that one up to a generational difference.

"So, we heard you paid a visit to Richard a few days ago," Frank pours gravy on his potatoes and lets it run over into his roast and green beans before looking up at Shep and me sitting side by side across the table. Frank and Billie have known Richard MacDougal since they were kids because everyone knows everyone here.

"Did they mention this on the news or put out an email newsletter or something? He lives across the road from us, not smack in the middle of town. How does everyone know about this?" I ask, shaking my head a little. I've lived in a small town all my life, and this particular one for nearly fifteen years-- you'd think I'd be used to this by now.

"I had lunch with Tammy yesterday. She said Carl mentioned seeing y'all a few days ago at Richard's. How is he doing?" Billie asked, spooning more mashed potatoes on Hayes's plate while he wasn't looking. Another generational difference we constantly run in to is our mothers being convinced our children are starving to death, despite the fact that they eat constantly.

"He's a little wound up about some developers coming to talk to him or something, but I guess fine other than that. He sure seems like an unhappy man, but there's not much I can do about that," Shep answers, shrugging. Shep is the most proactive man I've ever met, but he's also very aware of when action just isn't worth the fight.

"He is, but he always has been, really. Richard's been dealt a tough hand in life. He hasn't handled it the best, but boy, he's been given ten times what most people have had to handle," Billie laments, beginning to gather up some of the empty dishes to take them into the kitchen as the kids quickly finish and slip away from the table to play ping pong in the basement.

"Okay, I don't want to be a jerk, but like what? I know his wife passed away, but lots of people are widowers without being completely horrible to their neighbors who don't deserve it, you know?" I retort, probably leaning a little too much into victimhood. Billie pauses, setting her large Mikasa serving bowl back on the trivet underneath it.

"Well... when he was a child, he and his brother Charles were playing with their slingshots and Richard hit Charles in the back, like a total fluke, and that lodged into his spine and left him partially paralyzed for the rest of his life. He had a whole slew of health problems after that and passed away fairly young. I know Richard never got over feeling responsible for that. He was just miserable until our early twenties when he met Linda. She was the light of his life. He was pleasant for the first time in years, maybe even his whole life. Then about the time we all started having kids, she finally carried one baby to full term that died a few hours after birth, and then just had miscarriage after miscarriage. It turned out that she had very severe uterine cancer by that point and it had spread all over the place, so there was not a lot they could do for her. He was never the same after he lost her. He was alone again by the time we were in our early thirties and more miserable than before. He has definitely never minded his manners or been hospitable in the least, but man, it hasn't been easy to be him for seventy years," Billie explains, and Shep and I exchange looks as we both feel just a few inches tall at this point.

"Alright, I see your point. I'll be nice," I concede, feeling so guilty I'm not even hungry anymore. I push my plate an inch or so away from me, and look up to see Frank still going after his food wholeheartedly, seemingly unbothered by the vibe of the entire conversation. His fork loudly scrapes up the last of his mashed potatoes and gravy and Shep and Billie slowly turn to look at him as well as he cleans up the rest of his pot roast. After a few minutes, he finally notices we are all staring.

"It's not as good as the ground beef, but it's still good," He shrugs, standing to take his plate to the sink in the kitchen. "And Dick MacDougal is one of my least favorite people."

▭

"Where are you going with those?" A few days later, after making a triple batch of my famous chocolate chip cookies, I am packaging up a dozen or so on a melamine plate with saran wrap and a random gingham ribbon I found in the junk drawer. Billie's story about Dick MacDougal has been eating a hole in my soul, so I've decided to take him cookies as a good-will gesture to assuage some of the guilt I feel at my strong dislike of him for the last decade. I'm certain I'll be met with the same level of bile we have been for that amount of time, but it will at least clear my conscience that I did my part to be nice. We'd already eaten dinner, so I plan to run these over while the kids are finishing homework and getting ready for bed.

"I'm taking these to Mr. MacDougal."

"Did my mom make you feel guilty?"

"100%."

"Good luck. He's not going to like them."

"If he doesn't like them, I'm telling him it was your idea."

"Well, he seems to not like anything associated with me anyway, so what else is new?" Shep steals a cookie from the pile left on the cooling rack and tips it to me. "These are too good to share with someone who doesn't appreciate them."

"Well, that's very sweet, but I'm trying to mend fences. Maybe Jolene was right and that we will miss him when he's gone. I don't want us to have any regrets, you know?"

"First of all, our fences are solid, there is nothing to mend. Second of all, never say Jolene Casey was right again. You know how I feel about her. Third of all, I have no regerts. You know that," He winks at me, and I laugh at his reference to a Milky Way commercial that used to come on all the time when the kids were little. It featured a man with a tattoo saying "NO REGERTS", who obviously had regrets. We've referenced that dumb commercial for years anytime we talk about taking a step out in faith, or doing something that seemed iffy- just go for it so we have no regerts. It's honestly been a decent life motto despite the fact that it started as a joke. He hasn't taken the conventional way to get here, but he's done a damn fine job getting to where we are, and I don't regret any of it, either.

"Well, just because we have no regerts doesn't mean Mr. MacDougal doesn't. Maybe these will help him reflect on his life and how he's treated those around him for the last several years."

"Oh, Molly. For twenty years what have I been telling you? The root of all disappointment is..." Shep raises his eyebrows at me and takes a bite of his cookie. I roll my eyes and finish packing up my little care package.

"Unmet expectations!" I finally reply, grabbing my bag and keys to drive across the road.

"If you expect Dick MacDougal to be anything more than a dick to you, you are going to be disappointed!" He calls after me as I leave through the side door. I toss the cookies in my passenger seat and jump in the driver's side, mentally preparing myself for the venture ahead. For the last twenty years, there has been nothing more infuriating and more reassuring than the fact that Shep Jones is absolutely always right. And I'm not expecting that to change today.

A few minutes later, I pull to a stop in front of Mr. MacDougal's house. I take a deep breath, grab my cookies, and walk up the few sagging steps to his front door. I can see through the window in the door that his small, hunched shoulders are sitting in his recliner in the living room, lifelessly watching *Bonanza* on his old box TV. A large mug of beer is sitting next to him on an end table, just sweating condensation down the sides like a fountain. I quietly knock on the door and wait for him to respond.

If he hears me, he completely ignores me because not a single thing about the scene changes one iota. I knock again slightly louder and wait. Nothing.

"Mr. MacDougal? Are you home? It's Molly Jones from down the road. I have something for you," I call while staring at him through the door, gradually getting more irritated. *Alright, you old coot, open the door! I'm trying to be nice here!* I try to redirect my thoughts to my original intention in coming here instead of my growing annoyance. *He's had a hard life, he's here all alone, he's just a human.*

"Mr. MacDougal? I just came by to say hi and bring you some cookies. How are you?" I find that the door is unlocked and, unable to help myself, I make my way in. I slowly walk toward him with the cookies in hand, a little creeped out that he still hasn't moved since I've let myself inside. "Mr. MacDougal? Are you okay?" I ask quietly, stopping about two feet from his recliner, not comfortable enough to go any closer. He is wearing a beat-up pair of jeans, and an old white men's tank top that reveals his classic rancher tan: deep brown on the lower parts of his arms and face, and pale white on his forehead and scrawny biceps. The pale looks a little darker than normal, almost yellowish, and his eyes are about half open, making it difficult for me to tell if he is intentionally ignoring me or not. I lean over as far as I comfortably can, trying to discern if he is asleep, or alive, or what his deal is.

"What the hell are you doing in my house, girl?!?" He suddenly shouts, jumping up in his chair as fast as his run-down body will let him. I reflexively jump back, throwing up my arms and letting the whole plate of chocolate chip cookies fly across the room as he scares the bejeezus out of me. He yells a flurry of curse words as cookies rain down on him and I clutch the back of an old wooden dining chair near me to steady my heart rate before answering him. Once I can breathe again a minute later, I wait for him to stop cussing me so I can explain.

"I thought you might enjoy a treat, so I brought you some cookies. I was trying to be a good neighbor!"

"You interrupted my nap. I don't need your damn cookies; I just need to be left alone. What don't you people understand about that?"

"I'm sorry to have startled you. That wasn't my intention at all. I know you prefer your... privacy. But you know, everyone needs someone to care about them. I just wanted to see if you need anything." I glance across the table behind me to a handful of pill bottles and a plate and cup that look like dinner remnants. "If you ever need help sorting through any of your medication, I'm happy to help. You know, I used to be a pharmacist before we had the kids and moved out here. I know some things have changed, but I'd be glad to help you any way I can," I say, picking up a bottle labeled "Digitron" with the dosage and his full name and address written underneath.

"I am fully capable of taking care of myself, and I have

been for fifty years. There isn't a damn thing wrong with me; those are just my vitamins. I don't care what fancy pieces of paper you paid too much money for; I don't need you, and I want you out of my house!" He throws a nearby cookie in my direction and I smack the pill bottle down on the table and look back at him.

"Alright, that is it! This has gone on long enough. You are seventy-five years old and have worse manners than a disobedient toddler! What is wrong with you? I could see you being cranky if people were constantly bothering you, but literally everyone avoids you if at all possible *because* you treat them this way. This was me trying to do something nice for you because I felt sorry for how life has treated you. Well, now I know that you've been just as mean to life as life has been to you, so that's square and I can stay the heck out of it. Consider this my goodbye, and I don't plan to ever bother or talk to you again!" I take one last long look at his stunned face before turning on my heels and heading to the door. "Also, you need to talk to your doctor and your pharmacist to lower your heart failure medication dosage. You are turning yellow!" With that, I slam his front door and march to my car. He doesn't follow me, surprisingly, and I make it all the way home before trying to decide if that accomplished my intention and if my guilt is now better or worse.

When I pull up on the driveway, Shep is out on the front porch in his rocking chair with a cup of coffee and an *Angus Bulletin* in his lap. Our littermate Bullmastiffs Crabcake and Beignet laying lazily on either side of him. He has a small smile, his I-knew-I-was-right smile, waiting for me as I walk around the rock path from the driveway to the front porch and sit down in the rocking chair next to him.

"Are you and Dick best friends now?"

"Not even close."

"How bad was it?"

"I woke him up from his nap unintentionally because I thought he was ignoring me. He threw a cookie at me and told me to leave him alone, so I told him to stop acting like a petulant child and to have his doctor lower his Digitron dose because he's jaundiced. I also told him I was no longer speaking to him. I don't think he found that to be the insult I meant it to be."

"Holy hell. Do you have more realistic expectations now?"

"He's just a sour old man, Shep. Like I've always felt that way, but I think a part of me thought I could really kill him with kindness and win him over. That is really not the case. He's a mean old son of a bitch, and no one is going to change him."

"I'm surprised he's on heart failure meds. I don't see him going to a PCP, much less a cardiologist."

"It's probably because his heart is three sizes too small. The bottle had a label from one of those mail-order pharmacies some insurance companies use, so I don't know. Whoever prescribed it is going to kill him with that dosage though. He's already jaundiced."

"You went through his pill bottles?"

"Not really. They were all out on the table and I glanced at them while he was cussing me out."

"If you were waiting for him to wrap that up, I'm sure you had plenty of time."

"I'm done feeling bad for him. And I told him that. It sucks his life has been so terrible, but that's no excuse to act like he does. No more sympathy from me. He can die alone and friendless and have only himself to blame."

"Did you at least bring home his cookies?"

"No, they flew all over his house. Who even knows the last time it's been cleaned."

"Oh, good call."

He sets his magazine on the square table between our

rockers and takes my hand silently. We sit and watch the sun go down over our rolling green pasture full of black cows and calves, and I think to myself that I'm as frustrated as I am with Mr. MacDougal because I'll never understand him. I can't possibly understand what it would be like to experience that much heartache in this life because I've been so overwhelmingly blessed.

chapter
three

"I AM NOT PLAYING with you. Get in this house this instant, young man," I demand, staring down the two large brown eyes trying to guilt trip me into letting him stay outside. "I'm not kidding. It's time for us to go, and you need to come inside."

A pitiful howl comes out of his mouth, and Crabcake moves just close enough for me to grab his large blue collar. He woefully follows me through the back door into the utility room to his spacious kennel next to his sister's. Beignet has been happily snuggled in her kennel for fifteen minutes while I chased down her brother in the yard because he is the most stubborn dog that has ever lived, except for when his sister decides to be the most stubborn dog. We've had Bullmastiffs for the entirety of our marriage and have never once regretted them, but this pair has been our first time to have two of the same age and there has been a learning curve. Mainly learning which one is going to be the center of attention for the day and which one is going to behave. We've had quite the menagerie of dogs over the years, but the current team seems to be the most unique. In addition to the bully bro-and-sis team, we have a border collie that is scared of cows, and a lab retriever that is so jacked up to retrieve he will retrieve water-fowl, plus anything else available on the water. If there's one thing that has remained steady in our marriage, it's that if we like something, we'll accumulate way too many until we question our life choices. And we like dogs for some reason.

"Mia, let's go! It's time for the bake sale!" I yell up the back stairs to the kids' rooms as I gather up my Bundt cakes into a large box for travel and head for the door. Mia comes running down in her cheer skirt and a team t-shirt with her blonde hair in a sweet simple ponytail. I reluctantly have on my team mom t-shirt with flowy linen pants and am wondering how delusional it is to hope we sell out quickly and hit the road before our shift is over. Or maybe, they'll sell out before we even get there, and we won't have to work it at all. Dream big dreams, friends.

At the local grocery store, there are three folding tables set up in a U just to the left of the sliding door entrance, covered with plastic blue and red tablecloths and various baked goods. Mia adds our Bundt cakes to an open space on one side before heading out to the parking lot to panhandle customers with the other girls. I take a spot behind the tables with one of my best friends, Amanda, mom of Emily. "How's it been going?" I ask as I stash my bag under a table and glance around to scope out the scene.

"Not bad, we've made about three hundred dollars so far. What is your time slot?"

"1:30-3:30. You?"

"We're doing 12:30-2:30," Mandy sighs, lining up a few individually wrapped brownies that are out of line.

"So, who's been here with you?" I ask, looking back and forth again as the automatic doors of the grocery store open and an orange-tan freight train with short platinum teased up hair rolls through the doors out to our table. She has a sour look on her face and a handful of singles and quarters, wearing a team t-shirt that looks like someone attacked it with a Bedazzler, along with denim cut-off shorts, and what looks like full stage make-up.

"Molly! So glad you could join us!" Becki announces loudly and nasally, and I briefly close my eyes to remind myself how much I love my daughter. I flick my wrist to look at my watch and see that we still have three minutes until our shifts start so I'm not really sure what Becki is trying to insinuate, but I'm also not surprised in the least.

"Wouldn't miss it for the world, Becki. Didn't know I'd get to work with you, though," I respond, flashing a tight smile and tucking a wisp of bangs behind my ear. Since the weather is warming up, I opted for my signature low messy bun to mostly keep my hair out of my face and off my neck, but it usually creates an unintentional nervous tick of me trying to tuck my bangs behind my ear with the vigor of tucking in a small child that needs to go to bed and won't stay.

"Oh yes, I didn't sign up for any specific shifts because I obviously need to be here to supervise the whole thing. Are those your cakes?" She asks disgustedly with her nose crinkled and pointing her finger with her arm shrunk against her body like she can't bear to get any closer.

"Yes. Is there something wrong?" *So help me, Lord, I will not murder this woman. She is not worth the jail time.* I clench my teeth a little, but remind myself to release so as not to mess up all the work my orthodontist did on my bite as an adult with Invisalign several years ago.

Mandy silently turns to walk to the other side of the booth with balled-up fists, and Becki lets out an exasperated sigh with a large poof of air. She delicately lays her change next to the cash box and picks up a Sharpie from the top of a pile of price stickers lying next to it. "Well... it's just... our goal is to make as much money as possible," She drones, tapping the Sharpie against her palm. "Those are just... not what I was expecting. I don't think we can sell those for as much as I planned." *I'm not kidding, Lord, help me not murder this woman. We're in our forties, why do women still insist on being just flat out mean?*

"I am so terribly sorry they don't meet your incredibly arbitrary and unqualified expectations. I'll just put a middle of the road fair price on them. Every little bit helps, right? If there ends up being that big of a discrepancy at the end, Shep and I can make a donation." I yank the Sharpie from her hand and scribble $35 on a few florescent stickers and slap them on the ribbon around the cellophane wrap of each cake as she stares at me dumbfounded. I've endured more than enough back-handed comments about being a doctor's wife over the years and what an easy road that must be financially. Ranching is obviously a different financial situation than medicine, but we can still hold our own with expenses and I'm apparently not above using it passive-aggressively when the need arises. I place one front and center on the table and turn back to Becki as someone walks up to the table and Mandy engages.

"Hi, can we help you find something in particular? All proceeds benefit the Buffalo Creek Junior High cheer squad to go to camp," she says meekly as the older woman peruses all the offerings. She moves past dozens of individually wrapped cookies and brownies to stop in front of my cake.

"What a beautiful cake! What flavor is it?"

"Looks like the tag says Mississippi Mud. That was made by our very own Molly Jones and she makes her fudge sauce from scratch," Mandy replies, winking at the customer.

"I had a cake of hers at a ladies' league luncheon a few months ago and it was delicious! I'll take it! And keep the change. I feel like you underpriced that, darlin'!" She hands Mandy a fifty-dollar bill and takes her cake away smiling. I stay facing the parking lot, refusing to turn around and make eye contact with Becki because the most important thing I've learned to do when you win is to act like you've been there before.

A little bit later, in a flurry of Ziploc bags, my other best friend Lucy and the twins arrive for their shift. Lucy and I tag team writing $.50 on sticker after sticker to slap them on the small bags filled with two large chocolate chip cookies each overflowing from a large leftover Amazon box. Mandy takes each one and stacks them out on the sales tables as they are priced.

"We have to get these out before our dictator boss comes back," I murmur, nodding toward the parking lot where Becki is out directing the girls on holding posters near the road where customers are turning in. "When did you manage to bake all these?"

"Girl, please. These came straight from the bakery section at Walmart."

"No way. Did you miss where she said homemade?"

"Nope, read it loud and clear. And said to myself 'kiss my butt, Becki' on the way to the store last night. Nobody is making ten dozen whatever from scratch."

"I did..." Mandy says quietly, and we all start laughing. Mandy Scott is a down-to-her-core rule follower, and will probably get along with Becki the best over the course of this season just because her people-pleaser nature will keep her in line with Becki's bossiness. Lucy Miller will probably fare the next best because she is so far the opposite in not caring one bit what others think of her that she will do what she wants without being bothered that it's not what she was told. I'm a rule follower insofar as it is logical and makes sense for the greater good, and am somewhat of a recovering people pleaser. My toxic trait is I can get really bristly when I feel like I'm being told what to do by someone not qualified to be telling.

And Becki Lane is one of the least qualified people I know at life in general.

Lucy and I continue to man the sales tables as Becki supervises the girls talking to people in the parking lot once Mandy and Emily finish up their shift a little bit later. Business is steady as the majority of town is coming in waves to get their weekly groceries, and if there's one thing a small town excels at, it's supporting kids. Just as we are wrapping up some of the last items, a single cab 90s era F-150 putters into the parking lot and gradually comes to a stop near us. A hunched little man slowly climbs down from the driver's seat and stops to catch his breath with his back to us as he closes his door. Lucy and I both watch as he turns to head into the store, bracing himself on the hood of his truck with his head down.

"I can't go anywhere without running into your good-for-nothing face!" Dick MacDougal has managed to look up from the ground long enough to find me in his eye line and growls at me, reaching out for the table to steady himself. He looks terrible, and I say that as the opinion of a former medical professional, not someone who just can't stand him. He seems just completely gassed trying to get into the store, and his facial features are sunken in and haggard looking. He takes a long look at the baked goods on the table in front of him and then looks back up at me. "Are you trying to swindle people here?"

"No, sir, this is a fundraiser bake sale for the middle school cheerleaders. Please don't feel obligated, you are welcome to head on in to the store," I reply calmly, hoping he'll drop it and not make a scene here in the middle of town. It's one thing for him to lose his ever-loving mind on us in private, but public-- especially small-town America grocery store on a Saturday public-- is a whole different ball game.

"Don't buy anything from her; her cookies poisoned me! I

threw up for days!" he raves, shaking a fist at me and struggling a little to stay steady. *Lord help me, it's always something.*

"Sir, I don't know what you're talking about, but I can assure you, I didn't poison the cookies I brought you. I didn't think you'd even eat them since they mostly fell on the floor," I point out, wondering why he is so delusional. He sneers back at me and swipes a hand across the table, knocking off the remaining brownies. I roll my eyes and stoop to pick them up, still wondering why people choose to be so mean. "Sir, are you alright? You don't look very well; can I call someone for you?"

"I don't need no one! Leave me alone!" He shouts and turns, running right into Becki waiting next to him.

"Is there something wrong, sir? I'd be glad to assist you if these ladies aren't doing a good job. All proceeds send the BCJHS cheerleaders to camp this summer! Go Warriors!" She beams into his face like an equally delusional lunatic and he stumbles back into the table a little to get away from her.

"You! You get away from me! I remember you and I told you and your little boy toy no! Get away from me!" He yells, wobbling back to his truck as quickly as he can and limping in. He backs out more swiftly than he should and drives out of the parking lot with quietly squealing tires as we all watch him with equal parts dismay and terror that he's actually driving out with other real people on the road.

Becki looks absolutely mortified. She keeps her head facing away from us as Lucy and I line the brownies back up. "Becki, he's just a crazy mean old man, don't worry about it," I attempt, reminding myself that Jesus loves her even if I don't, so I should probably put in a little more effort to get on His level.

"Obviously he was distraught at the terrible customer service he was getting! Any more issues like that and you'll both be relieved of your duties and will pay all camp fees out of pocket!" She snaps back and rushes inside the store, presumably to collect herself in the bathroom.

"Did she just say if we mess up again, we don't have to work here anymore? Where's the next customer? Don't threaten me with a good time," Lucy retorts, rolling her eyes and leaning against a table. "What is her problem? You were just trying to be nice."

"Who knows, but it's going to be a long year and it hasn't even really started yet."

Business significantly slows as the afternoon drags on, and the girls join us back at the sales tables. As Mia and I wrap up our shift late in the afternoon and head back to the car, I can't get this nagging feeling out of my chest. I sit in the driver's seat for several minutes arguing with myself before reluctantly unbuckling my seatbelt and turning to Mia. I adamantly meant it in my soul that I would leave Dick MacDougal alone after he lost it on me a few days ago for trying to be nice. But it's hard to face humanity that clearly needs help and willfully ignore it but still call yourself a good person. Besides, anyone who has that much enmity with Becki is probably a friend of mine. "We need to go back in and grab a few things from the store."

"I thought you got groceries a few days ago?"

"I did, babe. These will be for Mr. MacDougal."

"I thought we weren't allowed to talk to him?"

"You and Hayes aren't, but Daddy and I do when we need to. He's sick or something, and he wasn't able to get what he needed earlier because of us, so we're going to grab a few things to take to him so he has something, okay?"

We head back in the store and grab some basics: bread, milk, eggs, deli turkey and cheese, regular potato chips, and a bag of oranges because the last thing that old curmudgeon needs is scurvy. We wave at Lucy and the twins as we head back out and take our little care package back to our neck of the woods.

Twenty minutes later, Mia and I pull through Mr. MacDougal's circle drive and come to a slow stop. After grabbing the large brown paper sack with his groceries from the backseat, I tell Mia to wait in the car, planning to just drop these and leave as quickly as possible. I may have felt convicted enough to do this, but I still have a daily limit on verbal abuse I'm willing to endure. I make my way up the steps slowly and peek through the large glass window in his front door again. He is sitting at his dining table with his back to me, looking like he just sat down to dinner as his plate is full of food. I knock quietly and wait to see if he decides to ignore me this time. His body slumps down into his chair slightly, but there is no change in his body language other than this. Knocking again, slightly louder, I peer in to see if I can see any other perceivable change in body language. Obviously, someone isn't going to sit down to their dinner at the table and take a nap instead, so he has to be ignoring me or just unable to hear his surroundings well.

I take the chance that his hearing is likely not great and quietly let myself in the door, planning to just leave the groceries on the counter and slip back out, ideally undetected. The kitchen is behind him, so as long as I slip in quietly and he doesn't turn around, my plan should be feasible. I try to remind myself that we don't need to get credit for good deeds, and this is one case where anonymity is highly preferable anyway. Besides, with the current state of his mind, there's probably a decent chance he sees a bag of groceries on the counter, remembers he went to town, and thinks he got them himself, no questions asked.

Turning the knob as slowly and silently as I can, I slip through the smallest sliver of door I think I can fit through and creep to the kitchen about thirty feet away. My biggest nemesis in this plan is the loud crinkly brown paper sack, and my biceps and triceps are on fire as I hold the sack away from my body to help damper the rustling. I finally make it to the counter and gently slide the bag onto the faded Formica and move back toward the door.

But suddenly I stop, the mom in me taking over, unable to be suppressed-- there are cold foods in there. The last thing I want is for him to get up from the table and go straight to bed or nap in his chair and all the milk and eggs and cheese and lunchmeat just spoil for no good reason. He had his dinner dishes still out the other night, so he clearly doesn't always clean up after himself immediately. I glance back to him and he hasn't moved a muscle, so I tiptoe back, gingerly opening the outdated refrigerator. It is barren, aside from a dilapidated box of baking soda, and my heart breaks a little. No wonder this man is so mean. It's cruel to have to take care of yourself like this for this long with no one around to be with you or help you. Although, I point out to myself, we did try to help. You can only be as helpful as someone lets you.

I gently turn the paper bag on its side, and manage to slip the cold items out as quietly as I can and onto the shelves in the fridge. I delicately set the potato chips on the counter, and I'm down to just the oranges to take care of. I pull them out of the paper sack and set them on the counter, starting to step away to get the heck out. Just then, I see a rip in the side of the net bag, and pulling them out of the sack allows them to thump one by one on the chipped linoleum floor. I wince as each one drops, and brace myself for the rage I'm about to endure. After the last one hits, I slowly turn back to the table and see him still sitting completely still. For the first time, I stop to really survey the situation and notice that he not only hasn't moved to notice me, but he hasn't moved at all- not even to eat his food. I take a few tentative steps toward him. He wavers ever so slightly, and then falls face down into his plate. I gasp, and rush toward him, working to pull his upper body off the table when I get to him. Once I roll him out of his mashed potatoes, I feel his neck for a pulse, and my whole body runs ice cold. It's not weak, and he's not syncopal like I initially thought he probably was. He has no pulse. None. He's dead. He's probably been dead the entire time I've been in here, just putting away groceries for someone who doesn't need them. Because he's dead.

Oh my God, how did this happen?? I immediately panic that I have now potentially tampered with a crime scene. And touched a dead person. I whirl around looking to see where I set my phone before I realize I left it in the car with Mia. Oh, Mia. All she'll ever remember from her childhood now is that her mom found a dead person while she waited in the car. Talk about a therapy bill.

I gingerly lay Mr. MacDougal's head on the table away from his plate and back away. I back all the way out the still-open door and race down the steps to my car.

"Mom, what's going on? I could see you through the window. Is everything okay?" Mia asks worriedly. She's always been my worrier, my little one concerned about anything and everything. We used to have to give her a step-by-step itinerary of our days when she was little because she wanted to be completely prepared for everything coming her way. Her brother blazes through any and everything no questions asked, but Mia is my cautious, concerned, tentative child. She's also now my child who's seen a murder scene in real life. Didn't have that on my parenting bingo card for her, good gracious.

"Um, something happened, babe. We need help," I reply, finally locating my phone sitting in my console under the heads-up display. I hit Shep's name on my favorites and try to steady my breathing. "Shep, I need you. We're at Dick MacDougal's. He's been murdered."

chapter
four

"EXPLAIN to me one more time why you are here?" Shep asks, rubbing his temples and forehead with his right hand, leaning against the hood of my car with his left. He hasn't yelled at me because Shep is not a yeller. He's the most even-tempered person to ever walk this earth, but I can tell he isn't thrilled that Mia and I are in the middle of what looks at best like incredibly bad timing, and at worst, really suspicious. It's clearly well known around town that we had an altercation with Mr. MacDougal recently, and he is gone without a clear explanation now.

"Well, MacDougal came to the grocery store while we were having the bake sale, and he stopped to talk to us before he made it in the store. He and I had a little bit of an argument- he was shouting around the parking lot for people not to buy anything because he thought the cookies I gave him were poisoned," I start, wringing my hands a little. If we're honest, Mia is our worrier, and she got it from her mama.

"Did you?" he interrupts, looking like he is half serious, half joking.

"Did I what?"

"Poison him with those cookies?"

"Shepherd William Jones, are you serious right now? I touched a *dead man's body* twenty minutes ago," I shriek, raising my eyebrows at him. I know he is potentially trying to just lighten the vibe, but I'm also not really in the mood to be jokingly accused of poisoning someone.

"Just curious. You came home so mad, it's not completely out of the question," he replies, cracking a small smile.

"No. No, I did not. And let's not joke about that when the sheriff's department gets here."

"Alright, so Dick starts a fist fight in front of the grocery store. Did you come back here to finish it off?"

"So, he and I were arguing about the fact that the cookies I made him were not in fact poisoned, thank you very much, and Becki came up behind him and scared him so badly he got back in his truck and left without getting anything from the store," I continue, glancing over to the lawn chair across the yard where Mia is sitting. We were honest with her about what is going on, but also would like to protect her as much as possible so we set a lawn chair from the back of my car as far away from the house as we could and have her sitting there reading her book for English class.

"I'd run from Becki, too," he interrupts again, laughing a little, and I shoot him a look, and try not to crack a smile myself.

"Ha ha, very funny. So, I just felt bad that he didn't get whatever he needed from the store and is probably starving to death out here by himself. So, Mia and I grabbed a few staples and were just dropping them off."

"In his house?"

"I couldn't leave them on the porch because they were perishable! He wouldn't answer the door, so I was going to just set them on his counter, hopefully without him noticing. But then I didn't want him to ignore them and the cold stuff to go bad, so I put it all away as quietly as I could, still hoping he wouldn't notice. And then the oranges all fell on the floor, and that's when I really noticed that he hadn't moved at all since I'd been there. Like not a single tiny muscle. He fell in his plate, and I checked his pulse and figured out he's dead. I can't believe I touched a murder victim," I shudder, flapping my hands a little like they probably still have death cooties, even though I reek of vanilla and alcohol from drenching them in Brown Sugar Vanilla hand sanitizer.

"Okay, I've heard you throw the 'm' word around a few times, and we don't know that. He was an old man, Molls, this was probably natural causes. We can't start rumors saying he was murdered."

"Babe, he was murdered, one hundred percent. I just know it. Tough old coots like that don't just die on their own. He's too mean to go out by natural causes."

"Well, that's a very sturdy scientific explanation, but until the ME gives us details, let's refrain from using 'murder'. Especially since you were the one that found him. That makes you look pretty suspicious...." He pats me on the shoulder as Sheriff Cooper and a few deputies all pull into the circle drive. An ambulance follows slowly behind them, presumably to take him to the morgue. Oh man, who will plan his funeral? Did he have a will? What kind of mess has he left behind?

"Well, if it isn't the Joneses, back for more trouble with Dick MacDougal," Sheriff Cooper plops down from the driver's seat of his truck and waddles toward us looking slightly amused. "What do we have going on here?"

"Molly stopped to bring Dick some groceries, and it seems like he may have passed when he sat down to dinner a little before she got here, sir," Shep explains, calmly and concisely.

"Molly, are you alright? I know that can be traumatizing to see someone who is no longer in this realm unexpectedly," Sheriff Cooper asks philosophically, nodding at me sagely and reaching to put a hand on my shoulder. I try not to roll my eyes, not because I'm not totally traumatized, but because his ask felt so patronizing, he might as well have said he thinks I'm a small defenseless woman who shouldn't have to deal with these manly man things.

"Well, Sheriff, it might be preferable to having him yell at me again, if I'm honest."

He stares at me blankly, unsure what to say to me. As I've mentioned, his wife is one of the most demure and innocent women I've ever known, so I'm sure he's not certain how to handle this level of sarcasm.

"Alright then, should we head inside and see what we're looking at here?" Shep and I nod and follow him into Dick MacDougal's house. Sheriff Cooper moves around the first floor for a few minutes while I stand about ten feet inside the door. Shep follows in behind me and stops short next to me as I jerk my head in the direction of MacDougal's body, still lying across the end of the old worn dining table.

For the first time ever, I take a minute to really look around the MacDougal home. Furnishings are sparse, just as you'd expect of a man who has been living on his own for forty years. The living room furniture is just a collection of matching brown plaid couches and a recliner with a coffee table and end table set. There is one photo framed on the mantle: a faded, pale-colored, eighties-era 3" by 5" with a beautiful, petite, auburn-haired, younger woman, and a beaming, young Dick MacDougal in modest, plain wedding attire. The rest of the main living area looks like you could put it on the market today as vacant, perhaps even abandoned, and no one would argue. Cooper has made a slow round through the room and is now stopped and talking on the phone, speaking low and facing away from us.

"Well, Shep, you still got that medical license, son?" he abruptly asks, turning back around to us after ending his call.

"I beg your pardon, Sheriff?"

"Is your medical license still active?" he repeats slowly, like Shep must not have heard him the first time. He walks a few steps closer to us and waits patiently for an answer.

"Sort of. I mean, yes, but I haven't used it in a few years. It's set to lapse in a few months, but we aren't planning to renew it because I don't practice anymore."

"But you can legally still practice?"

"Technically and legally, but ethically I probably shouldn't. I haven't been keeping up with evidence-based updates since I started ranching full time."

"Dispatch just told me the county ME is out this week. His mom was diagnosed with pancreatic cancer and he's in Lubbock with her getting a second opinion. It will be hours before I can get another ME in from another county. I need you to pronounce this body so we can all go home."

"Pronounce it as what, Sheriff?"

"Pronounce it with a preliminary time and cause of death, son," he replies slowly and gestures to MacDougal's lifeless body like Shep just asked the dumbest question anyone could ever come up with. They both stare at one another for a long minute and I shift my attention back and forth between the two, wondering who will break first.

After a few moments of silence, Shep opens his mouth to say something but quickly closes it. "Shep, I just need an esti- mated time of death and what you think might have happened to him. Doesn't have to be perfect, but I need something preliminary to put on the death cert. Coroner can take it from there once we get him in," Cooper answers, moving close enough to nudge Shep toward the table.

"Sheriff, I was a gastroenterologist. I answered medical questions via a colonoscope. I think we're past the point of me shoving something up his hind end to get an answer, you know?"

"All I need is someone with a valid Texas medical license to sign this death certificate. You can say he was eaten by tigers for all I care."

"Yeah, it's not your license they'd take for malpractice for writing that. I have no idea why he's dead, Sheriff, and I'm not exactly comfortable signing my name to a guess in this department. Scopes and guts were my specialty, sir. You should remember, I did your last colonoscopy."

"How can I forget? I had the damn runs for days. And what do you care if they take your license if you aren't renewing it?"

Shep shoots him a dirty look and walks a little closer to MacDougal's body. He circles him with a wide berth, and then looks back at me and Cooper. "Coop, there are literally dozens of possible reasons this man is dead. Stroke, pulmonary embolism, heart attack, you name it. He was a mean old man full of anger who clearly ate a lot of red meat and sugar, so his blood pressure, cholesterol, and blood sugar were probably through the roof. I'd bet money he never had any screening procedures or yearly physicals, so his chance of undetected advanced malignancies is high. I don't know what you want me to say, Sheriff. The possibilities are endless."

I've always been a little dumbstruck when Shep starts speaking physician, but it especially catches me off guard now as it's been a few years since he has practiced consistently. I can say without a shadow of a doubt that Shep has had no regrets about leaving medicine and hasn't remotely missed it. His literal blood, sweat, and tears have gone into building Red Rock from just a dream and extensive research, and there's not a cell in his body that wants to return to that life of long thankless hours and a potential lawsuit waiting around every corner.

"Well, I heard heart attack, so natural causes/ cardiac arrest sounds good enough to me. Was probably within the last two hours, don't you think? Just initial off on that right here,

Shep." Cooper pulls out a file of papers from his vest and shoves them closer to Shep to sign off. Shep glances up at the papers, but ignores them, and continues to stare at the clump of pill bottles on the opposite end of the table. He nods for me to join him and we both look at the pile. "Look at this, Molls," he murmurs, lifting up a worn container. It's from a pharmacy in the next biggest town, with a local elderly family care physician's information listed on the side. The bottle contains a common statin drug meant for high cholesterol, refill 11 of 12. Next to it is the bottle of Digitron I saw the last time I was here, with a new looking generic online pharmacy label with few details. The other two bottles are for men's multivitamins, and vitamin C tablets. He and I exchange looks and turn back to Sheriff Cooper.

"Sir, I'm not comfortable signing that death certificate."

"Son, it's fine. It's not that big of a deal."

"Sheriff, listen to him. This man was taking a statin and a heart failure medication with a very delicate toxicity. It's a known interaction to prescribe them together: no pharmacist would dispense this knowingly. The heart failure medication is from a suspicious looking online pharmacy with no prescribing doctor or refill information, but the statin is from Baker's in Abilene from Dr. Green. He has no other drugs prescribed for heart failure, which is unusual as well. Heck, he has no other prescriptions, period, meaning he was a relatively healthy old man. I've noticed symptoms of toxicity from this drug with him over the last few weeks. I think Mr. MacDougal might have been poisoned," I explain, not sure if he'll believe me.

Cooper looks at both of us for a long moment suspiciously. "Why would anyone poison Dick MacDougal? He hated everyone, and everyone hated him," he reasons, like this is a perfect explanation. Shep and I exchange looks and turn back to Cooper.

"Sir, this isn't a coincidence; it has to be on purpose. No responsible medical provider would do this," I answer, wondering at this moment what we are getting ourselves into by not just moving on and letting it go down on the record as a natural death with no one involved. Like the sheriff said, the hatred surrounding this man is mutual, and no one will be sad to see him gone. What's it to us how or why it happened? Why does this feel like the hill I'm willing to die on suddenly?

Cooper pauses, looking like he really doesn't want to believe us, but we're just a tad too believable to ignore. He remains silent for another few moments before reluctantly sighing and reaching for the walkie-talkie clipped to his chest. "Hernandez, get homicide out here."

chapter
five

"OKAY, Mrs. Jones, let's take it one more time from the top," Homicide Investigator Cason Phillips flips to a new page on his notebook and I let my head fall to the table in frustration. I've been sitting at Dick MacDougal's table as far away from his dead body as possible for over an hour hashing out my same story while the detective writes it down every time. It hasn't changed, hasn't gotten any more detailed or more concise, and yet I'm on the fourth go round here. Cason is a local boy in his late twenties, and while he looks the part of serious homicide detective, with no-nonsense black rectangle glasses over his dark brown eyes and meticulously parted and combed dark blonde hair, I can only picture him as a quiet, shy middle schooler we saw occasionally at youth group when we first moved here.

"I'm not trying to be obstinate or anything, but can I ask why? We've done this three times. I, like Dick MacDougal, have not eaten dinner this evening and I'm starting to get a little hangry if I'm honest," I say, muffled with my head buried in my crossed arms on the table.

"Molly, the guys are here to pick up Mia," Shep says quietly behind me before crossing the room and heading out the open front door. I lift my head a little and glance out the window to see the ranch hand truck idling in the driveway, and our ranch hand duo, Roy and Cooter, helping Mia into the back seat of the truck.

Roy and Cooter are in their early twenties, and have both been ranching since they were in diapers. They are lifelong friends and cousins, and both graduated from a high school about thirty miles away before coming to work full time for us as a pair. We built a two-bedroom bunkhouse for them on the far end of our property, and they have lived there ever since then, joining us multiple times a week for meals and really just becoming part of our family. The kids have known them and grown up with them around since they were young, and it's like having two goofy ridiculous big brothers for them, and extra sets of hands for us. Shep left Hayes with them when he met us down here, and now they're here to get Mia home so she doesn't have to sit in her lawn chair across the yard anymore. I want more than anything to run out there to give her a big hug and tell her everything is fine before she leaves, but Phillips is staring at me expectantly.

"Mrs. Jones, it's just protocol to run through everything multiple times to get as much detail and consistency as possible. But I'm going to ask a few questions as we go through this time, okay?"

"Alright, you get me for one more recap and then I'm going home to my family. Any more questions can follow me there tomorrow morning," I reply, taking a deep breath to start all over. "Okay, we've interacted with Richard MacDougal, the deceased, over multiple occasions the last several years since buying the property across county road 439 from him. The last occasion my husband Shep and I both saw him was about a week ago when he called us over to pick up three estray cows that he accused of being ours, but were actually Asa Shoemaker's. When we were here to pick them up, he also accused us of trying to steal his land. Sheriff Cooper was here to witness the majority of that altercation and confirm that he was in good health when we left. A few days later, I returned alone to bring him a plate of cookies as a goodwill gesture…"

"Why would you bring him cookies if you didn't get along with him, though?" Phillips interrupts. "You've said that each time and I just don't understand why you would do that if you didn't like him."

"Honestly? Conviction from the Holy Spirit, Detective. I can't think of a single other reason I'd purposefully interact with that man on my own accord, other than the Lord's intervening hand multiple times. He works in mysterious ways, haven't you heard that? The Lord, that is. Dick MacDougal was as subtle as a hammer to the head."

He eyes me suspiciously over the top of his glasses as they slip disobediently down his nose, clearly not buying my explanation. "Mmmhmmm, my nana does all sorts of nosy things under the explanation of 'guidance by the Lord'," he nods, pushing his glasses back up and poising his pen back over his paper, waiting expectantly for me to continue. "But, proceed, please."

I stare at him unamused and purposefully take a longer pause than I should before continuing to let him know that I don't appreciate his commentary. "Like I was saying, I brought him cookies as a goodwill gesture, but call it whatever you want. Mr. MacDougal was asleep in his chair, and I startled him awake. He yelled at me to leave him alone and threw the cookies at me. I promised him I would never bother him again. It was during this visit that I noticed he seemed pretty jaundiced and overly fatigued. He had a prescription for Digitron, which is a very strong heart failure medication that can have very delicate dosing. I suggested he speak with his doctor about his dosage because he seemed to be showing early symptoms of toxicity. Earlier today, he came to the grocery store while we were there having a bake sale fundraiser for the middle school cheerleaders and accused me of poisoning him because he vomited after eating my cookies..."

"Did you?" Phillips abruptly interjects, smiling a bit devilishly as he sets his pen down.

"Detective, do you think I would push for this to be investigated as a murder if I was the murderer?" I ask sarcastically, feeling like I should be allowed to eat while doing this if people are just going to ask dumb questions to drag it out.

"Fair response. Not a straightforward one though. Plenty of murderers return to the scene of the crime or get involved in the investigation. The thrill of being close to the crime outweighs the fear of being caught."

"No, Detective, I didn't poison him, and I didn't put poison in my cookies. Vomiting is another symptom of Digitron toxicity."

"You seem to know an awful lot about this Digitron and how it should and shouldn't be used. A little suspicious, don't you think?"

"Or common knowledge for a pharmacist, which I am. I don't appreciate your tone, either, young man," I spat back, raising my eyebrows and leaning across the table to him. "I play Bunco with your mother. I'm sure she'd love to hear how you harass innocent witnesses." And that is the precise moment I became a hundred years old.

His eyes widen a little and he sits back, composing himself and starting over. "Okay, how long have you been a pharmacist?"

"Seventeen years, but I haven't practiced full time since our kids were born about twelve years ago. I worked part time while they were little and quit completely when we began ranching full time about five years ago and my husband quit practicing medicine. But I keep my license and continuing education current just in case."

"Just in case what?"

"Just in case I suddenly need an income to provide for my family. You never know what's going to happen, and I'd rather not be caught unprepared, you know?"

He nods silently in agreement. He ought to understand completely as his dad was injured in a farming accident when he was a child and his mom went back to teaching to support them along with disability insurance payouts. The small-town knowledge of everyone and their business can be the biggest nuisance or the biggest weapon, most of the time both.

"Alright, what happened after he accused you of poisoning him at the bake sale in town?"

"He was in the middle of a rant when Becki Lane interrupted him. He seemed genuinely surprised and a little scared to run into her. He got back in his truck and left after that without going into the store."

"Did she say anything to him? Seem menacing? You think they have a connection of some sort?"

"I mean, she wasn't any more menacing than her everyday demeanor. She asked if he needed help and told him the fundraiser was for the girls to go to camp. She acted very natural around him, but he acted like she was a ghost or something."

"Did he say anything that seemed unusual or important to her?"

"Um, actually something along the lines of 'I remember you', and 'I told you the answer is no'. He was adamant that he wanted her to leave him alone. Do you think she's a suspect? Can she please be a suspect? She could definitely be a murderer."

"What did Becki Lane ever do to you? Cut in front of you at drop off or something?" he asks sarcastically, rolling his eyes.

"No, I'm not that petty, thank you very much. Although, when the kids were in kindergarten, she used to blatantly ignore that the outside lane was for second and third graders and inside lane was kinder and first, and go through with second/ third because it was shorter. She's one of those, Cason. She thinks the rules don't apply to her," I answer with a matter-of-fact and self-satisfied tone. I realize it's nothing that will legitimately stick, but it could at least make her life a little crazy for a few days, and I didn't hate the thought of that, if I'm being honest.

Cason Phillips sets his pen down on the table and looks me straight in the eye with a sudden seriousness. "Are you messing with me?"

"Of course not! Isn't that heinous?!" I respond, equally as serious.

"That is the most middle-aged white-lady-Karen complaint I've ever heard as a detective," he smirks back, shaking his head and picking up his pen again. "Tell me why *you* ended up here tonight then, if he left on his own accord after interacting with Becki."

"That *is* heinous, just so you know, and it is clearly a symptom of a larger problem of rejection of authority," I answer pointedly, and he glares up at me. "Okay, okay, so I know you think the whole Holy Spirit conviction thing is bogus, but I felt really guilty that he didn't get anything to eat and was clearly in a bad way. Mia and I grabbed a few basics and brought them out here to him. When we got here, I could see him sitting at the table, but I thought he didn't hear me to answer the door. I thought I could just sneak in, leave his stuff in his kitchen and get back out. While I was putting every-thing away, the oranges all fell on the floor, and I thought for sure he would have heard it, but when I turned to face him, he started wavering, and fell over into his food. I checked him for a pulse, but he didn't have one. And now here we are," I wave my hand across the room like Vanna White and wait for him to catch up with a Barbie-like smile on my face, telling myself not to lose it if he says his favorite phrase again: take it from the top.

Cason leans back in his chair and ponders for a few long moments. "So, you're convinced he was murdered. What's the motive?"

I sit silently for a few equally long moments. "I don't know. I have no idea why. The sheriff is right: no one got along with him, which means everyone has a reason and no one has a reason. I don't know the why, or the who, I just know the what. This wasn't an accident, this wasn't nature, or disease, or coincidence. This was purposeful. He may have been the meanest man in this county, but everyone deserves justice."

"Yes, they do. But what you're also telling me is that you found him dead, have had multiple recent altercations with him, and have no alibi."

Another hour later, I drive the quarter mile back to our house with my hands still shaking a little, wondering what I've gotten us all into. We could have just signed off on a heart attack, left it at that and all gone on about our lives. They could have auctioned off his acreage, torn down that sad little house, and the world would have moved on from Dick MacDougal, no questions asked. But what do you do when you just can't shake the nagging feeling that you need to say something? Obviously that nag has gotten me into some trouble as of late, with this being the most substantial.

Despite my being an obvious suspect, Cason and Sheriff Cooper had no issue with me leaving once my interview was over. I am not to leave town without giving notice (joke's on them because ranchers don't go away on vacation), and I am supposed to be available for questioning whenever deemed necessary. Shep left about thirty minutes before me to make sure the kids made it into bed without any major issues and to answer any of their questions so they could get some sleep.

I park my car in the driveway and slowly make my way in the side door, unable to get my mind to slow down and stop replaying all the events of the evening.

"There she is! Our own Ms. Molly, ace detective!" As I walk into the kitchen, Cooter and Roy are seated at our island in front of remnants of a cooked frozen pizza, both with backwards Red Rock caps, stained jeans, and raggedy plaid pearl snaps still on from checking cattle earlier. Shep is standing in front of the sink in the island, holding a cup of decaf coffee and looking as tired as I feel. Cooter slides the remaining few slices of pizza onto a paper plate and pushes them over to me as I sit on a high back stool next to Roy.

"Hey, guys. How are the kids?"

"They're fine. I think they must be pretty tired because they both fell asleep pretty quickly. They are probably going to have a lot of questions in the morning," Shep responds, handing me a napkin from the drawer next to the sink.

"Don't we all," I reply, picking the pepperonis off the top of the room-temperature pizza and taking a bite.

"He's really dead? Like really dead?" Roy asks quietly, like he's not sure if he should believe any of the events of the evening.

"He really is. Don't ask me why or who. I think I have a decent grasp on the how, pharmaceutically speaking, but nothing else beyond that."

"There's a dadgum killer among us," Cooter says somberly, and I struggle in that moment to stifle a chuckle. His exaggerated accent has always amused me, but there's something about the seriousness of his tone that just gets me. I start with a low, quiet giggle, and before I can stop myself, I am doubled over, falling out of my chair, full-out laughing.

"There *is* a dadgum killer out here! What are we going to

do?" Roy says loudly over my laughs, looking worried that I've maybe lost it.

"We're going to let the sheriff's department handle whatever is going on, and we're going to stay out of it and go on about our daily lives, right, Molly?" Shep gives me a serious look, and I suck in my laughter and try to get solemn.

"I'm sorry, I touched a dead man today. I don't think I've fully processed that, if I'm honest. But y'all are right. Someone around here was willing to kill him."

"Who gets his land if he dies?" Roy asks innocently, pushing my plate to Shep to toss in the trash can drawer of the island.

"It ain't an "if" now, Roy. Who gets it now that he *is* dead?" Cooter corrects, overly confident as usual.

"Don't know, guys. Don't think it's us, though, so I'm not going to worry about it. Y'all want a ride back to the bunkhouse, or are you good to get there on your own? I think it's time we get to bed," Shep answers, nodding to the side door and staring down Cooter and Roy.

"Nah, we got it, Shep. We'll see y'all tomorrow after church to start prepping for branding," Roy replies, pulling the ranch flatbed truck keys out of his jeans pocket. He and Cooter exit, lights flashing across the open shuttered windows in the family room as they drive by back to the bunkhouse.

Shep pulls me in for a long hug, and I just stand there and try to relax in the embrace. He moves to let go and I hold on a little longer. "Squeeze chute me," I say, and he squeezes his arms around me, in reference to the somatic calming that happens when the torso is compressed. This typically occurs with a hug in humans, but can also be mimicked for cattle by a cattle squeeze chute.

"You good?" He asks quietly, and I nod into his chest.

"I've never touched a dead person before."

"Well, now you have. It's a weird club to be in."

"Have you?"

"Uh, med school. I've sawed a dead person open."

"Ah, forgot about that. What do you think happened? Who would do that? Clearly someone was playing a long game to try to slowly poison him."

"I don't know, but I was serious when I said the sheriff's department will handle it. You can't get in the middle of this."

"Kinda too late now."

"Okay, any more in the middle of it."

"I'll do my best."

And my best somehow led me right back to the scene of the crime bright and early the next morning.

chapter
six

AFTER A LONG NIGHT of drifting in and out of unrestful sleep, I roll over and stare at the digital clock on my nightstand. A few years ago, after Shep stopped practicing medicine, we started charging our phones in our bathroom at night to help with more restful sleep since he wasn't worried about missing calls from the hospital anymore. These days, nothing ruins a good night of sleep like a random middle-of-the-night alert from the Little League team group text because some inconsiderate parent wants to ask about the practice schedule at 12:34 AM like a psycho. But, with no phones, we had to bring back the old-school alarm clocks so we could keep time and have alarms in our room. The dimmed numbers read 5:23 AM, and I lay there a few seconds longer before glancing over at Shep's side of the bed. He is buried under his comforter, softly snoring. We've each used our own set of covers on the same bed since we married because it helps us sleep better and right now it's making it even easier to slip right out of my side of the bed without waking him up. I tiptoe to the bathroom, and after retrieving my phone and changing into a thin faded Buffalo Creek Warriors sweatshirt and black Lululemon knockoff leggings, I pile all my hair up in a messy bun on the crown of my head and quietly slip out of our bedroom.

"I'm going to go check the south pasture bulls, be back in a little bit, bye, love you..." I quietly whisper as I silently close the door behind me and head out to the mud room to find my keys and sunglasses.

There are orange cones haphazardly scattered across the county road between our main driveway and the MacDougal ranch. I come to a slow stop in front of the lackluster barricade and jump out to do a little rearranging. After giving myself some room, I continue down the road and do a slow roll past MacDougal's. I'm not really sure what I'm looking for or planning to accomplish by being out here, but I just can't help it. I need to know more and see what is going on.

As I approach MacDougal's driveway, I see a bored-looking deputy leaning against his tan county truck blocking the gate. He perks up a little when he sees me driving and jumps forward to stop me. He looks all of twelve years old and like he wants to be really in the thick of it, but the thick of it is likely more than he can handle.

"Ma'am, this road is closed for a pending investigation. We ask that you go around to avoid interfering," he says with an official tone to his voice. I'm getting the idea that he may be new to this job and it hasn't exactly been the whirlwind of activity he had in mind.

"Yes, I'm so sorry, but we live just right there across the road, and I was just headed down this way to check some year-ling bulls we have in a pasture over there. I'm not here to mess anything up," I say sweetly, giving him a big smile. It's clear they haven't told this kid a single thing about this investigation so he will not have one semblance of detail to share.

"Across the road? Wait, are you the lady that found him?" he asks excitedly, glancing around to make sure he wasn't going to get caught gossiping like a blue-hair at the beauty shop instead of serving and protecting.

"Yes, it was me. Anything new going on in there… Harris?" I check his name on his badge, and address him directly as I push my sunglasses up into my messy bun to get a better look at him, wondering if this will help me get any further. Honestly, I probably know more than he does at this point, but it doesn't hurt to ask.

"The tox screen came back. You were right: he had an unusually high level of that medicine in his body… I shouldn't tell you this, but the sheriff is freaking out. This is our first homicide with no obvious perpetrator in twenty-seven years," he whispers through my open car window, and I stifle a laugh. There's nothing more reassuring about having a murder investigation across the road from you than knowing Barney Fife is on the case.

"Let me tell you something, Harris. Moms are always right. Never forget that," I advise him, digging through my cupholders and coming up with a crumpled Chick-fil-A receipt and a green washable marker. "This is my phone number. You hear of anything you think I might need to know, shoot me a text."

"Yes, ma'am," he replies reverently, folding the receipt up with care and slipping it into his front pants pocket. "What exactly might you need to know?"

This boy is handsome, and we all know the Lord doesn't give with both hands, so I try to think of a way to spell out what I'm after without getting me and him in trouble. "Just anything that might seem important or like I might be able to help more if I knew, you know?"

"Yeah, sure thing," He nods, and I know it's really a toss-up whether he actually understands what I'm getting at, but it's worth a try.

"How long have you been with the department, Harris?"

"I started last week, ma'am."

"That's what I figured. Is the sheriff still up there?"

"Nope, the sheriff is right here," A gruff voice interrupts us and I jump in my seat, knocking my knees into my steering wheel. As I curse my short legs for being so close to the wheel, Harris scurries back to his post like the spot he'd been standing in suddenly burned the bottoms of his feet, and Sheriff Cooper darkens my window. "Molly Jones, what in the world do you think you are doin'?"

"Are you making brownies? Brownies for breakfast? That has GERD written all over it," Shep asks when he finally makes it down to the kitchen an hour later, seemingly unaware of my early morning field trip. I'm pulling a pan of "Death by Triple Chocolate" brownies out of the oven and onto a trivet on the island. After narrowly escaping Sheriff Cooper, I figured I ought to make good on my excuse. These brownies can go to the potluck after services even if we don't. I've got to keep my reputation intact if I have any hope of getting any more insider scoop around there.

"No, brownies for the potluck after services," I reply, and hold up a hand to keep Shep from protesting. "No, we aren't going, just the brownies. It's a thing for Sheriff Cooper. Also, we need to leave ten-ish minutes early because we'll have to go over to 317 and around because 439 is blocked around MacDougal's and they don't want thru traffic."

Shep stops in the doorway of the pantry and turns to me. "Why do you know that?"

"Just do. I'm going to take a shower and get ready. I'll get Mia up if you get Hayes." As I head out of the kitchen, I see Shep shaking his head as he grabs the protein powder from the bottom shelf to make himself a shake to go with his usual eggs and bacon.

▭

"And do we have any additional prayer requests?" We are at the point in our church service that announcements are wrapping up, and the floor is open to prayer requests. Our congregation is truly too large to have an open floor like this, but against all logic, they still operate like a smaller congregation and do this anyway. We're near the end of services, and all you can mainly hear is shuffling bulletins, kids demanding crayons in loud stage whispers, and the occasional baby fussing. An arm shoots up like it's been shot from a cannon as soon as it's allowed and Jolene Casey's nasally voice fills the auditorium. "As most of you probably already know, Richard MacDougal, our dear friend and neighbor, was found dead last night. Prayers for his family and friends during this obviously difficult and devastating time." Shep and I pop our heads up from reading through the bulletin announcements in our laps to look at each other and then Jolene's self-satisfied smirk as hushed murmurs fill the room. Anybody who's been around Buffalo Creek any amount of time immediately knows all the holes in her story: he was not a dear friend to anyone, he lived fifteen miles from them so hardly a neighbor, and he had no family or friends, especially none that would think this is difficult or devastating. This is classic Jolene, and classic church lady-- share the latest gossip as a "prayer request" and get all the attention. The congregation all looks around at one another with confusion as this has actually not been made public yet, and I immediately start working through who might have leaked to Jolene.

"Uh, yes, we can add that. Richard MacDougal's... friends and family," Lance Miller, Lucy's husband, agrees confusedly, making a notation on his paper from the pulpit where he's giving the announcements. He shakes his head a little like he feels like that's kind of a dumb statement, but moves along with it anyway. "Okay, don't forget there is a potluck lunch set up in the fellowship hall immediately following services this morning, and please join us even if you didn't bring anything. We'd love to get a chance to get to know you if you are visiting. If there are no more announcements or prayer requests, we'll be led in our closing song and prayer, and then dismissal. Thank you." Lance steps down from the stage and heads back to his seat next to Lucy and their kids. We rolled in just in time for services to start, so I didn't have a chance to talk with anyone. Not even Lucy knows my involvement as far as I know. As soon as the final amen is said, Lucy makes a beeline to our seats.

"Okay, has Jolene completely lost it? What in the world is she talking about? We just saw Dick MacDougal yesterday afternoon! He was ornery as ever, definitely alive and kicking." She laughs and playfully smacks my shoulder waiting for me to agree. I take a glance at Shep, and he looks back at me with unease. The sheriff's department didn't specifically tell me not to talk to people, but they did repeat several times that the investigation would be compromised as more people get involved. Although, Jolene blew that up with her verbal vomit grenade ten minutes ago.

"He's dead; I'm the one that found him last night," I mumble to her as I cut my eyes to glance all around me, trying to be discreet and keep everyone around us from hearing.

"What?" The crowd seems to have gotten louder than they were a few moments ago as families are meeting up with one another to head over to the fellowship hall for lunch. Lucy leans over the pew in between us to try to hear better as I answer her again.

"I found him last night; he's dead as a doornail!" I reply

too loudly as the crowd hits a lull at that exact moment. Several heads turn to look at me inquisitively and I immediately look in Shep's direction. He hates crowds, and now he looks like he'd really like to just disappear under the pew altogether. I smile nervously and look for our quickest and easiest option to exit the auditorium. I turn and herd Mia and Hayes out of our row and out the back left door to the foyer with Shep, Lucy, and Lance on my heels. Once we are out of the main crowd, we stop and form a small circle.

"Mia and I went to take him groceries last night after the bake sale, and he was dead sitting at his dining room table with his dinner in front of him. He was poisoned with heart failure medication," I quietly blurt out, feeling some relief in just letting it out. I realize I told everything multiple times last night to the investigators, but there's a different kind of release in letting it fly to people that you maybe aren't supposed to tell. Lucy's eyes grow wide as saucers and Lance's jaw drops.

"No way. He was murdered?" Lance whispers and I nod emphatically.

"He was found to have a toxic level of this heart failure medication in his system and the prescription looks suspicious, but there is no proof that someone purposefully gave this to him in order to kill him. The toxicity was the cause of death, but they don't have any clear suspects or motives at this time to officially call it a homicide," Shep interjects and I look up at him in surprise.

"Who told you that?"

"Sheriff Cooper, when he called this morning to tell me to keep an eye on you after he found you past the barricades engaging a junior deputy in unethical behavior," He responds, slowly turning to me with a raised eyebrow.

"Unethical behavior with a junior deputy? Do tell," Lucy giggles, hoisting her large overflowing bag higher on her shoulder. The twins are their oldest, and they also have a five-year-old and three-year-old, so she is still in the thick of bringing coloring books and quiet activities with them to church.

"It was not unethical behavior. I just exchanged contact information with him, and told him that we could share mutually beneficial information."

"Well, there is no such thing as mutually beneficial information because you are not part of this investigation. You have shared everything you have with them, and they have no need to share anything else with you," Shep answers sternly and I stare at him stubbornly for a few moments.

"I am too part of this. They interrogated me for hours last night. They wouldn't even realize he was murdered if it weren't for me."

"Molls, don't be a Jolene Casey. Don't put yourself in the middle of things that don't concern you and act self-important. You did your part, but we need to let the professionals take it from here. You are not a detective. We can't interfere here."

I know Shep is right, but I've got that same nagging feeling in my chest that I need to do something. I obviously have no idea what that something is, but I know this isn't the end, and there is more to it than this. They are going to miss something and it's up to me to help them find it for some reason, I just don't know why. But rest assured, I'm going to figure it out.

chapter
seven

"GOOD EVENING, ladies and gentlemen. The Crawford County Rodeo Association would like to welcome y'all to the 56th annual Crawford County Cavalcade, presented by First Texas Bank."

Bud Jenkins, known mainly as the Voice of Crawford County as he is the announcer for all high school sports, the annual spring rodeo, and the Christmas parade, is seated directly behind us in his wooden press box with his loud, deep drawl booming across the open-air ring. The vast majority of Buffalo Creek has descended on the county fairgrounds, filling the old wooden stadium seating around the dirt arena. Some cities have carnivals, some have county fairs, some have festivals, Buffalo Creek has the annual county cavalcade rodeo and anyone who is anyone doesn't miss it. Shep started buying a sponsor's box a few years ago when Roy and Cooter started working for us because they compete in the team roping together every year. The cavalcade is one of our favorite events because the boys have won for the last four years running and we always have a big crawfish boil to celebrate after it's all over.

"When is the team roping?" Mia asks, pulling the program book out of my lap. A lot of rodeos in Texas are through the summer when it's unbearably hot, so I appreciate that ours is earlier in the year to cut down on heat stroke and armpit sweat stains, but it's still warm enough that I am using a second program book to fan a slight breeze in my direction. It rained earlier in the day, so there are mud puddles all around the fairgrounds, and the humidity is unusually high as patches of sun keep breaking through the remaining clouds and moisture hangs thick in the air.

As Mia flips through the pages of the program she grabbed, I thumb through my second book looking for the order of events, stopping at each page to look at the ads. Shep and Hayes are down in the barn area with Cooter and Roy helping them prepare, so Mia and I are holding down our box seats waiting for them, the Millers and Scotts to join us.

"Looks like it's about halfway through, right before breakaway roping," I reply, pointing to the schedule. The grand entry was just about to begin, meaning the boys are maybe an hour or so from competing.

"Hey, hey, sorry we're late. What did we miss? Not Guthrie's prayer, right?" Lucy and company all tumble into the box in that moment and she dumps a large bag full of activities in the back of the box as Luke and Lily, their five-year-old and three-year-old, head to their seats. The twins and Mia huddle into a corner of the box, all comparing phone screens and speaking in hushed tones as Lucy takes the chair next to mine.

"Nope, just in time. Where's Lance?"

"He ran into Shep and John Peterson down at the pens on our way in. The boys are all saddled up, they look like they're ready for a five-peat."

"Oh, it's Guthrie time," I nod to the arena as a large older man with a long, full, white beard and full 1800s cowboy attire dramatically rides into the ring with one arm held high in the air looking for applause and fanfare and the other arm trying to hang on to both riding reins and a waving Texas flag. He circles the ring a few times riding to the pomp and circumstance of the *Magnificent 7* theme song before settling in the middle of the dirt and adjusting his Britney Spears headset microphone. It squeals briefly, which works to quiet the crowd as Crockett Daniel Guthrie, local historian and Crawford County history enthusiast, begins his annual Cavalcade soliloquy.

"Ladies and gentlemen of Crawford County, welcome to the historic, the unparalleled, the unbelievable Crawford County Cavalcade! I am Crockett Daniel Guthrie, and I will be heading off our festivities this evening with a moment of silence and optional word of prayer to our almighty Heavenly Father, followed by the singing of our beloved national anthem. Please stand and bow your heads with me," he booms like a televangelist, as the crowd gets up from their seats and look around at one another before removing their hats and bowing heads as he begins his show of a prayer.

"Almighty Father, it is by your divine providence that we are all together in this place this evening, and we are so very thankful. We know that nothing happens without your guiding hand, and you have guided us all here to this time and place to watch these amazing feats of athleticism and heritage played out before our very eyes this evening. Daddy God, the powers that be in this country have decided that they will not endorse our public prayer to You on these public county grounds, but they cannot censor our hearts and minds. Lord Baby Jesus, in this upcoming moment of silence, hear the prayers of our inner workings!" Lucy and I peek our eyes open as Guthrie pauses his dramatic speech for all of a brief 30 seconds before launching back in to his monologue. "Benevolent loving Prince of Peace, cover these competitors with your all-powerful hands, and keep them all safe as they ride and rope for Your glory. Let every eight second ride, every calf roped, every barrel navigated be in Your name, Abba!"

Crockett Daniel Guthrie is probably somewhere in his sixties (no one has ever actually cracked open his shell to find out his real age), and is a lifelong bachelor, mostly because he is a Texas history, particularly Crawford County history, fanatic. Like he dresses daily in period attire, likes to pretend that technology doesn't exist, runs the local historical village fanatic. He swears left, right, and sideways that his lineage traces back to Davy Crockett (apparently through his mother's side), hence his name and his diehard affection for all things Texas history. He is mostly harmless: the worst that happens is getting cornered by him and getting some sort of history lecture. Meeting him is a bit of a Buffalo Creek rite of passage as all the elementary school kids take his tour through the historical village in the first grade. If he could convince someone, anyone, in Buffalo Creek to participate in some sort of Texas Revolution reenactment scenario, he would accomplish his life's greatest work. His Super Bowl every year is opening the Cavalcade, and his opening speech and "prayer" gets more and more over the top each time. He's not the events announcer-- that will be Bud Jenkins until the end of time-- but he takes what he can get and makes the biggest show of the opening ceremony and grand entry as possible.

As Guthrie waxes on poetically and nonsensically, I peek an eye open again as the Scotts, Mandy and Brett, Emily and Carlisle, quietly shuffle in next to us trying to be reverent as they shuffle. Guthrie finally wraps it up long enough for them to sing the National Anthem, and then we all sit as he launches into his yearly speech about 'The Cowboy'.

"The Cowboy, ladies and gentlemen, is more than just a person. He's more than the man that rounds up the cattle for branding; he is a way of life," Guthrie is pacing his horse up and down the middle lane of the arena gesturing and speaking dramatically as the line of competitors weaves back and forth across the dirt to form the grand entry parade. Just as we spot Roy and Cooter slowly ride in one after another, Shep and Hayes slide into the box and take the last two open chairs.

"Are they ready?" I ask quietly, leaning over to Shep. He nods silently, and we turn our attention to the end of the grand entry line finally making their way into the arena.

The rodeo kicks off with bronc riding, followed by steer wrestling and bull riding, all things that make my entire body cringe. Something about watching bodies slam to the ground, or narrowly dodge a hoof with two thousand pounds of force above it in real time just does that to you. After about an hour of competition, we arrive at what we came for: the team roping. There are six pairs ahead of Cooter and Roy as they scored the best in the prelim rounds, so we wait patiently through each set of competitors, with me holding my breath each time another duo flies out of the wings.

Just as I take a deep breath to prepare for holding it during their run, Cooter and Roy take their places behind the tape and give the guys at the gate a nod. A buzzer sounds and they both fly out into the arena with a young steer calf running ahead of them. Cooter swings his rope in a loop above his head and throws toward the calf's nubby horns and catches around them. As he turns everything to the left, Roy starts looping his rope and throws it toward the feet, and it lands just an inch away from the feet. His rope lies limply on the dirt as the calf continues running forward, still caught by the horns by Cooter. In five years of knowing these boys, Roy has never missed as a heeler. His horse slams to a halt as Cooter briefly holds his rope before letting it go when he realizes they've been disqualified. Times are not recorded if you miss either the head or heel, as they have. And just like that, the five-peat vanishes into thin air.

Shep and I instantly jump up and fly down the stairs to

the pens where they hold competitors after they've finished competing. We make it to their pen just in time to witness the world's most ridiculous argument.

"You missed! How could you miss, it was five feet away!"

"I don't know, I thought I had it. I'm sorry, man!"

"How could you be such a dummy!" Cooter has dismounted by this point and is angrily walking right up to Roy, so close they are touching foreheads, and he is poking a finger into Roy's chest accusingly.

"How could *I* be such a dummy? Well, at least I don't have a completely dumbass name like Cooter!"

"How dare you, you know I'm named after my grandaddy!"

"Your grandaddy has a dumbass name, too!"

Cooter pauses briefly, and then cocks his arm back like he's about to take a wild swing at Roy just as Shep jumps in between them.

"Guys, guys! Both of you take three steps back and a deep breath," he loudly interjects as he uses both arms to push them away from each other. As I stand there and watch uselessly, I have flashbacks to when the kids were younger and would still get into physical squabbles. Shep was always the one to step in between them and break it up. He was also known at times to make them hug it out until they apologized to each other, so I wait patiently to see if he plans to employ that technique here as well.

Cooter and Roy both stand silently, the only sounds between them their heavy breathing. "Guys, you both know you are more than just competitors in this event. You are both good men with good hearts, and you don't want to say anything you might regret to one another. You know as far as Molly and I are concerned, you are members of our family, and one of our family rules is to be kind or be quiet." He tentatively takes a step back from directly in between them.

They continue to stare angrily at one another, both refusing to speak.

"Would it help if I said we can still have the annual celebratory crawfish boil? There's no reason not to still have a party. I mean, we can't eat forty pounds of crawfish by ourselves," I add, stepping up and pulling them both into a hug with me. I can feel that they are both still pretty angry. I don't blame them; this is immensely disappointing as they had no reason not to win, and both expected to win. Roy is honestly probably madder at himself than Cooter is, and this one is going to sting for a little while.

We stand in silence for a few more minutes before Cooter takes a deep breath and seems to release some of his anger, finally hugging me back a little. "It's okay, Roy, we'll get 'em next year."

Shep and I both smile and Shep claps both of them on the back, like he's proud they chose the high road over beating one another up in the holding pens. We turn to head out of the open-air barn with Cooter and Roy on each side of us when we hear Cooter's inquisitive voice speak up. "Hey, Boss?"

"Yeah, Cooter?" I reply. It's been a long-running joke that I am the "boss" (because I'm typically more of the buzzkill and fun squasher), and Shep is one of them and their friend, so they took to calling me Boss a few years ago.

"Can I borrow a hundred bucks? I bet True Walker that we'd beat him and his top hand. I thought that was a safe bet." He halfway shoots a side-eye at Roy, and I try not to laugh. Leave it to these boys who want for nothing-- free room, board, meals, transportation, and clothing-- to try to make easy money that they don't really need off what should have been a done deal.

"Sure, you can. I've got a backyard full of Crabcake and Beignet piles with your name on 'em."

"Dang it, Roy. I always have to do gross stuff 'cause of you."

———

"So, have they figured anything out yet? What's the latest update?" A few days later, Mandy and Lucy are both seated at our island with cups of coffee and a plate of shortbread cookies in between them. I pour myself a cup of coffee over frothed salted caramel creamer as I look out the kitchen window into the backyard. Cooter and Roy are both milling around the backyard begrudgingly picking up dog poop with shovels and dumping it into an old five-gallon bucket lined with a trash sack. Crabcake and Beignet are laying at the opening of their large dog house shaped like a log cabin in the corner of the yard with big drooly grins on their faces, like seeing Cooter and Roy do their bidding is one of the funniest things they've ever seen.

The girls are out in the barn turned workout gym/ basketball court practicing cheers, and Hayes and Carlisle have taken fishing poles down to one of our bigger ponds on the property, so just us moms are getting a little coffee chat without constant pre-teen interruption.

I lean against the counter on the opposite side and take a sip of coffee. "Not that I've heard. But I think I'm out of the loop at this point like Shep said. They have no reason to share any info with me. I feel like someone has to know something, but I haven't quite figured out who that someone might be, you know?"

"Maybe it truly was like an accidental coincidence? Like the doc that prescribed the Digitron didn't know about the statin and it was an honest mistake?" Mandy offered, ever the optimist. She offers a weak smile and a shrug, and I take a moment to admire her naïveté.

"Maybe. I think they're trying to believe that because it's a lot less work than figuring all of this out. But, that's part of the suspiciousness: no one can find the prescribing doctor of the Digitron. It's not on the pill bottle."

"Isn't that illegal? Like doesn't it have to have certain information on the label for it to be a legit prescription?" Lucy points out, ever the pessimist. Hanging out with these two is about like hanging out with the two different versions of your conscience on your shoulder telling you two opposite points of view.

"It's been so long since I've dealt with that, I don't even remember." I pause for a second and then perform a quick Google search just to allay our collective curiosity. "Okay, this says prescriptions are required by the FDA to have the pharmacy information, doctor information, description of the drug, instructions for use, number of pills, dates for use, number of refills, and pharmacy prescription ID number."

"Okay, what do you remember being on the label?"

"Well... like a sketchy online pharmacy name, and his name. Maybe a number of pills," Lucy pulls a sheet of scratch paper from pad of sticky notes in the middle of the counter to take notes. Mandy hands her a Red Rock Cattle pen from the cup on the counter of the built-in buffet to her right as I try to remember as much as I can. "Oh, wait! I snapped a picture when they weren't looking!" I dive for my phone and flip quickly through my pictures until I find a shot of the pill bottle from in between interrogations while Cason Phillips took a potty break.

I frown as I try to read the details of the label, zooming in and out, but not gleaning as much as I hoped because it's so blurry. I rummage through the basket of random items in the junk drawer under the coffee bar and come up with a pair of readers that might help.

"Since when do you wear glasses?" Lucy asks incredulously, her eyebrows shooting up as I set clear square framed glasses at the tip of my nose to try to get a better look.

"Since 1996, aka sixth grade. But Shep and I both got Lasik while he was in residency. Now it's starting to fade, and I'm needing readers, which is truly cruel. Anyway, I don't think I can make anything out after all that. What do y'all think?" I slide my phone across the counter, and Mandy and Lucy crowd around it. After a few seconds, Mandy holds out a hand and I pass the readers on to her.

"We did residency Lasik, too." She rests them up on her nose, and furrows her eyebrows. Mandy's husband Brett is an ear, nose, and throat physician. We initially met in a group for physician's wives and became fast friends because our kids are the same ages and genders. They have a side business running Airbnb's in the area and hope to have Brett out of medicine in the next few years, just like Shep.

"That looks like maybe E-Z Scripts? What do you think?" Lucy asks, sliding it closer to Mandy. "Is that a thing?"

I cross the kitchen and pop into the office to grab my laptop off my desk. After opening it and booting it up, I open an internet browser and google the possible pharmacy name. "It's a real pharmacy. Does that have his DOB?"

"No, but I think his obit did," Mandy replies, pulling out her own phone for more googling. "This says March 17, 1949."

I grab the cordless landline off the cradle and punch in the 1-800 number listed on the contact page for this online pharmacy. "What are you doing?" Lucy stage whispers, as I wait through a series of rings until someone picks up on their end.

"Yes, hi, my name is Dr. Molly Jones, with Baker's Pharmacy of Abilene, Texas. We have a patient here with a prescription from your pharmacy needing a refill, and we just need to verify how many refills are available on this script." Mandy and Lucy both give me impressed looking nods, and I hold my breath a little to see if this is going to work.

"Ma'am, you will need to check with the prescribing physician for that information," A bored-sounding, nasally voice drones through the speaker. "Is that all?"

"That's just the thing, ma'am. There is no prescribing physician listed on this bottle. There are several key required pieces of information missing from this label. I was hoping you could answer this for me without me having to file a complaint with the state board of pharmacy." I clearly enunciate the last four words, hoping to get my point across. My peanut gallery continues with their nods, and adds small, silent golf claps.

There is a long moment of silence. "Full name of the patient."

"Richard Francis MacDougal- M-A-C-D-O-U-G-A-L."

"Date of birth."

"3-17-1949."

"One moment, please." The line abruptly cuts to an aggressively peppy hold music and I look up to see Mandy and Lucy dancing a little in their seats. I try not to laugh, and focus on what they might ask me next.

"Ma'am, are you still there?" The whiplash of going back to the operator's loud, irritated drawl from the upbeat music makes me almost drop the phone, and I take a second to regain my composure before answering.

"Yes, still here."

"I think you called the wrong pharmacy. We have no record of a patient by that name."

We all sit in silence for a moment, dumbfounded. "Are you sure? I clearly have a pill bottle here with a label from E-Z Scripts, for Digitron with that name, but no other information, including refills or dosage. Where else would this have come from?"

"Ma'am, I'm not authorized to give out patient sensitive information, but I can tell you we do not have a patient by that name in our system, which means that prescription did not come from us."

"What does that mean?"

"Sounds like your patient there is a bit of a pill popper and took someone else's prescription and put a fake label on it, if you ask me. It's not rocket science to steal someone's logo off the internet and make a label, ma'am. But if my supervisor asks, I didn't say that."

"This isn't a narcotic or any other medication someone would want to take; what is the point of taking someone else's heart failure medication?"

"Beats me, ma'am. Why don't you ask the patient since he's there trying to get a refill? Is there anything else I can help you with?"

I sigh and try not to sound as defeated as I feel. "No, I think that's everything. Thank you anyway." I hang up the call and return the phone to its cradle. I slump against the counter, looking at my two shoulder guardians wondering what we're going to do next.

"Well, I think that answers a big question," Mandy says softly. Lucy and I both look at her confusedly.

"How so? That didn't tell us anything about the doctor or dosage or where he got this medication. She was less than help-ful. Maybe you should file that complaint after all," Lucy griped, plucking a shortbread rectangle off the stack and taking a bite sulkily.

"I hate to be negative, but Lucy's kind of right. She didn't really tell us anything. It sounds like anyone can make a fake label for a pill bottle. Although, I don't think it's grounds to get her in trouble," I reply, giving Luce a bit of a raised eyebrow. Mandy shakes her head with increasing intensity as a slow smile spreads across her face. She has always been quiet, timid, and reserved, very rarely asserting her opinion, even when she is completely right and everyone around her knows it. I like to think she's gained a little confidence since she became friends with us, and hopefully not that Lucy and I dampen her self-assurance with our more outspoken personalities.

"No, she told you exactly what we were wondering: this wasn't a coincidence or an accident. That's not his prescription. Someone gave Mr. MacDougal those pills on purpose and he didn't need them. That is the confirmation. He was for sure murdered."

"WAIT, WHERE ARE Y'ALL GOING?" I ask, tossing bottles of water into a Yeti backpack cooler as Shep refills his travel coffee mug. Despite the fact that it's four in the morning, Shep is bright-eyed and bushy-tailed in starched Wrangler jeans and a deep red Game Guard button down shirt with the double R Red Rock brand embroidered in white on the left chest pocket. This is basically his official ranch uniform, the sign that he is about to go out and do some real ranch work. Since becoming a full-time rancher, he has leaned into the rancher diet: coffee all day long, including a cup as soon as he gets up, and one for heading out the door. Through the open kitchen window shutters I see headlights, then Cooter and Roy jump out of their Red Rock truck with the horse trailer attached and head toward the side door into the house.

"Mornin', Mrs. Molly," Roy says quietly as he and Cooter head straight for the coffee bar. I've set out foil wrapped breakfast burritos filled with sausage, eggs, and cheese next to the half full pot of coffee and the boys each grab a few after filling their thermoses.

"Good morning, boys. Where are we off to ranch this

morning?" I ask again, noting that the boys are also in their Red Rock embroidered shirts and jeans not completely covered in stains.

"True called and said they secured a new lease property and they need help gathering their large cow/calf herd to drive to the new place. When we finish there, I've got fifteen recip heifers that are ready to transfer," Shep replies, nodding toward the back room of our house, known as the 'lab'. A few years ago, Shep went through courses in artificial insemination, ultrasound, and embryo transfer, and now regularly flushes embryos and transfers them to recipient cows and heifers to improve genetics more quickly. "What do y'all have going today?"

"It's Thursday, just a normal day of school drop off/ pick up. Will y'all be through here for lunch?"

"I'm going to plan on it, but we'll see how long this drive takes. If we end up looking like we won't make lunch, I'll call," He kisses me on the cheek as he heads out to his truck. Roy and Cooter both give me fist bumps as they follow him out to their truck. A few minutes later, I see both trucks head out the long gravel driveway and west toward the Shoemaker ranch.

Time to get to work.

Later that morning, after dropping the kids at Buffalo Creek Intermediate School, I take a slow roll through our small local coffee shop for a salted caramel latte, and head down to the county records and appraisal district office. The question of who would get Dick MacDougal's land if he were gone has loomed large in my head for the last few days, and I am hoping the fine people of Crawford CAD can help me out.

"Good morning, Rhonda!" I bounce through the front door up to the reception counter to find Rhonda Avett, a redhead in her mid-fifties, seated at a desk a few feet back from the counter in front of an older desktop computer, clearly scrolling social media. It's only 8:15, and she's obviously checked out for the day already. Rhonda was the secretary at the elementary school for a few years when our kids were there, so I got to know her a little bit just from volunteering, checking kids in and out, and dropping off forgotten lunch boxes. She decided small kids were maybe not her cup of tea a year or so ago and moved over to county records where she likely has to do very little actual work and can do a decent amount of exactly what she's doing right now.

"Molly Jones, what are you doing here? I haven't seen you in forever! How are you, girl?!" She jumps from her seat to give me an awkward hug over the counter and I am silently relieved she still seems to consider us pretty good friends as this will hopefully make this slightly easier.

"I'm doing well, how about you?" I reply, maintaining my upbeat smile while rehearsing my story in my head. I set my tote bag on the floor and lean on the counter as she perches herself back in her little nest of a desk chair.

"Oh, I'm doing good! You know Hunter graduated last year and is up in Denton for now, but he's thinking about transferring to Lubbock next year. How are your littles? I can't believe they aren't in elementary anymore!"

"I know, time has just flown by! They are doing well. Mia just made cheerleader for 7th grade next year, and Hayes is locked in on baseball season right now. You know how that goes. I'm honestly surprised y'all aren't busier this morning! I was expecting a long line and wait!"

"Oh, girl, it is dead in here all the time. Nobody comes in here except the week we take property tax appraisal protests.

Whatcha need?" Rhonda minimizes her social media screen and looks up at me expectantly.

"Well, I'm hoping you can help me out. Shep and I are looking at leasing a few properties a bit to the south of us, but we were wanting to look up the tax appraisals just so we can make a fair offer for the leasing. Is it possible for me to just pop in the records room and take a peek? It's a handful of different properties so I don't want you to have to look it all up for me and take up all your time." I am hopeful that my promise of doing any requested work for her will be enough to convince her to let me have free rein in the room alone. She hesitates, like she knows she probably shouldn't let me back there unattended, but there is what looks like a bodice ripper romance novel laying open spined on her desk, and a half-eaten sleeve of powdered sugar donuts sitting next to a large mug of coffee that seem to be calling her name. "I promise I'll be super quick! I just told Shep I'd knock this out today so he can send over the offer by the end of the week."

She hesitates again for another brief moment, and then nods and comes around her desk to the small hip-height door connecting the counter to the wall. She unlatches it and winks at me before pointing to a narrow hallway to the right of the door, with dingy gray and brown mottled carpet leading to the records rooms. "Records are in order by county road number or alphabetically. Just put everything back where you find it and I'll be right here if you need anything." She points back to her desk before moving around it to sit back down. I nod back with an equally conspiratorial wink and head down the hall.

I flip an old, yellowed light switch inside the property records room and a dim overhead bulb weakly lights up. The medium sized room is lined with vertical, dark wood paneling and wide floor-to-nearly-ceiling filing cabinets. I run my eyes along the small, neatly-typed labels on each drawer until I find the one that has documents for our address, and theoretically, the MacDougals' across the road. I carefully roll out the large drawer and walk my fingers down the file labels until I come across 1820 County Road 439, our address, and then back up to 1235 County Road 439 and pull the file.

There is a small, round, honey wood table in the middle of the room, and I pull out one of the heavy matching chairs to sit while I scan over the MacDougal file. Nothing seems much out of the ordinary-- the original MacDougals homesteaded that property in the 1860s, just as Mr. MacDougal said, with total property size of 11,520 acres, approximately 18 sections. The current owner listed is the MacDougal Family Trust, with beneficiaries/ current owners listed as 50% "heir(s) of Richard Francis MacDougal" and 50% "heir(s) of Charles Thomas MacDougal". That's interesting, since neither one has heirs that anyone knows of. How are imaginary and unknown people current owners of 18 sections of land? Also, 18 sections! It's a well-known ranching faux pas to ask a rancher how many head of livestock or how many acres of land they own-- that's essentially asking their current net worth. While everyone was semi-aware of MacDougal's land borders, the exact acreage has always been a decent mystery. This is also further evidence of what a miser he was: 18 sections of land could support 450-500 head of cattle. He hadn't ranched in at least five years and could have made an easy living leasing the grazing rights, not to mention really helping many ranchers who need more space to graze, but he called the sheriff the second anything four-legged accidentally stepped on his property.

I snap a few pictures with my phone of the paperwork in the file and slowly close it. Are there any MacDougal heirs? Or is this a mistake or shortsighted planning by previous genera- tions that didn't actually come to fruition? After sliding the property file back in its spot, I make sure the rest of the room is tidy, and peek my head out into the hall. Judging by the different music or narration about every fifteen seconds, Rhonda is clicking through short videos on social media again, flipping from recipes to "get ready with me" videos to videos meant to be joking skits. I feel comfortable rolling the dice and making it a few doors down to the birth and death records room.

I quietly open the old wooden door marked "BIRTH AND DEATH RECORDS 1968-1988" and let myself in, only partially closing the door behind me to help me keep an ear out for a change in Rhonda's location. This is such a curveball that I stand in front of the filing cabinets lining these walls and take a minute to figure out what I might even be looking for at this point.

After taking a deep breath, I start out around the 1980 mark of the birth records and flip through to the M section, as records are organized by date, and then alphabetically by father's name. Nothing in 1980, 1981, or 1982. I hear a brief pause in Rhonda's noise, and move to quickly put everything away, but the cacophony of social media noise starts up again. I skip through rapidly to 1983 and am actually shocked to find something: the birth certificate for Evangeline Lily MacDougal, born on February 12, 1983, to Richard and Linda MacDougal. This must be the baby Billie mentioned that passed away a few hours after birth. Then, a little further back in the file, there is a faded birth certificate for a baby boy born to Charles Thomas MacDougal and Wendy Foster, with the given name of Thomas Foster Hodges, on December 21, 1983. I snap a quick picture of this and push it back in the drawer before flying across the room to the death certificates. *Did Charles MacDougal know he had a son? Did Dick and Linda know they had a nephew? Where is Thomas Hodges now? Does he know he's a 50% heir to 18 sections of ranchland? Does he become 100% if there is no heir on Richard's side? Why does he have a totally different last name than either of them?* Questions pinball around my head as I quickly run fingers through the death certificate drawer, working forward from February 1983, knowing he would have at least been alive at that time for conception of this pregnancy. After about a minute of searching, I stop at May 1983 on a certificate for Charles Thomas MacDougal, date of death May 28, 1983, cause of death as primary pneumonia. There is no spouse listed, with his marital status marked as single. I take a second to do some quick mental math while snapping a picture of this as well. *So, whoever Wendy was, she would have been about two, two and a half-ish months pregnant when Charles passed away. Did Charles know? Or did she even know at this point? Billie made Charles sound like a total invalid that passed young, but the death certificate says he was 26 years old, almost 27 at the time of death, and clearly could somewhat get around. Was Wendy a known girlfriend, or just a fling?*

I slide the death certificate back in its file and take a moment to process as I make sure all the drawers are slid back into their cabinets and the room looks undisturbed. I think I have enough information to start moving in the right direction and want to get out before I overstay my welcome and get caught. I quietly close the door behind me and head back to the front counter, hopeful that a short, unobtrusive stint here will potentially buy me more time here later if I need it.

"Thanks so much for letting me look, Rhonda! I'll see you later!" I say chipperly as I let myself out the door and into the lobby, hoping she doesn't ask any questions or want to pry any information about what I was supposedly looking for or found.

"No problem, girl, any time!" She replies, waving a donut in the air while keeping her eyes locked on her computer screen. I head back out into the parking lot, and check my watch. It's about 10:30, which means I have about an hour to get home and get lunch put together before Shep and the boys should be back. I'd better get a move on if I want to get all that done without anyone realizing I took a little unexpected field trip this morning.

As I drive out of town and head toward our house, I let my mind wander to the known facts as I accelerate down the highway. I'm jolted from my thoughts by my car briefly stuttering as I speed up. I frown at the dashboard and pull my foot off the gas, and then put it down a little more to see if the ol' girl will do it again or keep speed. As it shifts from 5th to 6th gear, it stutters again for a brief moment, and then moves on through up to 10th for the rest of the drive. Well, here's hoping I can ignore that until it goes away.

⬛

"Alright, boys, chicken bacon quesadillas and chips and dips. Roy, whatcha want to drink?" I ask, setting a Fiestaware platter of quesadilla triangles on the island counter next to a large bowl of tortilla chips flanked by three smaller bowls full of salsa, queso, and guacamole. I tried years ago to get away with quick lunches: sandwiches, salads, etc., but these boys were not having it. They prefer a full cooked hot lunch, and my current season of life is being their lunch lady, so we all compromise-- I cook something hot, but it's not usually a full-blown meal for the most part unless I really feel like pulling out all the stops. With my little extracurricular activity in town, I was short on time, so leftover grilled chicken and left-over bacon became quesadillas today. Roy and Cooter eagerly grab melamine plates from the cabinet and help themselves as Shep fills a few glasses with ice from the ice maker.

"I'll take tea if you have it, Mrs. Molly," Roy replies with his mouth half full of quesadilla already.

"Me too, Mrs. Molly," Cooter agrees, and I pull a flower-print pitcher full of freshly brewed sweet tea out of the fridge to add to the glasses Shep just filled. After they are settled, Shep makes his plate and sits at the counter with them and I slide him a glass of tea. I usually wait until they are finished to eat so I can scroll social media while I eat in peace, especially since they are all usually finished eating in ten minutes flat and on to the next activity. My goal with today's lunch scroll is seeing what I can find out about Wendy Foster and Thomas Hodges.

"Did y'all get the Shoemaker cows moved?" I ask, taking a sip of tea as I watch them all devour their lunches silently, just trying to make conversation. Three heads nod and I can tell they'd rather eat than chat, as usual. "Where is this new lease place they got?"

"On 420, kind of catty corner to the east," Shep replies, grabbing another handful of chips from the bowl.

"Like south of MacDougal?"

"I think so? The fences aren't great, but it's got pretty good grass, which is what they need. I didn't realize how bald that place was until we went in to start gathering and moving."

I pause, staring absently at the framed photo of a topographical map of our property hanging on the wall near the door to the office. Knowing what I know now, does MacDougal's 18 sections actually stretch to County Road 420? All this time we assumed the land along that road belonged to someone we didn't know because we didn't know the true size of MacDougal's place, but could it have just belonged to him this whole time? Did True just take over the bottom section of MacDougal's with no one to argue or debate him?

"Molly? Molls? Hello?" I startle back to the conversation when a tortilla chip hits me in the forehead. I turn and Cooter, Roy, and Shep are all staring at me expectantly.

"Uh, sorry, I kind of spaced out a little. What were you

saying?" I smile weakly, wondering exactly what I missed that necessitated hitting me in the face with a chip.

"We need a box of shoulder gloves and some b lube before we can do the transfers this afternoon. The truck is still hooked up to the trailer, so can I take your car up to Allen's to grab some?" Shep looks at me slightly concerned, but I nod and slide him my key fob. "What do you have going on this afternoon?"

"Not much, just paying bills and then school pick up. Will you be back by 2:45?"

"Yes, I need to start transfers by 2, so I'll be back," he replies, jumping up from his stool and kissing me on the cheek before heading out the side door. Roy and Cooter finish the last of their lunches a few minutes later and head into the lab room to start prepping the rest of the supplies they will need. I peek out the front window shutters and see tail lights at the end of the driveway. I know Shep is gone, and the boys are out of my hair, too, so I can safely start googling and social media stalking Thomas Hodges and his mom.

I sit down in front of my computer a few minutes later with a plate full of "girl lunch": fancy crackers, muenster and gouda cubes, sliced strawberries and grapes, and rolled slices of deli turkey and roast beef with another full glass of tea. A quick Google search reveals what I anticipated. A whole slew of Fosters and Hodges pop up, meaning some in depth investigation is going to be needed. I debate back and forth who would be the best initial target, Wendy or Thomas, and decide that Wendy might be able to tell me more about the nature of the situation with Dick, Charles, and Thomas's birth before I jump into questioning Thomas about all he stands to gain with Dick out of the way.

Very little comes up on Facebook about Wendy Foster, just a few posts about the Buffalo Creek Class of 1978 reunions over the years that have more than thirty profiles tagged. But, hers is grayed out like it no longer exists. Just as I take some notes of people she might know that I could potentially ask about her, I hear the side door slam, and Shep appears in the doorway. I quickly minimize my windows and smile at him, wondering why he looks harried and unsettled.

"How long has the transmission in your car been acting up?"

"My what?"

"Your transmission. It dropped out looking for a gear while I was driving and I almost got t-boned pulling out of Allen's because I couldn't get it to move. Has it been acting slow for you?" Shep drops the fob in the large wooden bowl on the island counter and returns to the doorway.

"I guess, but I hadn't thought much of it. It would mainly kind of bottom out for a second then jump back in first thing in the morning taking kids to school. I just thought I wasn't warming it up well enough before we take off. You think something's going on with the transmission? That sounds serious."

"Yeah, hopefully it's just that the fluid or filter needs to be changed. I called Donny and they can take it after you pick up kids from school. Mom is going to pick y'all up from there and you can borrow her car while they are looking at it."

I open my mouth to protest, but Shep has already jogged up the back stairs to change to start his transferring. I glance at the large clock hanging on the wall and see that it is 1:45, so he has to get going. Because of heat cycles and other variables, they are on a very strict schedule to get these transferred to have optimal success.

I frown, staring back at my computer screen, frustrated that my afternoon now looks completely different than I planned. I pull my computer windows back up and scroll back through the posts Wendy Foster has been tagged in, and suddenly a lightbulb goes off as I stop on the post about a forty-year reunion a few years ago. There, next to a grayed-out Wendy Foster's name, is a hyperlink to the profile of Billie Bailey Jones, which is rarely, if ever, used, despite the time I invested to set it up. Looks like my little ride this afternoon could be pretty productive after all.

chapter
nine

"SCOOT OVER, I don't want you to sit that close to me!" Mia screeches as Hayes slides as close as humanly possible to her in the backseat of Billie's powder-blue, two-door Ford Bronco as we prepare to leave the dealership service department a few hours later. I close my eyes and slump down in the passenger seat to help tune out their bickering and am silently thankful that this is happening post car seat era. I might have had an actual mental breakdown if I'd had to put car seats and subsequently tiny humans in and out of the small backseat of this two-door Matchbox car. After a few long seconds, I peek one eye open and into the backseat to see Mia holding Hayes at arm's length via a palm to his forehead and I swat an arm through the backseat at them silently as Billie gets back in the car. Billie grew up with Donny, the owner and manager of the local dealership, so getting her away from it in any manner of timeliness is usually difficult. Although, I'm glad she's taken at least this long so she misses the bulk of the arguing.

"Y'all ready to rock and roll?" she asks chipperly, turning to the kids in the backseat, who are now silent and perfectly content as far away as they can get from one another. I smile weakly and nod, feeling worn out for the day, despite the fact that I haven't accomplished all that much.

Billie exits the dealership and heads out onto the highway toward their house. We will drop her off, and then head back to our house in her car until they can diagnose whatever is going on with mine, and get it fixed. It is a blessing to have this and not be struggling to coordinate transport with Shep, but this is going to severely cut down on my anonymity as I investigate. Billie's baby blue ride is a bit legendary around town.

"Well, did y'all ever hear anything else about Richard? I think the last time I talked to Shep about it, they didn't have enough evidence to rule it any which way. Is that still right?" Billie ventures after a few minutes of silence other than the radio.

"Yes, I think that's the last we heard from Sheriff Cooper. Hey, by any chance do you know someone named Wendy? Wendy Foster?" I ask just as nonchalantly as I can manage. For the better part of twenty years, Billie has always been down to be my sidekick or accomplice in all manner of shenanigans, which are honestly usually shopping or college sports related, not murder. I can't get both of us in trouble with Shep and/or the law, depending on how things go down, but I do think her help could be valuable. Not that I'm planning to get in trouble with the law, but you know, who knows?

"Oh, of course, I know Wendy. We went to school together. Why do you ask?"

I pause and try not to physically cringe at my lack of forethought. *Why am I asking... Do I tell her straight up what I'm doing, or come up with a cover?* "How interested are you in what happened to MacDougal?" On a whim, I decide to go the Jesus route: answer a question with a question and see where it leads me.

She looks a little taken aback by my question, and pauses. "Well... I did grow up with him. It's hard to believe anything bad would happen around here, especially to him, but I am genuinely curious. What do you know, Molly Pop?"

I glance back into the backseat to see Hayes asleep with his head bouncing against the tiny back window, and Mia absorbed in something on her iPad screen with her puffy bright pink headphones over her ears. I have no idea how much they have picked up from all of this going on, or how much they even care, but I am trying to be mindful in attempting not to scar them for life with all of this. As I weigh my options in what to say, what to ask, and how to involve her, the heaviest item on the scale outweighing all the other considerations is the fact that Billie grew up here and knows just about anything you could think of about every living soul in this county. "Okay, I'll tell you what I know if you'll tell me what you know. You down for an adventure?"

▭

"Hi, Wendy? It's Billie! Billie Bailey! How are you, darlin'?" When we get back to Billie and Frank's, Billie jumps into action and looks up an old phone number she has for Wendy Foster. The longer Billie has known a person, the more exaggerated her drawl gets, and she sounds downright Dolly Parton-esque catching up with this mystery woman I can't wait to talk to.

Billie nods and hems and haws as they catch up, and I wait nervously at their kitchen table for her to give me some information. We sent the kids down to the basement to play games for a little bit upon arrival and Billie has jumped into sleuthing with me with both feet, which I appreciate. I've never seen her do anything halfway, and apparently being the Watson to her daughter-in-law's Holmes is no exception.

"Alright, hon, we'll see you tomorrow. 'Bye!" Billie hangs up the phone and turns to me excitedly. "Okay, we're having lunch with her tomorrow at Delilah's." She takes a seat with me at the table and scrawls out the appointment in her traditional cursive writing in the small generic datebook she keeps by her kitchen phone.

"That's great! Why are we meeting her?" I ask, wanting to know our cover story so I can practice and be natural, especially with any potential segue ways into what we really want to talk about.

"We're meeting her to talk about her involvement with Charles, hon," She responds, winking at me like I'm a little dense. I try not to laugh out loud to myself, thankful I've got such focused help.

"Yeah, Billie, I know that and you know that, but I figured we would have some sort of cover story to talk to her, not just everything out and about. I'm not sure I'm really supposed to be involved in this anymore, but clearly, they are not doing everything they should be doing, you know?"

"Oh, right! Well, she is a baker. She does those little sugar cookies with all the designs on them, and I told her you were interested in getting started doing that and I wanted to connect you two."

"That's actually a pretty good cover. Nice work," I comment, nodding approvingly as I take a sip of the sweet tea she poured me when we first got here. She beams from the approval and slides a plate of M&M cookies, her specialty, closer to me.

"Okay, tell me everything I need to know. I thought I knew everything, but clearly, I don't."

▭

The next day, Billie and I pull into the parking lot of Delilah's Café and Bakery, a renovated small cottage home, promptly at 10:45 for our 11:00 lunch date with Wendy Foster. I work to control my heartrate as I start to feel nervous-- more nervous than I have at any other point in this process. For some reason I've just about psyched myself out thinking that this will be my (our) one and only chance to talk with her, and if I mess it up or don't get it right, she'll be a dead end, despite being my current strongest lead. I think Billie can sense my nerves and she calmly pats me on the arm as we park and decide to go ahead in and get a table in the small coffee shop. I had mixed emotions about meeting at Delilah's. It's the best place for lunch in Buffalo Creek, and it isn't super open or loud inside, but there's never a time you go there and don't run into at least five people you know, either inside eating at one of the few tables available or picking up lunch to go. Wendy doesn't know my true intentions of our discussion, but there's a chance as we try to steer things toward more personal matters, she (and we) will be less comfortable in such a public place.

Billie and I settle into a small, square, light oak table for four in the corner of the front room next to the bay window overlooking the quiet side street. I nervously glance out the window watching cars putter by, reminding myself that I don't even know what Wendy looks like, or what she drives, so I won't be able to identify her whether I'm watching for her or not.

"Hey, gals, haven't seen y'all in a while! What are we drinking?" Carrie, daughter of Delilah and current owner/proprietor of Delilah's, rolls by our table as she finishes clearing a table across the room. She pulls a small spiral-bound notebook out of her quilted apron and a pen from over her ear, giving us a big smile. Carrie is in her late fifties, and has been the face of Delilah's for the last ten years but part of the café since she was a child and Delilah first opened the doors. They've kept the same menu of what Shep calls ladies' Bible study brunch food: chicken salad, dainty sandwiches, salads, and soups, for the café's entire life, but when Carrie stepped into a larger role, she brought her dessert expertise with her, and really elevated the bakery side. Large elaborate cakes, homemade cinnamon rolls, hand rolled croissants that are all meticulously made and delicious. I could honestly come here and just eat dessert, but the chicken salad croissant is pretty good too.

"How are ya, girl? I think we'll both have lemonade," Billie replies, popping up to give her a quick hug.

"Sounds good. Are y'all ready to order, or do you need a minute?"

"We have one more coming, so we may wait a few minutes. Do you have strawberry rolls today?" Billie asks, peering around Carrie toward the kitchen and the bakery case near the register with one eyebrow raised mischievously.

"We did this morning, but let me see how many we have left. How many do you want?"

"Just two or three to take home to Frank," Billie answers with a smile, and I silently flash her four fingers, also with a smile, indicating I'd like four to take home as well if she has them. Carrie's strawberry rolls are legendary, like a cinnamon roll, but filled instead with fresh strawberry filling and topped with swirls of homemade cream cheese frosting. I always get four to say I got one for each of us, knowing there is a low likelihood Shep will actually eat his, essentially giving myself two without having to look like a pig ordering two. Carrie nods in understanding and heads back to the kitchen.

I sit nervously watching the front door once Carrie leaves. Billie pulls out her phone and starts scrolling social media as we wait, calm as a cucumber. I stare at her for a brief moment, wondering how she is so nonchalant. In the twenty years we've known one another, calm is rarely, if ever, a word I've used to describe her. I think she can feel me staring at her, and silently puts her phone on the gingham table cloth and stares back at me.

"Molly, it's going to be fine."

"What if she doesn't agree to talk to us or tell us anything?" I quietly shriek back, my nervous energy escaping like steam from a tea kettle.

"Then she doesn't." Billie shrugs as she arranges her silverware set on the table and puts her floral napkin in her lap. I stare at her blankly again, wondering if she gets it at all. Or am I missing something? We are clearly not on the same page and I suddenly feel a modicum more stress than I did a few seconds ago.

Why is this so important to me? Clearly the authorities aren't concerned about it; why am I? It's not like Dick MacDougal was a very dear person to me, or like bringing his killer to justice will bring me immense closure about it all. Why has my Nancy Drew side suddenly kicked in and this is consuming me to the point that I think it's my full-time job and I need to solve this like my life depends on it. The sheriff doesn't even think there's anything to solve, so what am I doing?

Being a mom can be weird at times. It's like you know life can't happen smoothly without you- you find the socks, and pack the snacks, and sign up for summer camps, and know what is being served in the school cafeteria so you know if they need a lunch box or a tray. But at the same time, it's invisible work. It's work that isn't obvious work, typically goes unseen, and often feels unappreciated, even though you know pulling one thread of these things that sometimes feels trivial would collapse it all.

I never felt that way when I worked out of the home. I knew that my work as a pharmacist was noticed, valued, and mattered. It obviously had a different set of challenges, like constantly worrying about having childcare arranged, and having to beg for a few hours off to attend Valentine's parties, and feeling the crushing guilt that your children's precious childhood is flying by at warp speed and you are missing it because you're at work counting someone else's diet pills. That work doesn't feel so important then, but it was at least seen. My family is amazing, and I've never once felt like they don't appreciate me, but you do start to feel a little invisible in society as a stay-at-home mom. And maybe that's my why. To show everyone that us girls at home that few seem to notice can notice a few things of our own.

"I believe you that something is going on, Molly. And I believe that you are going to figure this out. If Wendy talks to us, that's great. If she doesn't, we'll figure it out some other way. You've always accomplished anything you've set your mind to, and if there is something here that others are missing, you are going to find it. Don't psyche yourself out that this is the only way," I tear up a little at Billie's encouragement, and just as she is about to continue, we hear the small tinkle of the bell attached to the front door.

"Hi, Billie, how are you?" A petite older blonde in neat linen pants and a striped knit sweater tentatively walks up to our table. Billie and I exchange a bit of a look; my face likely looks completely bewildered and hers is a solid look of "get it together, man!" as Wendy pulls out a chair and takes a seat at our table.

"Wendy, this is my daughter-in-law, Molly," Billie starts, gesturing toward me. Wendy flashes me a shy smile, and I stare at her for a brief moment wondering why she actually looks familiar.

"Yes, we've actually met," She answers quietly, waiting a few seconds to see if I'm going to figure it out.

"Do you work at the elementary school?" I ask, thinking this is the most likely and least troublesome place I can come up with, hoping I get it right on the first guess. Her kind eyes and quiet demeanor track for being an elementary teacher.

"I was the librarian at the elementary school for a while. I was married back then and went by that name, Wendy

Hodges. We divorced a few years ago, and I switched back to my maiden name a year or two ago. I retired just after the divorce so I think most people still remember me as Mrs. Hodges," She replies, nodding slightly as Carrie appears and sets down three lemonades on our table. "Hey, Carrie. I've got tomorrow's orders in my car. I'll grab them after we finish lunch."

Carrie nods, taking out her notepad to write down our orders. "What will it be, ladies?"

"I'll have the chicken salad croissant, please," I say, handing her my single page laminated menu. Billie and Wendy both agree, handing her their menus, and Carrie leaves to start on our lunch.

"How old are your kiddos now, Molly?"

"Mia is twelve, and Hayes is ten. They are finishing up sixth and fourth grade."

"That's wonderful. I remember Mia being quite a reader."

"Yes, she loves to read, although now we're in this fun stage where the books considered "young adult" are a little racier than I'd prefer. Hayes wouldn't touch a book with a ten-foot pole if he could help it," I laugh nervously.

"Oh yes, I had a boy like that," Wendy chuckles, and I instantly think *Thank you, Lord!* for such a seamless transition.

"How old is your son? Does it get better, or should I throw away his lifetime library card now?" I joke, trying not to nervously play with the paper straw in my lemonade. I realize in that moment that the bottom of the straw is disintegrating in my drink, and I frown a little as I pull it out and set it on a napkin next to me.

"Aren't those paper straws the worst?" Wendy comments, doing the same with hers. "My Thomas is forty, and I would say I learned early on that he wouldn't be an overly active library patron and it didn't really change. But he seems to have made something of himself, so I excused his lack of love for reading." She winks at me and gives me a kind smile. *Okay, Molly, time to get down to business. Your opening is right there.*

"Oh, he's about our age! Does he live around here, too?" *Play it cool, play it cool, don't be over-eager...*

A barely perceptible sadness comes over Wendy's face and she shakes her head slightly. "No, he went to the east coast for college, and then ended up wanting to live close to his dad. I was always the third wheel with them when he was growing up, and then after we split up, Thomas made it abundantly clear who he'd rather be closer to. They all live in Massachusetts. That's where Peter grew up and always wanted to go back."

I pause, trying to figure out all the details, careful not to reveal what I think I already know. "Peter is your..."

"Ex-husband. We lived in Ivy City for most of our married life, and moved back to Buffalo Creek a few years before the divorce to take care of my mother when her health started failing. She passed away a few years ago."

"Oh, I'm sorry to hear that, Wendy. Mrs. Foster was always so sweet to us when we were growing up," Billie offers. "Is Thomas an only child?"

"Yes, we actually jumped the gun a little bit, if you know what I mean, so we got married a few months before Thomas was born. We always meant to have more, but it just never worked out. After Thomas had been out of the house for a few years, Peter felt like we had nothing connecting us anymore and wanted out. Turns out you can be married to someone for thirty-five years and it still doesn't last. He went back to the northeast when we split up and Thomas joined him. We had moved to east Texas for a while when Thomas was growing up and came back here right after he graduated high school. That's when I started at the elementary school."

I take another moment of pause to process what I knew

prior and what she is telling us now. Her story is that she and Peter Hodges conceived Thomas out of wedlock and then married before he was born, no mention of Charles MacDougal at all. So why is Peter not on his birth certificate? I make a mental note to go back this week to see my BFF Rhonda at the records office to see if there is a corrected birth certificate somewhere for Thomas, or some other explanation.

"How did you and Peter meet?" I ask, trying to sound the most casual, but knowing it's a bit of a stretch. "Shep and I met at a study table at the library in our first year of graduate school. My guilty pleasure hobby is learning how couples met." I add on a timid smile, hoping she'll just go for it and it won't be as weird to answer as it's felt for me to ask.

She shoots me a tentative glance, like she's sizing up whether to trust me. I don't blame her; we are essentially strangers. I'm trusting her to trust me on the basis that she and Billie grew up together but essentially haven't been close in 15+ years.

"We met when we were teenagers. He was a cousin of my best friend growing up and would come down from New England to visit them in the summers. Do you know the MacDougals?" I choke a little on my lemonade and nod. *Do I tell her that we are in fact close, very close, to the MacDougals, or give it a little space to see what she says?* My only detective training is watching any and all episodes of *Monk*, *Castle*, and *Midsomer Murders* since I was a teenager, and I'm now feeling like that's not going to be enough to help me know what to do and say in this situation.

"Um, yes, our ranch is actually across the county road from the MacDougal homestead," I venture, trying not to say too much in hopes that she will fill in some blanks she doesn't know I already know.

"Oh, so you've been in the middle of all the investigation and mess with Richard's death lately, haven't you?" She tuts, and I inwardly cringe a little, not wanting to wander down that road. I know she wasn't friends with Richard, and I don't need to hear much about him right now.

Carrie appears just then with three plates of chicken salad croissants accompanied by homemade potato chips. After passing them out, she adds two boxes of strawberry rolls to the middle of the table, and disappears again. I take a few bites of my sandwich before jumping back in to our conversation.

"Yes, Richard's passing has been a little wild the last week or so," I start, not sure how to describe it. While I think we all collectively agree it doesn't suck that much that he's gone, that's really not a great look to be the one to actually come out and say it.

"He was always the absolute worst, and I'm honestly sure no one will miss him, darlin'," Wendy waves a hand toward me before picking up a potato chip between her freshly manicured fingers. I choke again on a small bite, once again initially shocked by her answer.

"So, I take it Richard wasn't your best friend growing up?" I squeak out, taking the opportunity to steer the conversation back to, fingers crossed, Charles.

"No, Charlie and I were two peas in a pod. I had a severe speech impediment as a child, and I went to private speech therapy a few times a week. Charlie was there almost every day for physical and occupational therapy after his accident, so he and I got to know each other there and stayed close as we grew up. I met Peter when we were about sixteen and he came to visit for a few weeks that summer. Peter's mother is Charlie and Richard's aunt, their father's sister. She was disinherited by their parents for moving away and marrying Peter's father."

"Oh, my goodness. That sounds like something that only happens in movies or soap operas," I interject, a little carried away in the drama. I mentally make notes that there would have been another heir included in the mix had Peter's mother not followed her heart. *Could there have been some jealousy that Richard and Charles ended up as the only named heirs? When's the last time either of the Hodges boys came to Texas from New England?*

"Honey, you don't know the half of it."

chapter
ten

"THAT'S IT, Warriors! Keep your eyes up!" A few days later, in the sweltering early evening spring heat, moms in assorted setups of lawn chairs and umbrella canopies line the chain link fence of the Buffalo Creek Little League field as the fourth-grade Warrior all-star team takes the field for the top of the sixth inning. Never a crowd to be quiet, the chain link peanut gallery is yelling all manner of encouragement and advice as the boys are one run down at this point. Most of the dads are seated in the covered bleacher seats on either baseline, or standing behind the bleachers around various coolers. Before my kids got into youth sports, I would have confidently said it's the dads that make scenes at sporting events, and to be fair, occasionally they do. But there's no mama bear like a youth sports mama bear, and no one is as opinionated as a youth sports mama bear.

Hayes has been playing baseball since he was three and could barely lift the tiny tee ball bat to make contact with the ball, but has loved it since then. He plays in the area Little League, and toward the end of the spring each year, an all-star team is chosen to compete against other area teams. This game kicks off the all-star schedule, and we'll melt at these all-star games for most of the summer.

Over the years, I've seen a lot of things, like personal tents, chairs with built in umbrellas, chairs that double as coolers, coolers that could be chairs, sleeping bags that you wear (which isn't typically needed by this time of year), and all sorts of unimaginable gear from the more experienced sports moms. I never played sports growing up, so I had no frame of reference going in with my kids, and with Mia being my first, I was spoiled to air-conditioned studios and auditoriums after years of ballet. Once Hayes got into baseball and we started 'lawn chair sports', I had to learn to handle the elements in a variety of creative and different ways. The in-fashion set up this year is the rocking lawn chair with an umbrella attachment just large enough that parents who choose to sit in the bleachers have somewhat of a hard time seeing over the spread. I just couldn't bring myself to wrestle that to the field multiple times a week, so Shep and I are seated on the top row of the metal bench seats in tastefully-sized stadium cushions, leaning against the chain link back stop behind us. Mia is unenthusiastically seated next to me, as she's already received the canned lecture about how many of her activities Hayes has endured over the years that she can repay him in kind. In typical pre-teenager fashion, she has chosen violence this day in the form of not speaking to any of us for having to sit out here.

I peer over the top of my Ray Bans to second base, where Hayes is slightly crouched over, preparing to field any ball headed his way. The opposing team's batter walking up looks like someone might have forgotten to check his birth certificate before the start of the game, or his parents have a really good forgery man on staff. I brace myself for this kid to hit an absolute slugger and pray Hayes grabs it if it makes it near him as the pitcher throws a ball for the first pitch. It lands in the catcher's mitt with a thunk, and I take a deep breath while I have the chance. *Strike one.*

I see a bit of a commotion happening behind the opposing team's dugout, but ignore it and focus on this high school freshman pretending to be a fourth grader in the batter's box. Our pitcher slings the ball a little wild, but it still lands in the strike zone with another thunk. *Strike two.*

One more, one more, one more. Some moms are the type that swear their kid can do no wrong, and make no mistakes. I love, adore, and support my kids to the end of the earth, but I am typically the one just praying fervently they do their job well and aren't to blame for any blunders. One of our parenting goals is to raise humans that are considerate, selfless team players. We're probably less successful at that than we'd like to be, but it's a lot easier when your kids are the hero of the team, and not the pariah.

Our pitcher winds up and lets a third pitch fly, and my stomach turns as I hear the crack of the bat as it makes contact with the ball and it sails toward second base. I close my eyes for a brief moment, and then peek one open as Hayes jumps and catches it from the air, then sends it flying to home. His catch was an automatic out of the batter, and his throw allows the runner heading home to be tagged out, preventing another run and ending the inning.

"Way to go, Hayes! Way to make the play! Let's get those runs now, boys! Get the bats hot; let's go!" I jump from my seat and start yelling to the field in excitement until I feel a hand take my hand and start to pull me down. I turn to see Shep silently trying to guide me back into my seat and I frown a little. "It's okay to cheer, you know. He just made an awesome play," I retort as I sit back down, a little huffy that I'm being semi-forcibly sat down.

"Cheering is good, but you were starting to cross into Karen territory. I don't think they need your advice on how to pull ahead," Shep chuckles, adjusting his Warriors baseball cap and giving a small wave to an older man a few rows in front of us who has turned to stare. I believe he is the longtime owner of the local cattle auction barn, and I give him a sheepish smile, hoping Shep reined me in before I truly embarrassed myself.

As the teams prepare to head back out from their respective dugouts, the commotion behind the opposing team gets louder. One of the assistant coaches is trying to calm down a platinum blonde facing away from me, but her tiny denim cut-off shorts look vaguely familiar. The coach looks progressively irritated as she increases her volume and hand gestures. Even Mia looks up from her FaceTime conversation with Emily and winces as the three of us are now more invested in this than our first batter heading to the box to kick off the bottom of the sixth. "This is so cringe. I feel so bad for Hainslee," she mutters to her phone, as she has turned her camera so Emily can see what's going on. She quickly ends her FaceTime after I give her a stern look.

"Hainslee? How is she related to this?" I ask quietly a few moments later, just as the coach pushes away from the blonde and she turns for me to see her profile. Becki Lane looks fit to be tied, and I have no idea why, but I'm suddenly really craving some popcorn in this moment.

"That's Hainslee's dad... Her bio dad." As if reading my mind, Mia digs through our baseball Bogg bag and hands me an individual size bag of Boom Chicka Pop before opening one for herself and pointing to the coach. "He lives in Ivy City and H said her mom was going to catch him this weekend when he is in town for this game. His son with his real family plays on this team."

"Real family?" I ask incredulously, because clearly, I don't know a dang thing about Becki Lane's life.

"Yeah, he was married when he got Coach Lane pregnant

with Hainslee. He and his wife worked it out and stayed together, and that's his son," she explains as she discreetly points to the short stop. "She has a half-brother and two half-sisters. Apparently, he's never really had any contact with her, but her mom is wanting him to pay some old child support. He won't answer her texts or calls, so H said she was going to make him talk to her today."

"I thought Coach Lane is married?" I say, taking a sip of flavored water from my large tumbler and trying to eat my popcorn daintily. Her husband is some sort of oil field salesman or something, one of those careers where he is gone often, and she never seems to act like they miss him.

"She is. That's Hainslee's step dad, but she tries not to tell people he's a step."

What in the Peyton Place is going on, and why do all these sixth graders know all this? I make a mental note to text Mandy and Lucy about this ASAP. He clearly adopted her at some point because they all have the same last name, so why would she be pestering him for child support? I try for the life of me to remember Becki Lane's husband's name but I feel like I can think of every name around it that doesn't sound quite right. It's Troy. No...Travis. No, that's not it. It's...

"Your son is up to bat, just in case you're interested," Shep interjects, and I jerk my wandering attention to the batter's box. Hayes walks up confidently and crouches down in position with his bat hovering steadily over his right shoulder. The pitcher lets one go, and it's strike one.

"Eye on the ball, Hayes! You got this!" I yell out to him, sitting on my hands to keep them from flailing into everyone's faces as I try to calm my nerves. Shep gives me a look to remind me that my commentary isn't needed, and I wave a dismissive hand to him that I'll keep a lid on my crazy.

The second pitch comes out and it's a ball. We repeat this process three more times until the count is loaded-- three balls, two strikes-- and it's Hayes's last pitch. I hold my breath as the last pitch comes through and Hayes makes contact with it. It's a shallow hit to left field, but it's enough to get him to first base, and for me to breathe again. Once he is safely on first base, I see him search the stands and then give a small wave in our direction. I return in kind with a massive wave and double fisted thumbs up with a giant grin until Shep quietly puts a steadying hand on my thigh. "I'm sorry, these crazy baseball moms are rubbing off on me," I reply, taking a deep breath and sitting back in my spot. He nods silently, neither agreeing nor disagreeing, and keeps his attention on the field.

The Warriors manage to get three batters over home plate before three outs, and win the game by 2 runs. As we are packing up to head out, it seems that Becki is trying once more to accomplish what she came here to do. She has cornered this man against the backstop behind home plate, and is making quite a scene as both teams' fans are exiting the stands.

"Listen, Trent, you have a responsibility! I've raised her for twelve years without a dime from you, but we need it now, and it's time for you to step up! Stop ignoring me and do the right thing!"

"Becki, I told you before you had her that I was out. I have my own family, and I told you not to put me on the birth certificate. I signed away my rights, and she's your husband's now. Stop trying to hound me for a few hundred bucks from 2012. Get over yourself and quit trying to ruin everyone else's lives because you aren't happy." He slings a bat bag up on his shoulder and turns to walk away from her. She stomps a tiny flip-flopped foot in a rage and hesitates a few seconds before yelling after him.

"This isn't over!" Mia and I look at each other uneasily and wait to see if he turns around to answer her. He doesn't even flinch as he continues to walk away, refusing to acknowl-edge anything happened behind him. Shep has already walked on to go wait by the home dugout for Hayes, but Mia and I can't help but continue to stand and stare dumbstruck at the train wreck that has unfolded in front of us, arms full of snack bags and stadium cushions. Becki does a quick semi-circle turn to see most of the remaining crowd watching her, and angrily flees to her white Yukon Denali parallel parked on the curb next to the field. Now probably isn't the time to tell her that the Little League Association has repeatedly chided patrons for parking there and in that manner, but chances are she doesn't know and doesn't care. We all know how she feels about vehicle related rules.

Mia is a few steps ahead of me as I turn and walk to the home dugout to meet up with Shep and Hayes. As I walk behind her, my mind wanders back to the last time I saw Dick MacDougal alive. None other than Becki Lane was there, and she had some sort of connection to him. Clearly not a favorable one, as he was not thrilled in the least to see her. The lead of Charles's long- lost heir has some heat, especially after our lunch with Wendy Foster- Hodges- Foster but maybe the next thread I should be chasing is where in the world Becki Lane and Dick MacDougal make a Venn diagram. Who knows? It might even have something to do with this long overdue child support request and these obvious daddy issues.

"Hayes William, what a game!" I exclaim as I catch up with my three back on our side of the field. Hayes has quietly exited the dugout and I immediately envelop him in a bear hug. "We're so proud of you!"

"Thanks, Mom. Can we go home now?" He asks, extricating himself and heading in the direction of the truck with his bat bag hoisted up on his shoulders. Shep follows silently behind him, and I take one last look toward the opposite side of the parking lot before following Mia behind Shep and Hayes. Becki Lane's baby daddy (oof, I wish I had any other way to describe him!) is now having what looks like a heated argument with a different blonde, presumably his wife. This one is wearing the same neon green Ivy City t-shirt as him with black leggings, and her dark blonde hair is pulled back in a sleek ponytail. She looks less harried and more controlled than Becki, like she is skilled at keeping it all together without a big fuss. She has all the typical baseball mom accoutrements: a large tumbler, oversized sunglasses, a large stadium seat, and a Bogg bag full of snacks, sunscreen, and bug spray. By any other standards, she and I don't look all that different on the outside, but I'm suddenly washed over by a feeling of gratitude looking at her because Shep Jones would never put me in that situation. I know you should never say never, but Shep Jones would never. That woman chose forgiveness, for whatever reason, all those years ago, and her family has been putting together and holding together broken pieces ever since. Today, all those pieces were harshly exposed to light, and she has to now deal with the aftermath of everyone seeing inside their cracked, but repaired, façade. If we're honest, if this guy wanted nothing to do with Becki and Hainslee after she was born, there's a decent chance this isn't a well-known fact, and Becki just outed him in front of quite a few people he knows, and she now gets to deal with the secondhand embarrassment from this fallout.

I stand and stare for a few more seconds before I hear Hayes call back behind me. I snap out of my nosiness and hustle out to the truck in the parking lot. We didn't want to all squeeze into Billie's Bronco to come up here, so we're all piled in the ranch truck with Shep's collection of half-drank bottles of water and Yeti tackleboxes full of ear tags, tools, and other cattle equipment. As Shep drives home, I watch the small town of Buffalo Creek disappear through the window, replaced by rolling hills littered with mesquite trees and barbed wire fences. After living here for almost fifteen years, I thought

I knew everything I needed to know, but clearly, I'm just getting started.

"Hey, Donny, how's it going?" The next morning, as I stir creamer into my second cup of coffee, Donny calls to give me an update on my car. Ever an optimist, I'm hopeful he's calling to say that in a matter of just a few days they've not only pinpointed the issue, but also fixed it, and I can come rescue my car today. I've already done school drop off for morning, which included us holding up the line for longer than we intended to as Hayes's backpack got stuck as he climbed out of the backseat. He ended up on his butt on the sidewalk with his backpack wedged between the seats as it stayed and he kept going. After repeated yanking while I encouraged him to get a move on, he finally freed his bag and hurried into the school, more than a little embarrassed. Mia had exited the front seat several yards ahead of him so we're all lucky we didn't second-hand embarrass her and have to deal with her almost teenage wrath. At this point, I'm more than ready to be back to a vehicle with four whole doors and a backseat that can hold more than two small behinds exactly next to one another.

"Hey, Molly, it's going okay. Listen, I'm afraid I have some bad news for you," Donny replies, and I plop down on an island stool, preparing myself for this bad news. I should have known; of course this wasn't going to be simple. Shep slides through the kitchen from the side door, covered in some unidentifiable fluid on his jeans, and heads for the back stairs. I cringe, terrified of where he is planning to put those jeans, knowing in my absolute core that when it rains, it pours. "So, we thought we could just swap out this valve head in the transmission, but when we did that, it's still dropping out of gear.

I'm going to have to order a few more parts and work on it a little longer."

I pause and sigh. "That's fine, Donny, just do whatever you can do. Keep us updated, okay?"

"Will do. Do you want me to talk to Shep?" For years, I've had him explain things directly to Shep so nothing gets lost in translation. I always think I can relay everything with exact precision, and then the second I get off the phone, everything he said drops right out of my head and I botch it every time.

"Well, I just saw him come through, but he looked like he was headed to something important. I'll do my best and have him call you if he has questions."

"Sounds good, I'll talk to him this afternoon," Donny replies before hanging up. I stop for a second, realizing he just implied that I will definitely mess this up, and I frown at the insinuation. I mean, I probably will, but I don't need it pointed out to me.

After slowly climbing the back stairs, I timidly walk through the cracked door to our bedroom, hesitant to see what Shep is doing. I see an old towel laid out on the floor near the closed door to our bathroom with Shep's jeans crumpled on top of it, and I breathe a little easier. I should be able to wrap them up in the towel to carry them to the washing machine. Or the trash can, depending on how bad it actually is. As I kneel down to start picking up the bundle, Shep whips open the bathroom door, and I jump at the unexpected interruption.

"Who were you on the phone with?" He asks breezily, tucking his work shirt into a fresh pair of clean-ish jeans.

"Donny. Apparently, the new valve head wasn't enough and they're going to have to order more parts."

"I'll call him here in a little bit. Prepare yourself; at the rate this is going, I'm betting we don't make it out without a new transmission, and we're not doing that. You might want to start looking at new cars," he says matter-of-factly, and I deflate a little. A whole new car? That seems a little overboard for a simple stutter. As if sensing my hesitation, he continues. "It makes no sense to sink a ton of money into a new transmission knowing that we don't have good luck with transmissions. Do you not remember residency?"

When Shep was in residency, the transmission, inexplicably and without warning, died in his beloved truck he'd had for nearly fifteen years. We scraped together the money to replace it (believe it or not, residents are not paid very well despite their work load), and moved on. Exactly eleven months later (thankfully, as this meant it was still under warranty, whereas it would not have been after a year), the replacement transmission died. We had it replaced again, and saved up for about six months before just replacing his truck entirely with a new one. I know he's right; I don't want to deal with an unreliable vehicle any more than the next person, but I'm not entirely in the headspace to find something completely new out of the blue.

"Well, we'll see. What have you been up to?" I ask, looking from him, to the pile of dirty jeans, back to him.

"We were helping Hank AI some heifers and one got a little wild. There's always one, right?" At this, I grimace a little knowing the unidentified fluid is probably quite the mixture of things I don't want to touch. I've done better than most, in my opinion, transitioning from medical professional, to stay at home mom/doctor's wife, to ranch wife/assistant ranch manager, but regardless of experience, gross is gross.

"Always one. What's up next?"

"I need to finish up some EPD collections for those yearling bulls before lunch. Then we're headed out to brand this afternoon. What about you?"

"It's bedsheet morning," I say, gesturing to our stripped bed. Once a week I try to change and wash everyone's bedsheets while they are gone. "Then I need to work on banking some social media posts to lead up to the fall sale. I think after lunch I'm heading over to Wendy Foster's for a little bit to learn about decorated sugar cookies." I throw out the last part nonchalantly, hoping I don't sound too suspicious. Obviously, we have an open and honest relationship, but at this point, I don't want him to know too much. I'm not looking for another lecture on my place in this investigation.

"Why do you need to learn about decorating cookies?" He asks skeptically, and I know now the direction he's moving in: the direction of why am I taking on one more thing to do when I already have more than enough to do, and aren't always great about getting everything done.

"Oh, I just thought it would be a fun thing to learn for the afternoon, not like as a business or a hobby. This lady is one of your mom's old friends, and she's a little sad because she lives here alone, so your mom thought it would be nice to hang out with her a little."

Shep hesitates a minute and then nods understandingly. "Hey, who was that blonde lady we saw at the ball fields yesterday making a scene?" He asks off-handedly as he weaves his belt back through the new jeans to get ready to head back out.

"Becki?"

"Yeah, I think I saw her driving west on 439 when I was coming back in from Hank's. I thought I saw her turn toward Shoemaker's when I stopped to check the rain gauge."

Becki at Shoemaker's? Asa Shoemaker doesn't have any family, and she has no discernable connection to anything there that I know of. The plot thickens as I'm still trying to figure out how she knew Dick MacDougal as well.

"Why would Becki Lane be going to see Asa Shoemaker? Also, it's during the school day, why wouldn't she be at her job?"

"Beats me. How do we know her?"

"She is the sponsor for the middle school cheerleaders, and she runs the computer lab at the intermediate school. Her daughter Hainslee is Mia's age."

"Well, don't know why and don't care. Just thought it was weird," He shrugs and heads out of our bedroom. Sometimes, he is so useful, but so not useful all at the same time. I have loads more questions that he clearly has no answer to, so I might as well work on that solo.

"What EPDs do you have left to collect?" I ask, trailing behind him on the stairs with his dirty laundry wrapped up in my arms.

"Scrotal circumference."

chapter
eleven

"ALRIGHT, so you'll use your outline consistency to just run around the edge there," Wendy says, as we both lean over our respective flower-shaped sugar cookies. I have a piping bag full of bright pink royal icing, and she has yellow, and as she slowly gives directions, I move my bag around the outside edge of the cookie to outline it. It is just the two of us in her kitchen, surrounded by cooling sugar cookies and several bowls of different colored royal icings. I'm actually pretty thrilled my little ruse to get more information from Wendy is going to give me skills I've wanted to learn for years, although it is undoubtedly harder than those little relaxing videos on social media make it look.

"How do you keep your line so smooth? I feel like mine keeps breaking," I ask quietly, trying to keep intense concentration on the pencil thin pink line coming out of my piping bag. It looks like a series of dashes in parts, and I frown a little as Wendy's is coming out at the perfect rate around the scallops of her flower.

"Just keep even pressure on your piping bag, and keep that hand steady," She replies, absently gesturing to my non-dominant hand braced against my dominant doing the main work of moving. "It just takes practice. You can always use a tooth-pick to fill that line back together before flooding it."

I finish the cookie in front of me, and set it aside to dry before starting on another one. "How long have you been doing this?"

"I started learning about ten years ago, and it became my main interest after I retired from the school and Peter and I separated. I stay pretty busy with orders, mostly for birthdays and weddings. I also make a few different flavors of specialty cookies in large batches and Carrie sells those in the case at Delilah's."

"Wait... are the strawberry lemonade cookies yours?" I ask, feeling suddenly like my whole life has been a lie. For a few years now, Delilah's has had a soft pink strawberry flavored cookie with an almost cake-like consistency, topped with the most delicious cream cheese frosting with a hint of lemon. They are my weakness, my nemesis, and my favorite thing all rolled into one. All this time I've thought, and spread around town, that they were Carrie's genius.

"Yes, that was kind of the cookie that started it all. I tinkered around with one of my grandma's recipes, and that really jumpstarted my love of baking. I used YouTube tutorials and books to teach myself royal icing decorating because I know that's what really sells with cottage bakers, but the simple flavored cookie is my first love."

"Those are my absolute favorite dessert in the world. I had no idea they weren't Carrie's recipe." I start to look around her modest kitchen, and fall a little in love. It's a small cottage kitchen straight off the pages of *Southern Living*. Older cabinets painted a pale yellow are paired with white tiled counters around the perimeter. There is a white wooden table in the middle of the room that serves as her island, where we are currently standing to do our work. She has floral valance curtains edged in frills and lace over the window above the sink that match curtains covering the double French doors to the backyard. Along the walls are antique looking photographs, all sepia toned and framed in barnwood, like a visual family history through the ages. She has one modern looking picture in the room- a shot of her and Thomas at what looks like Thomas's college graduation in a small silver frame on the window sill. Next to it is a framed yellowed recipe card with worn edges and shaky cursive. I can see now that the title says "Strawberry Cake Cookies".

"I'm glad you like them. I get enough business through word of mouth and referrals that I don't really need to advertise in the case anymore. I just make my weekly quota and drop them off to Carrie for her to sell."

We go back to outlining silently, with Wendy periodically looking over to see how I'm doing. After several minutes, Wendy finally breaks the silence. "So, are you planning to go to the service?"

I pause, trying to figure out what she's talking about. "Service?"

"Richard's funeral service." She answers quietly, never breaking her icing line as it loops around the cookie.

"Oh, I didn't know a service had been organized. Who put it together?" I ask, realizing after it tumbles out of my mouth how nosy it sounds.

"Yes, Nancy came home. She put it all together."

I pause again, assuming that Nancy was Richard and Charles's aunt who'd moved to New England. She has to be in her eighties? Nineties? "Wow, she can still travel?"

"She's ninety-three, but you wouldn't know it. Rage and vindictiveness help a woman last longer," Wendy quips, setting the last of her outlined cookies on a drying rack and picking up her flood consistency icing like she is preparing for war. She twirls the piping bag closed and massages the icing to get it more fluid before snipping what looks to be a very precise amount to her off the tip. After it is ready for battle, she pulls her most dry cookie off the rack and starts pushing icing inside the outline, shaking it gently as she goes to help it spread naturally. I watch in awe as she floods the entire cookie in less than a minute and sets it to the side. "What are you waiting for? Get your flood bag there. Close up the end and massage it down. Now, cut one pinky nail from the bottom. Good, now just squeeze it smoothly into the outlined petals. Overflood a little so it doesn't get pits." I follow her directions to the letter and finish flooding my first complete cookie. "That looks pretty good, so let's get these flooded and move on to the detail work."

We flood cookies without speaking for several minutes as I work up the courage to ask her more details. "Is it going to be a pretty small service?" I finally squeak out, trying to be nonchalant. I can't help but think that a ninety-three-year-old woman who lives thousands of miles away wouldn't have put together too large of a shindig, but you never know.

"My former mother-in-law does nothing small. I can assure you it will be unlike any funeral you've been to before."

"Seriously?"

"Undoubtably."

I am obviously intrigued about attending what sounds like quite the hurrah for a man no one liked and who liked no one. But, if I'm honest, I am more excited about the fact that two highly suspicious persons may be coming straight to me instead of me having to find a way to talk to them from afar. "Does Mrs. Hodges fly alone? That's a long way to travel for your nineties, even if you are in good shape."

"No, she never flew alone even when she was younger. That's more of an etiquette thing, not an age thing. She has Peter accompany her on all her trips. Even when we were married, he'd have to fly to Massachusetts to fly her here, and then take her back. It was the most wasteful thing, but it was there to waste... Are your parents close by, Molly?"

"Part of the time," I reply, taken aback a little by her veering of the conversation. "They raised us, my brother and me, in Texas, but my dad is from western Nebraska. After they retired, they became snowbirds: winters here and summers there. We have a portion of our herd on a few thousand acres there and my dad manages it and a small herd of his own up there through the warm months. We bring them down here where we have grass for longer when it gets colder. They just left to go back up a few weeks ago."

"That's nice. It's good to have family close by. It's also good to have space from them," she says cryptically. *What in the heck does that mean?*

She finishes up flooding her stack of cookies and looks to me expectantly. I rush through the last few to catch up, still wondering how I can steer the conversation back to Peter and Thomas potentially being in the area. "We miss them when they are gone, and are always glad when they are back here. It's easier to handle them gone because we know they love being up there." I pause as she starts gathering the bowls of different colored icing to make piping bags for the detail work. "Did Peter always like living down here? Or was he always anxious to move back up there?"

She stops gathering, and looks at me, somewhat suspiciously. After a long pause, she decides she trusts me and finally answers. "I suppose he always wanted to be back there. He was a mama's boy through and through, and it was the main struggle of our marriage that he was so far from her. Somehow, in an attempt not to repeat that mistake, I managed to raise a boy that wants nothing to do with me, and everything to do with his dad, regardless of what I do. But, maybe now he'll see me a little more," She answers mysteriously. I open my mouth to ask what she means, and she quickly changes the subject as we start to clean up some of the kitchen to have more space for the detail decorating. "Well, are you ready to be a cheer mom for a whole year? That Becki Lane is something else." She begins organizing all the cookies onto racks for us to decorate, and then starts stacking up the dishes we aren't using anymore. I gather the stacks at the sink to begin washing.

"Oh, you know her?"

"I've known her for a long time, but what really left a bad taste in my mouth was when the girls were in elementary school when I was the librarian. That little girl of hers was constantly losing books or damaging them. Any time I would send a note home about her bringing them back or treating them better, she would come flying into the school to the principal saying I was harassing her and wrongfully accusing her daughter. I've never seen such spoiled entitlement in all my life. No wonder her husband left her. And I can say that because mine left me."

"Her husband left her? Like her current one?" I ask incredulously, accidentally dropping a dirty bowl in the sink as I turn away from my soapy water to look at her.

"What do you mean, her current one? Trevor Lane, her only one that I know of." Wendy replies, looking at me like I'm crazy. She stacks up the baking sheets and sets them on the counter next to me as I get back to work washing and rinsing the icing bowls.

"Trevor, that's his name! I couldn't for the life of me think of his name the other day. But I was in the right ballpark... Ha, literally, I was in the right ballpark. She came up to the Little League park to corner some guy from Ivy City who is apparently Hainslee's biological dad for child support at their game. But that guy didn't want anything to do with them, and told her to kick rocks. Apparently, he was married at the time, and they worked it out, so he's never wanted anything to do with her. I didn't realize Trevor wasn't Hainslee's dad because they've all had the same last name. He must have adopted her when they got married, so I'm not sure how she's petitioning him for child support."

"Oh, honey. Do you live in a hole?" Wendy gives me a look of sheer pity, and I stop the water running to give her a slightly exasperated look. I mean, I thought I was sharing some pretty decent gossip and she's acting like I'm way late to the party. Wendy hoists herself up on an island stool to watch me wash dishes, and apparently give me the scoop I've been missing.

"What do you mean?"

"Babe, they all have the same last name because the man that is her daughter's father that wants nothing to do with her is her 'step-uncle'. Becki married her baby daddy's brother." She rolls her eyes and hands me a glass measuring cup off the island to wash next that I have to work not to drop out of sheer shock.

"You're kidding!"

"I am not. We lived in Ivy City for most of our married life and those three went to school with my Thomas. She was head over heels for Trent, the baby daddy, their whole time in high school. They dated their senior year, and he dumped her right before prom for his now wife. When they were grown adults and he had been married for a few years, he and his wife had a short separation. I think their oldest daughter was maybe two or three years old at the time. Becki cornered him at the little bar down in Ivy City, got him drunk, and got him in her bed one last time, hoping to lure him back while she thought she had the chance. He woke up that next morning, realized what she did, and told her never to contact him again. He went to Jessica to beg her to take him back and they reconciled. Of course, Becki popped up a few months later "accidentally" pregnant, but they all knew it was on purpose to get him on the hook. He has been adamant since before day one that he was not having anything to do with them, period. Trevor was a year younger than them, and always a little bit of an outcast, in Trent's shadow. He saw, I think, what he thought was a chance to maybe one up his brother and be the "hero", so he married Becki. She never gave up hope that Trent would one day come back to her, so she gave their daughter his last name, which later became hers when Trevor married her. Despite all his moral shortcomings, Trent is fairly charismatic, and has had quite a successful career as a realtor. She only sees people for dollar signs and how she can use them to her advantage. Now that Trevor has finally realized he's only a meal ticket to her, he left her for a better job in the Midland/Odessa area, and she's going to have to fend for herself, which means hitting Trent up for child support he doesn't owe her. They have no custody agreement because he signed away parental rights of the daughter before she was even born. That was part of the restraining order he filed against her."

My jaw has to be scraping the floor at this point because I am in such disbelief. How in the world does she know all of this? I mean, I know exactly how: small towns. They are interesting and dynamic and, at times, fun, when the gossip swirling is like this. Not so much if the swirling gossip is about you, which I'm sure Wendy has also experienced.

"So should she have even been at the game if there is a restraining order?" I near-whisper, eager to hear more of this wild story, as I drip a little soap water on the wooden floor.

"No, darlin', she was not to have any contact with him, period."

"Well, that explains why the sixth graders said she was going to see him in person instead because he wasn't answering her texts or calls."

"That girl is hell on wheels, and I wouldn't want her anywhere near my daughter."

"You don't have a daughter."

She frowns in frustration, handing me a set of spatulas and nodding to get back to the dishes. "I mean, I just wouldn't want her in any position of authority over my child. Be very wary of her this next year. She's trouble."

"Did Thomas ever hang out with her growing up?" I throw out, hoping this is my "in" to swing back to Thomas and get some answers for the questions I came with.

"Oh, no. Peter saw her once at a football game when they were fairly young, maybe freshmen, and immediately deemed her white trash. Thomas took Peter's opinion as gospel, and never had anything to do with her."

"So, it sounds like Thomas and Peter are still pretty close. Did he know Richard at all?"

"I think they met a few times when he was a child, but he and I weren't exactly close, especially not after Charlie passed. Peter and Richard were always adversarial, and Charlie was the peacemaker between them. I think Peter is here for this service because, one, his mother required his presence and assistance, and two, I wouldn't be shocked if Peter spits on that grave, either metaphorically or literally."

"Gracious, that's a fun family dynamic. So, did Thomas come for the service also, or just Peter with his mother?"

"Yes, Thomas is here. He made an obligatory swing by here to give me a hug before checking in to the guest house at Brooksmith Ranch. That's where they always stay when they visit. It's the only place up to snuff around here." Brooksmith Ranch is a historic ranch on the west side of Buffalo Creek. Years ago, the granddaughter that inherited it turned the old ranch house into a small boutique hotel because she preferred to stay in her large home in the city, but didn't want to sell it. It's become a hot spot for well-to-do people passing through or looking for a weekend getaway. The original ranch staff run trail rides and other "ranch activities" that are just citified enough for city people to handle them while still feeling like they are experiencing the 'country'.

"Oh, I see. Do you get to see him for dinner or anything?"

"Maybe sometime in the next few days, but they have a standing tradition of dinner at Silver Spring the first night every time they visit. I would put big, easy money that Peter and Thomas will be sitting at the corner table by the fireplace at 7:30 tonight. That's what we did for thirty-five years before we divorced, and what they've done every time they visit ever since."

"Oh, funny. Silver Spring is our favorite restaurant in Buffalo Creek, too, but we haven't been there in a little while. We should maybe go soon," I reply, finishing up the dishes.

Bingo.

chapter
twelve

AT 6:23 THAT EVENING, Shep finally rolls into the driveway in the feed truck and parks next to Billie's Bronco. I know the exact time because I'm sitting next to the open shutters on the picture windows of our living room watching for him. He lets himself in the side door and I meet him in the kitchen as he sets down his keys on the island and hangs his worn-out straw Stetson work hat on the hook by the side door.

"Hey, Molls, what's for din-" He cuts himself off as he turns and looks up at me, dressed in a simple, dark red, sleeveless A-line dress that hits just above the knee. I've curled my hair, done my makeup, the whole nine yards. "Did I forget we have plans tonight? Where are the kids?" He looks around me to the empty family room and a small look of panic flashes across his tired face.

"You didn't forget, I just thought I'd surprise you! Mia had a project to work on with Emily, and Hayes has been asking to have a video game night with Carlisle, so they are both at the Scotts for the night. I got us a last-minute reservation at Silver Spring," I say nonchalantly, hoping he is excited by this. He looks briefly defeated, and I pull on a large smile to start the upsell. "It's our lucky night! The special this week is the surf and turf. And we don't even have to pay a babysitter!"

He looks to rally a little, and I am silently relieved. "What time is our reservation?"

"7:15," I reply, still with a Barbie upsell smile. That only gives him a little less than thirty minutes to shower and get ready. It was a gamble to pick 7:15 because there are times Shep doesn't come in until close to 7 or after, but I wanted to get as close as I could to what should be Thomas and Peter's reservation.

"Alright, I'll be down in a minute. Are you ready?" He asks skeptically, acknowledging that I am typically the reason we are running late.

"Yes, completely ready!" I encourage as he wearily ascends the back staircase. I double check that I have my necessities in a small clutch bag- phone, keys, small wallet, lipstick, and a digital recorder I dug out from my pharmacy school lecture days. I'm sure there is some way to record on my phone, but I feel like that would be way more suspicious than me turning on my recorder in my bag and trying to get it as close to the Hodges' table as possible.

"Alright, I think I'm ready," Shep says, coming down the stairs about fifteen minutes later. He has showered, and changed into a blue-striped Ariat button-down shirt and nice jeans with his hair still a little damp. He sits on the bottom stair leading into the kitchen and slips his nice Lucchese boots over his socked feet, pausing for a second before pulling himself up and heading for the side door to the driveway. I follow behind him quickly, tossing him keys when he turns back to me, and then he opens the passenger door for me to slide in.

"I feel like I'm in high school again going on a date in my mom's car."

"Hi, we have a reservation for 7:15, under Jones," I say, as we walk up to the ornate carved mesquite wood hostess stand. Silver Spring is best described as upscale Texas: everything is rich, worn-in leather, with European mounted deer and antelope, and large, intricate landscape paintings featuring ranchers on horseback and herds of cattle. Each table is polished mesquite wood with heavy upholstered armchairs and hand-turned wooden salt and pepper shakers on each one. The menu is what you would expect: large, prime cut marbled steaks, variations on typical side dishes, such as green chile mac and cheese, or balsamic brussels sprouts (my favorite!), and big, buttery rolls to start. This has been our go-to nice restaurant and date night spot since we moved here, and I'm on the website to get a reservation any time we remotely think we might have a babysitter. It makes complete sense that this would be the choice restaurant for the Hodges family if they are as bougie as Wendy has made them out to be.

I lean back a little to get a peek into the dining room as the hostess checks off our reservation in the book and stoops below the counter to grab us menus. The famed "best table in the house" is the two-top directly next to the large brown river rock fireplace. From here, I can see that it is currently empty, and even better, the table next to it is as well.

"Hey, Haley?" I say quietly, hoping she can hear me, but Shep maybe not as well. He has been texting with Hank since we arrived at the restaurant about setting up a time to vaccinate and tag a group of heifer calves the next day and I am thankful he is slightly distracted.

"Yes, Mrs. Jones?" Haley replies, setting our menus on the counter and looking at me, slightly annoyed. Haley is a senior in high school, and I've known her since Mia and Hayes were little and she babysat for us a few times. We haven't made it to

Silver Spring in a few months, so I'm unsure how long this has been her post, but she seems slightly bored by it.

"Would it be possible to get the table next to the table by the fireplace?" I ask sweetly, hoping she decides to use her perceived power for good and not evil. Something about the exasperation in her voice tells me she could deny my request just out of the not-goodness of her heart, and I'm hopeful she decides to be benevolent.

"Sure, Mrs. Jones," She sighs, and gestures to the dining room. "Right this way." I follow in behind her eagerly, and Shep jumps in behind us, sliding his phone into his shirt pocket.

We take seats at my requested table, me with my back to the fireplace table, but closest to it, and Shep facing it. I'm a little disappointed I won't be able to look at them the entire time, but potential quality of audio is more important to me than visuals at this point.

Our server arrives a few moments later with our bread basket, and we order drinks and the crab cakes, one of our long-time favorites, as an appetizer.

"Did y'all get your plans settled for tomorrow?" I ask, tearing a roll in two and reaching for the whipped butter and the tiny silver butter knife in the basket.

"Yeah, we're going to push his up about 7:30 and get them done. Then we'll get ours done and move them out to the northeast pasture," He replies, taking his own roll from the basket and buttering it.

"Sounds good. Are y'all working out in the morning?" When we moved out to the ranch and first got to know the Douglases, Hank casually asked Shep if he wanted to join his group that works out together at his home gym doing cross-fit type workouts incredibly early in the morning. Like 4:30 in the morning before any type of ranch work goes down. Shep agreed, thinking it would be a group of been-in-better-shape guys that provided a little accountability and mostly good company. What he found was that Hank is actually a certified Cross Fit trainer and he shows no mercy in writing legit workouts for them to do, along with accountability and good company. The self-dubbed "Dad Bod Squad" doesn't meet up every day, but a few times a week as their schedules allow.

"I think so, at least me and Hank. I'm not sure if David is back in town," He replies, referring to the third main member of the squad. "I think I'm getting the ribeye; what about you?" He closes his menu and sets it in the middle of the table for the server to pick back up after we order.

I stare at him blankly for a minute, and then jump into looking at my menu because I actually have no clue what I want. The last several times I've taken a break from getting steak with the nightly special, so I flip through the book for the card they slip in the back listing the changing entrée options.

"The lobster ravioli sounds really good," I comment, running a finger down my choices. "I think I'd like that better than a salmon or a stuffed chicken. Are you getting a salad?"

"Probably not." I'm not sure why I asked because Shep has never been a huge vegetable fan. I could bet easy money that his steak will be accompanied by a loaded baked potato and the green chile mac and cheese. "How was your cookie thing this afternoon?"

"It was fun. I've wanted to learn how to do those for a long time, but never knew who to ask. I should have known your mom would know someone."

He nods silently in agreement. "How does my mom know her again?"

"They went to high school together. Apparently, she was also best friends with Charles MacDougal before he passed away," I say nonchalantly, hoping if I pique his interest ahead of time, I can potentially share what I've learned without it feeling like I've bombarded him with small town gossip.

"I thought he died when they were kids?"

"Um, no, actually, I found out that he was in his mid-twenties or so. Complications from pneumonia."

Shep shoots me a skeptical sideways glance, and I feel slightly busted. "Was this information provided from probing an unsuspecting friend of my mom's, or from another source?"

I pause for a moment, trying to decide how to answer, and am saved by the server bringing our drinks and appetizer. We order our entrees, and just as the server leaves and Shep looks to me to finally answer, Haley leads two very tall men through the dining room to the table by the fireplace.

"This will do nicely, Haley. Thank you," The older man nods approvingly at Haley, sliding her something discreetly as he moves to take his seat directly behind me. The younger man with him sits across from him silently, and I remind myself that I'm not supposed to know them, so staring is probably not ideal.

"I did a little of my own research," I respond, turning back to Shep. I am trying to be quiet so the Hodges men don't necessarily hear everything I'm saying, and also so I can actually hear them. I unhook my bag from the side of my chair and pull my phone out to set on the table to disguise me turning on my recorder before hooking it back on my chair as close to Peter Hodges as I can get.

"Does this little research of your own have anything to do with Richard?" He asks pointedly, placing one of the two crab cakes on his appetizer plate, along with a spoonful of the corn salsa relish that garnishes the dish.

"Maybe," I hesitantly answer, knowing that I don't keep things from him, and don't want to keep things from him, but also desperately wanting him to understand why this is important to me, and why I can't stop now.

He puts his fork down and stares at me for a long moment. "Do you really think something is going on?" He asks seriously, with the sincerest look on his face. I don't see that look often; it's reserved for things he's truly serious about, and he's typically such a jokester and so laidback. The last time I can remember that look was the night he sat me down a few years ago and said he was ready to quit his hospital job.

Shep and I met what now feels like many, many moons ago when he had just started medical school and I had just started pharm school. We met each other briefly at church through mutual friends, but the real connection came when we continued to run into each other at the health sciences education building. Of course, I thought he was (is) handsome, but he seemed quiet and very focused on school. I was an epic overachiever and solidified goody-two-shoes, so one night, as I was headed into a student government meeting (because all real goody-two-shoes serve on SGA), I spotted him studying at a table alone. I was also pretty quiet, but I decided to take a chance. I pulled out a bag of homemade cookies left over from a student scholarship bake sale earlier that day and set them on his table as I was walking by, telling him he looked like he needed some cookies. That started a chain of us dropping each other cookies on study tables for a little bit until he asked for my number and the rest is history.

Obviously, there is no comparison of something like medical school or graduate school to something like war, but in a way, seeing each other and supporting each other through that time was like a trauma bond. It's like we've always known that if we can make it through medical school, and then residency and fellowship, we can make it through anything.

When you make it through medical school, residency, and fellowship with someone, generally speaking, you think you'll be a physician's wife, and all that comes with it. Honestly, that wasn't really my scene, and we have been lucky to be in an area where I had plenty of other friends, and weren't really immersed in an overly toxic medical community. That was just Shep's job. And even though he was damn good at it, it just wasn't what he ultimately felt called to do.

Once we knew what area we would be settling in long term, we starting looking for acreage to buy for the purpose of hunting. At the time, Shep was an avid hunter, particularly waterfowl, and we spent hours through residency and fellowship at local ponds training labs to retrieve decoys to prepare for hunting season. The perfect property came up a few years before we were set to move, but we couldn't resist shooting for it, even though it was not exactly in our meager fellowship budget. After days of negotiating back and forth with an impressive amount of confidence, Shep got it within a doable price range, and through what I can only describe as providence from the Lord, the bank gave us financing for it. We officially became land owners.

Even though the primary purpose was hunting, to maintain a lower ag rate, we got a few cows when we moved here for good. And those few cows got Shep hooked. He wanted more cows, which led to us finding another larger property that we felt the same perfect feeling about as our first property. Through his first years as an attending, we slowly built the operation, adding in cows a few at a time to grow our registered Angus herd. After a few years, we built the ranch house, and moved out to be with the operation full time while Shep dropped to three days a week at the hospital. At some point during this time, we held our first bull sale, and did much better than we expected. It was another year or so after this that we made it to the night I can still see vividly- his earnest face telling me it was time. Time to move off into the deep end and do this full time. Since then, it's grown more and better than we could have imagined, with us getting to know other wonderful ranching families in the area, and adding Cooter and Roy to the family. It hasn't all been rainbows and sunshine, but the man I'm sitting across from now is exponentially more joyful than the man I first met in the beatdown of medicine.

I snap myself back from reminiscing to his waiting stare. "I do, Shep. I really do."

He stares at me for another long minute, and then exhales deeply, like he's slowly accepting the fate about to befall him. "Okay, then, let's figure this out."

I am thrilled that Shep is on the same page, but if I'm completely honest, the timing is not ideal as I have two suspects essentially within listening distance and I can't unload all the things verbally at this current juncture. I give him an appreciative smile, and glance around the room before giving a small point to his phone in his front shirt pocket. I pick up my phone and jot out a quick (hopefully not too cryptic) text to him.

Watch the table behind me. They are main suspects- Richard's cousin and his son cut out of fam estate. They are here from MA for funeral. Try to hear and see what you can.

Shep's phone buzzes on the table where he placed it from his pocket, and I wait anxiously as he reads through it. When he finishes, he looks up at me with a slight frown. "I should have known you didn't just randomly get a reservation to eat here with a very specific table request."

"Oh, you still get the steak you want, you're fine," I whisper back, holding back an eye roll.

"Is everything arranged for tomorrow?" I hear someone behind me ask, and I fight every urge in me not to turn around. I jerk my thumb to the left and then to the right to Shep to see if he can tell me if it's Thomas or Peter asking. Shep responds with a thumb to the right, so I know he means Thomas, and I try to keep eye contact with his very interested gaze as he gets a front row seat to this show.

"I believe it is, but I'm certain Mother will let me know if anything remains. Speaking of mothers, did you visit yours today?"

"I did, I spent an hour or so with her this afternoon. She gave me this envelope and told me to open it tonight with you at dinner. Apparently, it's for my birthday."

My curiosity has never been stronger, and I hold every muscle in my body as still as possible to keep myself from turning around. I've never been more jealous of Shep in my life being able to see everything without being obvious.

"Well, that's about like her. Nearly sixth months late, and not even wrapped," Peter chuckles, and I hold back another eye roll. I had gathered he was a bit of a jerk wad from Wendy, and it seems she wasn't wrong.

"I'm not sure I should open this here, Dad, not knowing what it is and it seems serious. What do you think?"

"I think..." It sounds like Peter has leaned over the table to respond in a whisper, and I've lost any intelligibility of their conversation. Shep gives me a slight shake of his head to indicate he can't hear anything either, and that we probably won't with their current set up. I try to nonchalantly scoot my chair back, moving a few centimeters at a time to be as inconspicuous as possible. Shep is calmly nodding in front of me like I'm backing up the cattle trailer to the loadout, so I continue to head back a little at a time until I hit something small on the floor blocking the chair leg from moving back. I can't see anything specific, and Shep is still nodding while sipping his glass of iced tea, so I take that to mean the object holding me up is not Peter Hodges's chair behind mine, so I push back with slightly more force to get over whatever hump is holding me back.

"Molly!" I hear Shep's voice in front of me but he is suddenly out of my sight line and I feel dizzy, like I'm flying backwards.

My chair's back legs stay planted where they are, but my slightly more force has tipped the front legs off the ground and propelled the back of my chair toward the floor. Before I can stop myself, I am lying in a heap looking up at the ceiling, plus Peter and Thomas Hodges peering over me. After a brief moment, Shep is also standing over the top of me, first pulling the skirt of my dress down, and then helping me up. Both Peter and Thomas glance back to our table, I assume to check to see what type of alcohol I've had and how much, which is none, much to their disappointment.

"Are you alright, ma'am?" Peter asks with a clip to his voice, like he's asking out of obligation, not true concern. He's clearly not lived in the south any time recently because any true Southerner would be all up in this situation trying to get details and gossip under the guise of being helpful, not looking on like it's an inconvenience. Or looking like there's a rather large and uncomfortable stick stuck up where my husband used to screen for colon cancer.

"Twenty years and I'm still head over heels for him!" I chuckle, trying to make light of things as Shep sets my chair upright and sets it back at our table. "I'm fine, thank you. I was just pushing my chair back to get up to go to the ladies' room and I think I hit that little wrinkle in the rug right there. I apologize for interrupting your dinner," I give a small embarrassed wave and linger for a few seconds in front of their table and see a thick cream envelope with Thomas's name on it that he has started to open. I gasp in a little breath, feeling like whatever is in that envelope is incredibly important, but not knowing how in the world to hang out here long enough to see what it might be.

"I'm so sorry, you look so terribly familiar! Are y'all on the Buffalo Creek Education Foundation?" Words just spill from my mouth and I glance back to see Shep looking at me with horrified eyes.

Peter Hodges has a look on his face somewhere in the three-way intersection of amusement, pity, and condescension. It turns my stomach a little and I flash a nervous smile waiting to see if one of them will answer, or if I'm going to have to slink back to our table defeated.

"No, ma'am, we don't live here. You must have us confused with someone else. I grew up not far from here, but we've lived in Massachusetts for several years now." Thomas gives me a kind smile, or at least one kinder than his father's, and I wish there was a way to siphon him off to get some answers. He is clearly less conceited than his father, but obviously admires and follows him in a way that means it would be hard to turn them against one another.

"Oh, my mistake! What brings you here from Massachusetts?" I ask, just one hot second from starting a soft shoe number to keep this show alive.

"My father's cousin passed away, and we're here for the service," He answers politely, tucking the envelope back into the inner pocket of his sport coat. I flash him a tight smile and nod.

"I'm so sorry for your loss. Anyone I might know? Everyone knows everyone around Buffalo Creek."

Thomas hesitates, glancing back to Peter, who is sipping a bourbon on the rocks with an incredibly bored look on his face. There is no indication in this exchange whether Peter gave Thomas permission to share any details, so Thomas hesitates again briefly, before nodding and answering. "Richard MacDougal? He and my father were first cousins. My grandmother and his father were brother and sister."

This time, I pause, debating with myself how to play this. *Do I jump in and let them know that I know way more than the average person, and I'm on to them? Or do I play it cool and see what they share organically?*

"Yes, of course we knew Richard. We've lived across from him for several years now. Just a shame what happened," Shep interjects, moving a little closer behind me and joining the conversation. Now, that's what I'm talking about! A little double-team action might get us somewhere.

"Oh, no, were you the neighbor that found him? We were told a female neighbor found him while bringing him groceries. Was that you?" Thomas asks, suddenly looking concerned. I admit, I appreciate the credit because it's all fun and games to know someone who has died recently, but it's a whole different ball game to be the one touching a dead guy.

Now it's our turn to exchange a look, and Shep's eyes tell me it's okay to tell them the truth and just see what happens. "Um, yes, that was me. We had a few run-ins with him in the weeks leading up to that where he didn't look or seem well, so I felt like I needed to check on him and make sure he had food to eat and was doing okay. Are you all his closest living relatives? We knew his wife and his brother passed away a while back but we didn't know if he had any other family still living that would be around to have a service." I choose not to mention the fact that he had exactly zero friends that would be willing to help out of the goodness of their hearts. Maybe for an inside scoop at some gossip, but definitely not out of friendship or kindness.

"Yes, at this point, my mother and I, and Thomas would be his closest living relatives. He had no children, or nieces or nephews, so we are the closest as cousins. My mother was very fond of Richard, despite his argumentative demeanor. She felt like he wasn't easily defeated or persuaded, and she appreciated that about him." Peter sets his bourbon on the table, like he's pressing pause on enjoying his evening until he can be rid of us.

"That is true, he was very... tenacious. We were surprised to find him on heart failure medication. He didn't seem like the type to go to the doctor, especially not to be on a very closely monitored and precisely dosed medication," I say off-handedly, looking to Shep as he nods in agreement casually.

"I honestly couldn't tell you anything about Richard's health. We hadn't seen or spoken to one another in over ten years. He and I weren't exactly ever close, especially after Charles passed. My mother may have been fond of him, but I found him insufferable and obnoxious and had as little to do with him as possible once we were adults and no longer forced to interact at family gatherings."

"Really? This is an awfully long way to travel for a funeral for someone you didn't care for very much," I reply softly, looking between him and a sheepish Thomas.

"If we're still being honest, I'm not here for Richard. I'm here because it is important to my mother, as is the reason Thomas is also here. He really should be working, but we've done our best to be here for Mother."

Now we're getting somewhere. "Oh, how kind. Thomas, what is your line of work?"

"Pharmaceutical research."

"Oh, what a coincidence! I'm a pharmacist! Well, I'm licensed to be, but I stay home with our kids right now. Do you have a wife or kids?"

"No, not yet," He ducks his head bashfully, and takes a sip of his drink. It looks like a mixed drink of some sort, but I can't really tell what. He winces a little at what is likely the bitterness, and sets it back on the table.

"Well, that's really interesting. Do you work with a specific drug class or condition?"

"I used to work mainly on drugs for high blood pressure, but they've recently moved me to heavy research on heart conditions, particularly heart failure."

chapter
thirteen

"GOOD MORNING, Donny! Are you calling to tell me good news?" The next morning, I cradle my phone between my shoulder and ear as I dump a few tablespoons of creamer in my second cup of coffee and give it a few stirs. We got in semi late from Silver Spring last night, but I've already taken kids to school and sent Shep and the boys off with breakfast sandwiches and full thermoses of coffee to give a group of heifers some hormone shots to start the artificial insemination process. I'm about to sit down and work on the layout and verbiage for the catalog we produce and mail out to customers for our large annual bull sale in the fall when Donny's call pops up. I take my mug and park myself in my upholstered office chair in front of my computer. After grabbing a felt tip pen and a pad of large lined sticky notes, I'm ready to take notes to share with Shep, but there is a pause on the other end of the line long enough to make me really nervous. "Donny? Lay it on me, man. What are we looking at now?"

"Well, Molly, I'm not sure it's good. We've gotten the extra parts, and we're going to start putting them in today. We'll see if this gives it a fix, but we may have to order more than what we initially thought."

"How much more, Donny?"

"Can't say just yet, Molly. We'll get you taken care of, though, don't worry."

I exhale the breath I didn't realize I was holding and let my head sink a little. "I know you'll get us taken care of, but is my bank account going to feel used and abused?"

"Probably."

"What would you do, Donny? If this were Shelly, what would you do?" I tap my pen on the desk in nervousness, knowing he would be honest with me regardless, but bringing his beloved wife into the mix takes it to a whole new level. I get another long pause, along with a heavy sigh.

"You might start looking at your options. I'm not saying you need a whole new car, but I'm saying the end of this road is a new transmission. This isn't the first time we've seen this with this model."

"You're kidding. We started with a simple stutter, and now it needs a new transmission?"

"I didn't say that. Not yet. But it's always something simple. Until it isn't."

I smack my forehead and try not to groan. He's not wrong. Shep used to tell me all the time about patients he'd see in clinic or the hospital that would come in for one small, simple thing. Some seemingly harmless ailment. But pulling that small string would begin the unraveling, and before they knew it, they were being diagnosed with some large-scale cancer, or heart failure, or some other life altering disease. All it takes is pulling some small, otherwise insignificant string to change everything.

"Alright, I'll let Shep know. Thanks for the update," I toss the pen up on to the desk and take another big gulp of my coffee.

"No problem. Tell Shep I'll be around this afternoon if he wants to call."

"Will do." I hang up and sit in my chair for a few minutes trying to decide what to do. Do I go tell Shep now, or wait until they come in for lunch, and use Cooter and Roy's presence to lighten the mood?

Before I get a chance to decide, I hear the side door open and close and Shep rush into the office a little dirty and frantic. He has some dirt stains on the bottoms of his jeans, and a smear of something on one shirt arm. After shuffling through a stack of papers on his desk, he comes up with a typed sheet of two columns of numbers. "I forgot our breeding group record. I know we have a few in this group that need to be sorted out to go to embryo transfer, but I want to double check them against my list here." He folds it lengthwise and tucks it into his shirt pocket before turning to head out, only stopping briefly to look back at me. "Are you okay? You look a little pale."

"Donny says I need a new car." As soon as I say it, Shep also pales, and I regret not tempering my words before letting them fly right out. No one can accuse us of not being honest with one another, that's for sure.

"When did he say that?"

"I just got off the phone with him. Technically, he said they had ordered new parts, and were going to try them, but there is potential that we'll need additional parts, and the last stop on this road is a new transmission."

"We'll start looking for you a new car," He replies instantly, confirming his quick choice with a confident nod. I sigh for the umpteenth time this morning, despite the fact that it hasn't been that long of a morning yet, and look between him and my computer.

"How do I start that journey? I don't even know what I want. I'm not really prepared to make a huge decision like this right now."

"We'll go walk the lot at Donny's this afternoon and just see what he has and go from there."

"We can't go this afternoon; they are having the visitation for MacDougal at 2:00."

"Why do we need to go to the visitation? I think we've visited him more than enough the last few weeks."

"That is a prime place to investigate! I still need to find out what Wendy gave Thomas for his birthday in that envelope, and see if there is more of a connection between him being in pharm research and MacDougal dying of a pharm related occurrence. I can't believe Peter just cut Thomas off last night from talking to us."

After Thomas revealed his current line of work, I was all jazzed up to ask many a follow up question, but was immediately cut off by Peter claiming they didn't want to interrupt our dinner any longer, and would get back to theirs. Clearly, they felt like we were overstepping their meal, but did that back-handed thing of making it sound like it was their fault so we'd get the hint and leave. We returned to our table and tried to overhear what we could while we finished our food. It seemed like they were on to us, or at least suspicious, and talked in much lower voices the rest of the time they were there. They finished their meal a good ten minutes ahead of us and left while we were waiting for our server to bring our check. My only solace was hoping that my recorder caught something while we weren't able to hear, but when I checked it in the car, apparently, my body slamming it on the ground in flipping my chair crushed it and it wouldn't even turn on anymore. Nancy Drew at her finest, obviously.

"Visitations are come and go. Do you plan to park and stay while everyone else comes and goes to get what you're looking for? Call me crazy, but that seems a little weird."

I pause, knowing he is right. It's not exactly a place I can just go hang out and see what I can run across. I'm riding a fine line of needing to be around enough to get the information I need, and not so much that I raise suspicion and the family shuts down.

"Okay, maybe give me 20 minutes there? I'd like a chance to at least meet Nancy Hodges before the funeral. Maybe linger around her a little to see what she might say."

"I'm this weird mix of proud of you and creeped out right now."

I stand and follow him out of the office to the side door. "I appreciate it. It's my life's calling to make you proud and keep you on your toes."

"We'll be done putting in CIDRs about noon, then I'll come back and clean up and we can go," he says, opening the side door and heading out.

"Okay, sounds good. I'll have lunch ready," I give him a quick kiss on the cheek, careful to avoid the unidentified smear on his arm. Somehow, he's a germaphobe about humans, but cattle? No so much. He nods and heads to the ranch truck to get back to the breeding work pens.

I feel a little untethered as I wander back into the office, wondering what to do with myself for the few hours I have until game time. I sit down in front of my computer and find myself surfing through the inventory on Donny's website, seeing if anything strikes my fancy, not having a clue what I'm looking for. I love my car, or maybe I should say loved, because my love starts to wane when reliability starts to wane also. *Do I want to take the chance on the same thing? Do I want to take the chance on something completely different and new?* As I ponder, the list of available cars starts loading in front of me, with the first being a vintage 1965 Mustang convertible in the classic cherry red. I laugh to myself and start devising a plan to convince Shep that is the car I can't live without this afternoon just to have some fun.

Soft strains of slow instrumental music and blasts of air conditioning drift out the front double doors of Blevins, Whaley, and Cusack Funeral Home as they open and close to let people slowly trickle in that afternoon. Shep and I are walking up from the back of the parking lot along with what appears to be most of Buffalo Creek, as there are more cars than the lot has room for comfortably. For someone that no one wanted to be around in life, Dick MacDougal has certainly pulled a crowd in death. I sigh nervously, wondering if all of these people are going to be a help or hinderance in finding anything out.

We enter the double doors and stand in the vestibule for a few minutes as the line in front of us signs the guest book before moving into the main viewing room. I'm not sure there is anyone that is completely comfortable in funeral settings, but I find this practice particularly morbid. Nothing gives me the creeps quite like just standing and staring at a lifeless body that you knew before death. I think it's hard for the mind to wrap itself around death. I hate the weird feeling of anticipation that swells in your gut thinking this person that you've typically only seen lively will jump up from this stillness and scare the bejeezus out of you at any minute. Obviously, that's never happened, but that gut swell happens every time anyway.

"Hey, sugar, how are you?" I look up from signing us in on the guest book to see Jacquie Welch, a longtime Buffalo Creek resident, and longtime friend from church standing in front of us in line. I give her a hug and a somber smile, and move from in front of the guest book into line to wait to see the family. Shep follows behind me, striking up a conversation with David Southerland behind him in line, another longtime friend and fellow member of the Dad Bod Squad.

"I'm good, Jacquie. I haven't seen you in a bit; how are you?" I ask quietly, wondering why this line seems to not be moving at all. My wardrobe is funeral light: a pair of black skinny ankle slacks and a classic black and white striped blouse, and I'm thankful I chose to pair this with red cushioned ballet flats instead of heels like I originally planned. Many moons ago, pre-kids, I would work the pharmacy floor for hours in stilettos, but those days are long gone, and I don't see a revival happening any time soon.

"Oh, I'm good, darlin'. What have you been up to lately?"

"Not much. Hayes is deep in baseball season right now, and Mia is gearing up for next year as a cheerleader. Shep and the boys just started prep work for breeding the spring calving herd. Nothing out of the ordinary," I say, trying to think if anything else is going on. Obviously, the biggest thing I'm up to is trying to figure out who murdered the man in the casket thirty feet away, but that's not exactly polite small talk conversation material, and I don't exactly want to blow my cover.

"I bet y'all are just having so much fun. I remember our kids at that age, and it was just so much fun. You know our Diane was a cheerleader at Buffalo Creek. Is Lisa Davies still the teacher for that?" Jacquie was a math teacher at the high school for decades and previously knew everyone that was associated with the school in the slightest. She retired a few years ago, and her connections have started to fall away as teachers leave or also retire. Lisa Davies was a wonderful, kind hearted English teacher who was an All-American cheerleader in the 80s that sponsored the girls for fun the last few years. All good things must come to an end, and she moved the last year when her husband took a head coaching position at another school, and Becki weaseled her way right in. I would have killed for Lisa Davies over Becki Lane. I mean, I would have vastly preferred her to Becki; it's probably a little gauche to say I'd kill for that given the current circumstances.

"No, she and Bryan moved to Staunton. The sponsor now is Becki Lane. Do you know her?"

Jacquie's eyes widen a little bit and she stammers for a second. "Uh, well, I don't know her well. I've just seen her around recently when she visits her uncle."

"Her uncle?"

"Yes, her uncle, Asa Shoemaker. Do you know Asa?"

"Yes, of course. They are just up the road from us, next to the MacDougals. She's his niece?"

Jacquie nods again, giving me a look that she's slightly concerned about what is probably an unhinged look developing on my face. "Wait, what do you mean, visit? He's not at home?"

"No, he took a bit of a fall a few weeks ago, and he's in the rehab facility on the edge of town. I volunteer there a few times a week. She blows in a bit like a diva a time or two a week to 'visit'. Asa is still basically all there, but I get slight grifter vibes from her. You know he doesn't have any kids of his own to inherit, so I think it's down to her."

What is it with all these people not having normal lines of inheritance? Was there something in the water around here that no one has kids fight over the inheritance like a normal soap opera?

Just as I open my mouth to ask some follow up questions, I hear a bit of a commotion behind me and turn to see the fuss. It sounds like two men are trying to jump the line and people are mostly being polite, but also a little annoyed that someone would bother to cut in line at a funeral visitation. After a few long seconds, Cooter and Roy appear in my sight line with large grins, and I try not to visibly drop my head.

"Hey, Boss, how long you been waiting?" Cooter asks, wedging himself between me and Shep in line, with Roy trying to squeeze in behind him.

"Uh, about ten minutes. What are you doing here?" I hiss,

gathering up all patience and trying not to catch anyone's gaze from behind me because they are likely not kind looks.

"Why, Mrs. Molly, whatever do you mean? We're here to pay our respects to the recently departed," he says, a tad bit too loud, like he's a bad actor in a stage production. "Also, Shep said we were having an early dinner at the Dairy Queen after this," he adds quietly to mainly me. I roll my eyes and turn to Shep, who just shrugs and nods with a slightly guilty look on his face.

"It's right next to the dealership, so I figured that was a given," he shrugs, like this all made logical sense to him. Truly, it is Shep logic, and I'm not surprised at that part, just mostly surprised that Cooter and Roy joined us so early in the lineup of festivities. I turn back to ask Cooter that very question and find him extending a hand to Jacquie.

"Coudreaux Phineas Cogburn, pleased to make your acquaintance. You can call me Cooter," he explains as Jacquie daintily shakes his outstretched hand. "This here is my partner and business associate, Roy Gary Blackburn. You can call him Roy." She giggles nervously, shaking Roy's hand also, and I step a little closer to try to explain.

"Jacquie, Cooter and Roy are our ranch hands. They are team roping partners," I say, shooting Cooter a raised eyebrow. "Is there a reason you decided to join us at this particular time instead of at Dairy Queen?" I corner him a little between Shep and me, and he gets a little wide eyed and defensive.

"I gotta make sure that old snake is really dead. If anyone can claw back from the depths of hell, it's gotta be him," he whispers back, dead serious.

"You have got to be kidding me," Shep mutters, shaking his head and turning back to finish his conversation with David. I take a deep breath and turn them to face forward in line. Jacquie stifles another giggle and gives me a knowing wink before turning back to her husband in line ahead of her.

"Richard MacDougal is really dead. He is not a ghost, he is not a demon, he is not whatever other imaginary nonsense you've concocted. Now behave in this line, or no Blizzards after dinner."

After another thirty minutes in line, we finally make it to the family and casket, giving solemn nods and handshakes to Thomas and Peter Hodges, and then introduce ourselves to Nancy MacDougal Hodges.

"Hi, it's so nice to meet you. We are Shep and Molly Jones, we live across the county road from Richard," I say, giving her a wide, hopefully not crazy looking, smile. She gives me an uneasy look, and I immediately know we've been discussed after our run-in at Silver Spring last night.

"Lovely to meet you both. I believe a thank you is in order for everything you've done for our Richard," She clips back, smoothing her black tweed skirt after shaking mine and Shep's hands.

"Oh, just being neighborly is all. Is everything going alright over there? We're just across the road if you need any help with anything," I reply, not knowing if she'll tell me anything about the state of affairs there or not. Thomas and Peter are both clammed up on either side of her, so this might be the dead end Shep predicted after all.

"Coudreaux P. Cogburn, very pleased to be making your acquaintance, ma'am," Before Nancy can answer, Cooter elbows through and shakes Nancy's hand with a vigor she seems unaccustomed to. Her face is a mixture of shock and disgust she's trying to temper with manners, but Cooter's vintage plaid pearl snap and dark wash jeans with his eager demeanor don't seem to be meeting her approval.

"Lovely to meet you," she squeaks out, trying to yank her hand back.

"You can call me Cooter," he answers confidently, giving her what should be a charming smile, but it seems to just repulse her more.

"I beg your pardon?"

"You can call me Cooter, not Coudreaux, ma'am. It's my nickname. That's like a shortened version of my name, so you don't have to use the long formal one," he explains, enunciating clearly, like she doesn't understand how formal names versus nicknames work instead of the truth: that she's so affronted she can't wrap her mind around what's happening in front of her.

"Um, alright. Thank you for coming, Mister... Cooter." She gulps out his name, like it is borderline offensive to her and she is trying to get it out of her mouth as fast as possible because it tastes bad. I turn back to Shep with a discreet hand over my mouth and try not to laugh. Maybe them being here isn't so bad after all.

"Oh, ma'am, we wouldn't miss it, no sirree. Ol' Dick was meaner'n a bag of rattlesnakes, but I reckon we still gotta pay our respects to the dead, y'know?" He is pouring it on thick and I stifle another laugh. Cooter is country, but not this country. And that's when it hits me. That's the real reason they came: to get a northerner's goose. Shep must have told them this morning that Richard's remaining family is here from New England to do this, and he thought a little prank was in order. There's very little a southerner loves more than to poke a little fun at a northerner.

Nancy stares at him blankly, like she is still in disbelief at everything she just heard. Peter looks like he might be ill, but Thomas looks to be suppressing a laugh himself. Cooter moves down the line a little and straightens Thomas's tie for him as it is slightly askew. Thomas stands speechless as he is put back in order like a small child by Cooter. "Boy, that's real nice. You just look... dandy. Like a real Yankee Doodle Dandy, my good man."

"Well, we are so sorry for your loss. We'll see you tomorrow at the service," I say, quickly gathering Cooter and Roy, and hurrying them out of line. We make it just outside into the parking lot before Cooter and Roy dissolve into giggles. I stop short and give them both stern looks that stop their laughter in its tracks.

I don't actually say anything, just continue to give them my "you know better" look, before starting toward the car again. Shep walks silently with me, no expression on his face, and the boys trail behind trying to keep up. Along with clicking boots on the pavement, I hear Cooter's tentative voice behind me.

"Hey, uh, Boss? Is that a yay or a nay on the Blizzards?"

chapter
fourteen

"I DON'T KNOW, Boss, I think you should just go for the convertible. You'd look pretty slick in a convertible," Cooter dunks a chicken strip in his bowl of gravy, and nods convincingly. Roy gives us a thumbs up with one hand while also dunking a chicken strip, and I stifle a laugh. The only thing I need more than two ranch hands who like to act out SNL skits is two ranch hands who are the ultimate hype squad.

Shep and I walked the dealership lot after leaving the funeral home, mainly looking at the full-size SUVs, but I did take a few minutes to try my plan of convincing Shep the convertible was my heart's desire. He didn't believe me for a second, but Cooter and Roy did jump on that bandwagon just for fun, too. The joke has continued all the way to Dairy Queen as the four of us enjoy our early dinner of chicken strip baskets.

Shep shoots them both a cease-and-desist look, and we eat in silence for a few minutes. We looked at probably seven to ten different vehicles and I feel completely overwhelmed at this point. Part of me wouldn't hate the convertible just because there's only one and it takes all the decision making out it. Even among the full-size SUVs the possibilities are endless-two-wheel or four-wheel drive, cloth or leather seats, captain seats or bench seat, regular length or extended length. The nice part of being in a small town is that you can hit one family of dealerships and see several different makes and models without having to tour around town and be accosted by all manner of salespeople.

"I don't think the convertible meets my seat number requirements, but thanks for the vote of confidence I'd be slick in it," I reply, wiping the corners of my mouth and finishing up my dinner. "What did you think of the Suburban?" I ask, turning to look at Shep so they know it's his opinion I'm after, and not anyone else's.

"It's different, but I'm not opposed. I have a hard time getting the same thing if there are known issues with this, you know?"

"I agree. Did you like that better than the Yukon?"

"I like the price tag better. Plus, the Suburban is the color you want."

"Well, it would just be weird to not have a black vehicle, you know?"

Shep nods in agreement and starts to gather up all our trash. As he walks to the trash can, Cooter and Roy both finish their dinners and look up at me expectantly. I stare stone-faced back at them for a minute or two, then relent, pulling a twenty out of my purse. "I want a mini brownie Blizzard and he wants a chocolate milkshake." Cooter snaps the twenty out of my hand with a giant grin and he and Roy jump up to head to the counter for dessert.

Shep joins me back at our table, sliding into the booth next to me and wrapping an arm over my shoulder. "Don't feel bad. We've done the best we can raising them, but nature might be stronger than nurture," he says to me quietly, and I laugh out loud. While they are obviously employees that are essential to our operation, they are also a little bit like two extra big kids that seem to need raising just as much as our other two. Our ice cream populates the front counter as they finish making it and Cooter and Roy return to the table once it's all ready. We eat dessert in mostly silence for a few minutes until we hear the chime of the front door and a group of guys walk in.

"Oh, no, look what the cat dragged in!" Cooter crows, as True Walker and his handful of ranch hands step inside. True looks up to see us sitting in the corner, and he grins as he heads over. Shep stands, and greets him with an outstretched hand.

"Well, I heard the Dairy Queen had rats, but now I can confirm in person. How are y'all?" He asks, clapping Shep on the back and shaking Roy's, then Cooter's hand.

"Good to see you, True. What are y'all up to?"

"Oh, just living the dream. We just moved a smaller heifer group to that new lease place, so we're grabbing a quick dinner before we go back out to check calves in that other pasture."

"Seems like y'all are getting quite a few moved. Are y'all planning to move all the herds?" Shep asks, returning to his seat. True jams both hands in his jeans pockets and shifts his weight from boot to boot, looking a little sheepish. I try not to visibly frown, wondering why he seems a little cagey. I get an uneasy feeling in the pit of my stomach, like there seems to be much more to this situation than we know, or that he wants to share.

"Uh, probably. We've overgrazed our pastures a little, so we're trying to let them rest. We'll get the rest of the smaller groups moved over the next week or so."

"Sounds good. I'm glad y'all were able to find something to move to, especially so close. That was pretty good timing and luck," Shep chuckles. Cooter and Roy stand to say hi to True's hands at the counter after they finish ordering, and I gather up our dessert trash to get ready to head out.

"Yes, if you have any tips or tricks for finding lease places, please share. That has been just about the hardest thing in all our time ranching. Leases are harder to find than gold," I joke, staring him dead in the eye just to see how he reacts. He gives me an uneasy smile, not far off from a grimace, and lets out a strangled laugh.

"I don't really have advice, just the right place at the right time, thankfully." He accepts his drink from one of his guys before they all head to a table in the middle of the dining room.

"Oh, by the way, we just heard that Asa is in the rehab hospital. Is he okay?" I ask, hoping the sudden change of topic might throw him off guard a little and get more of a reaction out of him.

It seems to work because True's eyes widen a little and he stammers out his answer. "Uh, he is fine. He just had a little accident."

"Jacquie Welch said he fell. What happened?"

"He, uh, he missed one of the stairs going up to his room and fell down about half the flight. He broke a leg and dislocated his shoulder, but he's a tough old bird. He's doing rehab and should be back home in a month or so."

"You're kidding, he fell down the stairs? It's a miracle that didn't kill him!"

"Yeah, it was a miracle for sure. Well, I better get to eating so we can get back to work," he flashes us another tense smile before shaking Shep's hand and heading over to their table.

"There's something going on there," I whisper to Shep as we head to the door. He glances back at True and his boys before opening the door and holding it open for me, Cooter, and Roy to walk out into the parking lot.

"I think you're right. That sounded a little like the only accident is that Asa survived."

"Hey, babe. How was Nana and Gramps'?" I ask as Shep and I walk in the side door a little while later to find Mia sitting at the kitchen island deep in math homework. I take one look at the paper full of equations and gesture for Shep to take his stab at it while I pull a few bottles of water out of the fridge to pass around. We all have our spiritual gifts, and math is not mine, so Shep is in charge of helping with math and science while I cover English and history.

Billie grabbed the kids from their after-school activities, so we could go to the funeral home and then look at the car lot. She fed them dinner and gave them a ride home, so now Mia is pushing through math homework that looks like one of my worst nightmares and Hayes is reading his required reading library book on the couch in the family room.

"Nana made hot dogs and hamburgers. She and Gramps played us in ping pong before we came home. They almost won, but we pulled through at the end," she answers, shoving her list of math problems over to Shep and dropping her pencil. Of all the qualities I could pass on to my girl, it seems a disdain for math has been one of them. He shoots her a look, and she reluctantly picks her pencil back up and tries to seem interested in her work.

"Sounds like fun. How much more do you have?"

"Like five problems."

"Any other homework?"

"No, I already finished my book for English."

"Good girl. Wrap up that math so you can get ready for bed. Hayes, you finished?"

"Just about."

"Alright, go take a shower when you finish up so you can go to bed, too."

As Shep and Mia knock out her last few problems, I clear some clutter from the island and organize bags from earlier activities. I pull out Mia's ballet leotard, tights, and cover up to throw in the washing machine, along with Hayes's dirt-stained baseball pants and socks that smell like something died in them. As I come back through the kitchen headed to hang bags on the hooks in the mud room, I hear my phone ping as my smart watch also vibrates with a notification. I flick my wrist to see who it is and the Buffalo Creek ISD logo lights up my watch screen with NEW GRADE POSTED flashing underneath. The school moved to some sort of online gradebook system a year or two ago, and I'm not typically one to micromanage grades, but I somehow ended up with notification alerts for every new grade posted. Normally I ignore them, and normally it's not that notice-able until the end of the grading period when there is inevitably one teacher that posts all the grades for the grading period in one sitting and it seems like my phone/watch is having seizures and meltdowns with how much it dings.

I have a spare minute, so I grab my phone and click through the notification to the app to see what was just posted.

43.

The header is History, and the line item says Chapter 18 Test with yesterday's date and a recorded grade of 43. My kids aren't the smartest in the world, but they are generally hard workers and know we don't tolerate anything lower than Bs without proof of significant effort that something lower was the best they could do.

"Does someone want to explain to me how they got a 43 on a history test yesterday?" I screech as soon as I register that the number is real and out of 100, not a much smaller number.

"43? Like 43% out of 100? Out of 100%?" Shep stammers, jumping up to grab the phone out of my hand and see for himself. I pass the phone off to him to look as I stare at my children waiting for one of them to respond. Hayes quietly closes his book and gets up from the couch.

"I'm finished with my book, Mom, so I'm going to go take a shower. Also, uh, wasn't me," he says, shooting me a finger gun and scurrying off to the front stairs to head up to his room. I immediately shift my gaze to Mia, who has her head slumped low to avoid eye contact.

"Amelia Beth Jones, what happened? You don't make 43s. Is this because of cheerleading?" I walk over to stand directly across the island from her, and Shep returns to his seat next to her. Big crocodile tears well up in her eyes and she starts sobbing.

"Kinda," She blubbers, and I maintain my patience. I've learned over the years not to believe every crying sob story because more often than not, they are in a mess of their own making, but I do try to hold grace at the same time because they are human, and we are also human.

"What do you mean, "kinda"? Did you study for this test, or were you goofing off doing cheerleading stuff instead?"

"No, I studied. I knew all the material," she heaves, a few hiccups interrupting her words.

"Then how did this happen? You know if you don't pass your classes, you can't cheer anyway, so skipping studying for that is futile."

"I know. That's part of it."

"Okay, so tell us what happened? If you knew the material, why did you make such a poor grade?" Shep asks, passing her a tissue to help calm her down. He shoots me a pointed look, like I need to maybe calm down the one lightbulb interrogation tactic. I take a deep breath and nod that I'll calm down. A little.

"I can't tell you the truth because I don't know if you'll believe me."

"Mia, we will always believe you. You've never given us a

reason not to believe you, right?" I come around the counter and sit on her other side, patting her back and looking her in the eye. "This is not like you, and we know that. But you have to tell us the truth if you want us to help."

Mia takes a big gulp of air and regains some composure.

"I threw the test."

"You what?" Shep asks, looking at her with confusion. I have to say, I don't really understand what she means either, but I try to look like I do.

"Hainslee Lane is failing history. She knows my average is a 97 because Mrs. Watson announced it to the class after the last test. No one got a curve on the last test because I made a 100 and she told everyone. The day before that test, Coach Lane cornered me in the computer lab and said that I needed to let Hainslee copy off me for this test so that she could raise her grade and not get kicked off the squad. She said if I didn't, she'd tell Mrs. Watson that I was cheating with stolen test materials and get me kicked off. I let Hainslee copy, but I purposefully chose mostly wrong answers. I can afford one bad grade and still get an A in the class overall."

I pause, looking her dead in the eyes, and let her words sink in. After a few minutes, I wordlessly get up from my stool and head to my laptop across the counter.

"What are you doing?" Shep asks hesitantly, looking a little nervous about what I might be about to do.

"It's fine, I'm just going to email Mrs. Watson about this grade. I'm not going to embarrass anyone."

"Mia, did you talk to Mrs. Watson about this?" Shep asks, turning his attention back to her, but cutting his eyes back to me every few seconds to make sure I'm still behaving.

"No, Coach Lane said no one would believe me in my word against hers."

I immediately suck in a large gasp of air and heave it out loudly to keep from screaming. I step away from my computer for a brief moment, and then return to my screen to start on my email.

"Molly," Shep tries to make eye contact with me and I angrily keep my eyes on my computer instead. I realize there are likely still many facets to this story, but at this point, I'm ready to make more heads roll than Henry VIII.

"Mom, seriously, please don't say anything. My grade will recover, and it won't be that big of a deal. I don't want it to blow up into this big drama where everyone gets in trouble. Please," Mia has big, pleading puppy dog eyes, and I relent slightly. I don't want to make her life hard at school, but I absolutely don't want either Lane girl to think they can threaten my girl and get away with it.

"Mia, I'm not trying to make anything harder for you, and I'm not trying to take anything away from your friends. But there is right and there is wrong. And this is wrong. I appreciate that you've set yourself up to weather this well, and to see the good. I think you came up with a pretty creative solution to a really bad situation. But what happens when they come back expecting the same for the next test? Or you get more threats because you didn't really do like she told you to do and Hainslee will still be failing? We can't establish you as a doormat that can be forced into things you know are wrong just to keep the peace. That isn't peace at all."

Mia holds back more tears from her ocean blue eyes and I try not to cry with her. Motherhood is such a weird intersection of feeling like you would take a bullet or wrestle a bear for your child, or at least slap a fellow mom for hurting them, while also knowing sometimes the best thing for them is to not fight their fight. I'm planning to fight for her, but it looks like I'm going to have to pull in a little more finesse and diplomacy than my gut instinct first recommended.

"I'm not going to go in guns blazing, I promise. I'm just going to start with talking to Mrs. Watson about options, and to gauge if she thought this was unusual or out of character. I'm not going to name drop or accuse anyone... Yet."

Mia visibly exhales and nods in agreement, and I walk back around the counter to hold her in a hug. Shep wraps his arms around her from the other side and calls out, "Squeeze chute!" before squeezing both of us tightly until we all start giggling.

"Alright, go ahead and get ready for bed, okay?" I kiss her forehead and we send her up the stairs as I gather up all her homework papers and put them in her notebook. After slipping her notebook back in her backpack, I sit back down next to Shep. He puts an arm around me and remains quiet for a few minutes.

"Are you really going to go into this calmly and not make a scene?" He finally asks, turning to look at me. I sit still and quiet for a few more moments before I nod, probably not convincingly.

"Becki Lane is up to something: something with Asa, something with that baby daddy of hers, something with her husband. Whatever all that is, that's one thing, but I'm going to make sure she knows that she better not be up to something with our girl. Or she can deal with me."

chapter
fifteen

"I STILL DON'T UNDERSTAND why you made me wear dress pants! Shep is wearing jeans. Every other guy we know here is wearing jeans," The next afternoon, Lance is pouting as we all walk into the funeral home together for Dick MacDougal's service. Lucy apparently convinced him that he absolutely needed to wear black dress slacks, and he's not wrong: every other male Buffalo Creek citizen I've seen is wearing jeans, from the ultra-dressy and ultra-old-school super dark wash, to the more modern and trendy super light wash. I have no doubt that the Hodges men will be in dress pants, but I'm thinking that's not the side he will want to look in an alliance with.

"You look handsome, that's all that matters," Lucy dismisses him with an off handed wave as we walk up the handful of front steps to the chapel doors to head inside. Shep opens one side of the double doors, and after we step inside and let our eyes adjust to the lighting of the chapel, we see that there is hardly a seat available anywhere. Lucy and I turn to look at one another as the guys come in behind us and also survey the scene.

"All this for the meanest old bastard in Crawford County?" Lance whispers behind us and Lucy promptly elbows him in the ribs. "What? Where's the lie?" He asks, rubbing where he will likely be bruised tomorrow.

"I think this just goes to show that small towns care just as much about the gossip and not missing out on something as they do the actual people," I say, as we shuffle behind the back left row to see if we can spot any openings. It's still thirty minutes until this is supposed to start, and people are already starting to fight for seats, and give each other disdainful looks about saving sections of pew.

"I would have never bet in any lifetime we'd be opening the overflow room for Dick MacDougal." Two funeral home employees, a grumpy older woman, and a rotund middle-aged man, are trying to elbow their way through the crowd to the double doors on the back right side that feed into a side room with more seating and a big screen TV that shows the pulpit speaking in closed-circuit. They stall out in the middle of the crowd, unable to get around the people trying to see any open seats and not willing to move in the off chance that it puts them in a weaker position to jump on anything that becomes available. The older woman, wearing a matronly long black skirt and black vest over a white button down, snidely comments on the crowd to her counterpart when they stop next to us. The middle-aged man, with thick dark hair combed over and a dress shirt struggling to cover his belly, makes a snorting noise in agreement before addressing the gathering crowd.

"Ladies and gentlemen, if you will create a path and allow us through, we will open the back overflow room. We have plenty of seating if you all will just part the way, please!" He receives a variety of dirty looks in response, and a few people start reluctantly moving out of the way to allow them through. The crowd at large is slow to relent because no one really wants to be relegated to the overflow room. I'd be willing to bet the overwhelming reason the majority of people are here is not to watch the pulpit speaking, but to watch the crowd that has assembled, and the overflow room crowd just isn't as enticing as the real deal. If I'm honest, I'm not really interested in the overflow room, but I steal a quick glance at my extremely crowd averse husband and count down in my head waiting for him to suggest we take seats in there.

5...4...3...2... "Look, there are four seats right there on the front row next to the aisle. I think that's our best option," He points through the newly opened double doors and immediately takes off for them before anyone can protest. The four seats are in the back corner closest to the vestibule, so they allow a partially obstructed view of the main auditorium in addition to the closed-circuit screen. He and the salty male funeral home worker exchange a nod of understanding with one another as he stands at the aisle and waits for Lance, Lucy, and me to slide in ahead of him.

"I should have known you'd be BFFs with Bernie over there and get us VIP funeral seats," I laugh, waiting for Shep to sit down after me. He surveys the crowd and nods to himself that this is likely our best option, so I go ahead and get comfortable and pull out my program to read while we wait.

The front page is the typical funeral information: time, date, place, name, and birth/death dates. The inside pages have an order of events, along with a cheesy poem about not missing someone when they are gone because they are always with you. I frown in slight disagreement because I'm hoping I don't ever have to deal with him again, but I suppose that only applies if I'm missing him. Which, honestly, I'm not. The back features his obituary, and I can tell it was written by a doting aunt who likely spent very little time with him. Words like "beloved" and "sorrowfully missed" are dolloped on like mountains of spray whipped cream, high and superfluous.

We have a great view of the front door, and watch over and

over as the doors open and we see faces visibly fall when they clock how many people are already here, and that the overflow room is their best option. We wave to random people from town that we see, as I periodically check my watch to see how much longer until this show gets on the road with the next 30 minutes ticking by slowly.

Finally, with about five minutes to go, the funeral director lightly taps on the microphone in the pulpit. "Ladies and gentlemen, the family of Richard MacDougal would like to thank each of you for making time to attend this memorial service today. We will be beginning shortly, so we would ask that you all take your seats so we can begin bringing in the family. Thank you." He exits the pulpit pedestal and disappears through a side door toward the family parlor. The crowd noise roars again as there is still a decent amount of pushing with the last guests frantic to find seats. The overflow room is now to the point of overflowing, and in front of our seats, there is discussion between Grumpy and Grumpier, funeral home workers extraordinaire, about opening the lobby and wheeling in another closed-circuit TV to lessen the crowd. After a minute or so of watching people jostle, they stall out with paralysis by analysis and decide not to do anything instead.

"I can't believe there are this many people here," Lucy whispers to me as the last of the crowd crams into the few remaining seats. We both do a slow scan of the auditorium to see who is here, and I think the list of Buffalo Creek residents who aren't here is probably a shorter, if not non-existent, list. Frank and Billie are a few rows behind us, and several friends from church and town are scattered through the audience. But there is one notable missing person to me: Wendy Foster.

Just as I start to scan the crowd again to make sure I didn't miss her tucked in between anyone, the door directly across the auditorium from us opens. The funeral director walks out solemnly, and stops a few feet from the door, gesturing for those behind him to walk ahead.

Nancy MacDougal Hodges emerges in a full black skirt suit ensemble, complete with a black fascinator atop her teased helmet shaped bob. She waits for one moment outside the doorway before Peter immediately steps to her side and gives her his elbow to help escort her to the family pew at the front. A few beats later, Thomas appears, but everyone is so focused on Nancy and Peter that he barely gets any billing. They all reach the front pew, and Peter nods for Thomas to slide in first so that he can have the outside seat. There is a visible disappointment on Thomas's face, but he quickly scurries in and gets situated before the elder two shuffle in and take their seats.

"That's it, that's all the family?" Lance whispers across Lucy to Shep and me, and we nod silently. "I figured with all the hoopla we heard it would be bigger."

"That's what she said," Shep whispers back, maintaining eye contact with the carpet in front of him. Lucy and I work hard to hold in our giggles as Lance reaches over us to fist bump Shep.

The funeral home director dims the auditorium lights, leaving the podium illuminated, and a hush falls over the crowd at an abnormally rapid pace. Everyone is waiting with bated breath to see which local minister drew the short straw to perform this service. Obviously, people want to hear good things about their recently departed relatives, but at the same time, no one wants to break the ninth commandment. After a few lingering moments, the back door behind the pulpit opens slowly and dramatically.

"No... way..." Lucy whispers, her jaw dropping in disbelief. My eyes lift from reading my program for the ninetieth time, and I let out a shocked gasp.

Moving slowly through the door is Crockett Daniel Guthrie, clad in a worn leather pioneer outfit, head to toe, trimmed in what looks like racoon fur, topped with a traditional Davy Crockett cap with the tail. His long, bushy beard glistens in the bright stage lights, with what I hope is some sort of hair care product and not sweat. He is using a tall, whittled, mesquite-wood walking stick to take about one step per minute, and at this pace, he'll be up to the pulpit podium by next Tuesday.

"He's never gonna make it at this rate," Lucy whispers and I nod in agreement, double checking the program to see if this was written anywhere and we just missed it. Nowhere on this half-folded sheet of paper is the name Crockett Daniel Guthrie, so we'll never know if this was intentional, or a last-minute substitution. After what feels like an hour, but is more literally like seven minutes, he reaches the podium and stands there surveying the crowd for a few more long moments.

"Good afternoon, ladies, gentlemen, fellow Texans," he booms into the microphone, and most of the crowd jumps in surprise at the volume. He adjusts the height on the microphone and rests his walking stick next to the podium before beginning again.

"We have assembled here this afternoon to memorialize a man. A man. A Texan man. A Crawford County man. Richard Francis MacDougal," He gestures to his left, where Richard's casket is immediately illuminated by a spotlight over the top of it. A large floral spray is covering the majority of the highly polished wood, with an easel set up to the right holding a poster size print of a young Richard in a military uniform.

Crockett proceeds to monologue for an hour and seventeen minutes. Not about Richard specifically or any of his life, but an hour and seventeen minutes about the history of Crawford County, and how the MacDougals were one of the first families to settle there, and Richard dying ends an era of the family maintaining their stake of Crawford County. By the time he wraps it up, Lance is asleep on Lucy's shoulder, Shep is using his Angus Association app to pretend breed our cows to different bulls, and the crowd as a whole is looking beat down. Funerals aren't typically ever a hot place to hang, but this is about the worst one I've ever sat through.

"And if there is one thing we can learn from this man here, it's the power of a loyal family legacy! The MacDougal family would like to thank you all for attending this afternoon. Good night!" He finishes up with his arms spread wide to both ends of the pulpit and a dramatic gaze to the ceiling before quickly folding into a bow. A few people tentatively start clapping, while the majority of the crowd looks around confusedly at one another. This feels like the strangest combination of a boring history lecture and a weird one-man show, so no one really knows what to think or do now that it's over.

The funeral director takes the podium back after Crockett uses his walking stick to slowly hobble back through the door he emerged from. "At this time, we'll begin the recessional," he announces, and nods to dime store Bernie at the back of the room near the doors. The back row of the overflow room is released first to walk past the casket and family before exiting a side door into the lobby, moving to each row from the back to the front.

After a steady flow for about ten minutes, our row stands and joins the procession line. We slowly make our way up the main aisle to the casket where everyone pauses for an appropriate few seconds before turning to acknowledge the family on the way to the side door. As we turn, I see that Nancy Hodges is softly crying into an embroidered handkerchief while Peter quietly comforts her, giving diplomatic looks of thanks to each person passing by. When he sees us, he adds a small dash of disdain in with his thanks and sorrow, and I try not to frown back at him in response. I get the feeling he doesn't care for us very much, and quite frankly, he doesn't really have a good reason to feel that way as far as I can see it.

Once we make it through the side door to the lobby, I try to casually glance around to see if there is anyone I know hanging around that I need to talk to. It feels like all manner of random suspicious information has hit me in the last few days, but I'm a little lost about where to go with it. As I look around, I see someone I haven't gotten a chance to meet up with yet, but could potentially be quite helpful.

"Mr. Shoemaker! How are you? It's been a long time!" Asa Shoemaker is sitting in the corner near the door in a wheelchair. He is alone for the moment, and when I speak to him from a few feet away as I approach, he perks up and looks around for a second until he matches my voice to my face.

"Molly Jones, how are ya, girl?" He rasps out, smiling at me with a sweet look of recognition in his eyes. I've only been around Asa a handful of times since we moved to the ranch, but he always struck me as a kind, gentle man, and a real cowboy. He hired True when he became considerably less mobile than he wanted to be, and essentially turned operations over to him, but we still saw him out petting and spending time with his cattle every day until he moved to a townhouse in town. He had a stint of colon cancer that he took chemo for, and it was much easier to be in town instead of going back and forth. As far as I'd heard, he has been in remission for the last year or two, and started staying back at his ranch house on the weekends, which is, I assume, how his "accident" down the stairs happened.

"I'm doing well, thank you for asking. It's great to see you, even if it's not the best circumstances."

"What do you mean? I'm not sad, are you sad?" He asks quietly, giving me a bit of a devilish grin. "It's okay to say he wasn't a very nice man, Molly. He's not going to get you like the Boogeyman."

"Alright, fair enough. What have you been up to? I heard

you took a little spill recently," I ask, pulling a nearby parlor chair closer to him.

"Yes, they tell me I passed out and fell down a few stairs, but I tell you, I just haven't felt myself the last month or two. I broke a few things here and there when I took my tumble but they got me patched up and I've been doing physical therapy. The girls down there are real nice, even if it does hurt like hell, pardon my language. When you're my age, you just don't work like you used to, I guess."

"I've heard getting older isn't for sissies. Do you still live in your townhouse or did you move back to the ranch? We miss seeing you when we drive by."

"Oh, I'd started staying out there a little more, but you know how it is to stay in a house no one keeps up. It's getting more and more run down, not as nice as it used to be, and it's easier to just keep up one house, if I'm honest. Really, I've been staying in the rehab place since my fall and it's been nice not to keep up anything. I've thought if I'm going to live in town anyway, I might have to move to one of those places that just does it all for me."

"I'd never turn down a place that cooks, cleans, and does my laundry for me. Do you have someone that checks on you?" I try to phrase that as delicately as possible because the question I'd really like to ask is, *can you make your own decisions or has someone taken over everything and you can't make decisions for yourself anymore?*

"I have a niece that looks after me from time to time. She had actually come out to check on me the day I had my fall. Lucky for me that she and True were both there, otherwise I'm not sure I would have made it to the hospital, you know?"

"Oh, yes, that's pretty lucky. It sounds like the Lord was looking out for you," I laugh, thinking to myself that He definitely was; it sounds like he was probably not supposed to survive that fall but did. "I know Jeannie Miller really loves it at Cinnamon Court," I add, knowing Asa should know Lance's mom from growing up. They moved her into assisted living a few years ago when Lance went to drop something off to her one day and found a small fire in one of her frying pans on the stove as she worked on her crocheting in her living room chair completely unaware. She is now living her best life playing bingo and doing chair Pilates in the rec room and safely not cooking any meals for herself.

"I haven't seen Jeannie in a while, but she is good people. Where's that rancher of yours? You leave him at home?"

Just then, Shep peeks around Lance and Lucy and spots us in the corner. He pats Lance on the shoulder and shakes his hand as Lucy gives me a little wave and nods her head to the door. I nod in reply and Lance and Lucy head out as Shep joins us.

"Mr. Shoemaker, good to see you," he says as he gives Asa's worn hand a shake. His skin looks thin as tissue paper, with purple bruising and veining blooming across it, and his fingers look a little warped and mangled. He is missing one or two knuckles off a thumb, likely an old roping injury, one of the main reasons I was always terrified for Shep to get into roping. Shep pulls himself up a chair and sits as Asa smiles kindly at him.

For whatever reason, it seems like a common theme for humans is just having a hard time rooting for each other. When Shep first made steps to move from medicine to ranching, we heard our fair share of backhanded comments and criticism. From our experience, money seems to cloud judgment, and when you say 'physician', all people take from that is 'big paycheck', and have no grace or understanding for why someone would want to leave that. And obviously, Shep made a good living, and it was really scary to let that go in a way. But that big paycheck came with big work and big responsibilities. I spent longer than I should have very naïve to what his days really looked like, not realizing that it wasn't uncommon for him to give someone a cancer or a major disease diagnosis. He was changing lives: usually for the better, but sometimes not, and that is a stress no one really sees or understands. Top that off with people that like to complain more than problem solve, take the shortcut or easy way, and make their issues everyone else's fault, it's really easy for me to see why he prefers cattle over people these days.

Buying the ranch and our first several head of cattle was a big step that we were excited about, but it was a little clouded by feeling like the small-town court of public opinion was judging us. Despite what they said, Shep wasn't "playing cowboy" and had done more research than anyone could have imagined. Luckily, despite all the noise, we had a handful of supporters encouraging us through the years we had to grind it out: mainly Hank, but also Asa. Shep would see him out with his cows as we were getting started and would always stop to talk, and Asa was always kind and reassuring. We learned that the real tried-and-true, love-it-with-all-their-hearts ranchers understand the dream, and have never been discouraging.

"I hear you've been around partying and got yourself in trouble," Shep teases, patting him on the shoulder and gesturing to his wheelchair.

"You know me, I just can't help myself," He teases back, his voice getting quieter and quieter. He looks tired, like he's packed more in his eighty-something years than they could hold, and they are catching up to him. In that moment, looking at his worn-down face and body, I'm suddenly so hopeful that it's just age making him seem subdued, and not anything extra or sinister.

"Are you hanging out here for a while, or do you want to hitch a ride back to the rehab hospital?

"Well, my niece dropped me off here, and she's supposed

to be picking me up, so I guess I'll wait for her. You all are kind to wait here with me," he slowly heaves out, sounding more labored with each word.

"Any time. So, how many head they let you keep in your room there at rehab?" Shep jokes, and Asa lets out a surprised laugh.

"Now, I will say, that's the one downside. I miss looking out my window and seeing my girls."

"I get that, for sure." Asa's eyes start to droop a little, and I start to feel increasingly suspicious and anxious. There is something wrong with him, I know it. I messed this up the first time; I let Richard die knowing in my gut that he wasn't okay, and I can't let that happen again. I shoot Shep a look of panic, and as he meets my eye, I can tell he sees it, too.

"Mr. Shoemaker, you doing okay?" Shep asks, slowly getting up from his chair and sliding next to him. Asa barely bobbles his head with his mouth starting to turn to the floor.

"Don't... let them... do this... to me..." He struggles to get his words out as the left side of his face continues to droop and his speech slurs. He slumps to his left side in his wheel chair and his eyes flutter closed.

"Shep, he's having a stroke," I blurt out, fumbling for my phone in my purse and trying to quickly dial 911. Shep nods in agreement and starts wheeling him to the door.

A Buffalo Creek Medical Center ambulance is at the door within minutes and we get him loaded up with EMS. When they ask about family or next of kin, I hesitate, but after a few long seconds, reluctantly give them the phone number I have for Becki Lane.

As the ambulance starts to drive off, a familiar white Yukon Denali with a temporary handicap placard swinging jauntily from the rear-view mirror careens into the parking lot and double parks crookedly in front of the funeral home lobby doors. As Becki gets out, she spots us and gives us a look that could kill before heading inside.

"Becki! Becki, wait!"

She completely ignores me as she shoves her way through the crowd trying to exit the funeral home, but I try to keep up with her.

"Molly, did they get him situated? Are they headed to BCMC?" Jacquie Welch and her husband are heading out the door as we are jostling in, and she stops me, as it seems word of Asa has already spread through the lobby. Becki manages to push her way in and does a quick circle in place in the crowd before realizing she doesn't see Asa.

"Where is my uncle?" She spats, turning back to me and staring me down with hateful eyes.

"He's headed to the hospital. He was having a stroke."

"You had no right, you aren't-"

"Young lady, your family is very lucky that the Joneses were here. They caught this at the onset and probably saved his life. You should be thankful," Jacquie intervenes, shooting Becki a look of warning. Becki looks like she wants to argue but also like she's a little scared of Jacquie. "Mike and I are going to head over there to make sure he gets settled." Jacquie heads out the door after giving her another stern look with her husband following behind a few seconds later.

Becki shoulders her way back to the door and I put a hand on her arm to stop her. "Hey, Becki?"

She whips around to look at me, her white blonde hair smacking me across the face. I push it all away, resisting the urge to yank the bejeezus out of it like she deserves.

"I'm on to you. And you won't get away with it."

sixteen

"THANK you so much for meeting with me. I just about had a heart attack when I pulled up Mia's test grade the other night," I slide into a desk in the front row of Mrs. Watson's sixth grade history class early the next morning and set my purse and coffee cup on the desk next to me. Mrs. Watson is in her late thirties, with long dark hair, and a matter-of-fact demeanor. Her husband is a banker at the local bank, and neither one is exactly the life of any party, but thus far in the school year, she's been consistent and firm with expectations, and we haven't had any issues. Her planning and conference period is the first one of the day, so after I send Mia and Hayes to class, I check in at the front office and make my way down the sixth grade hall to Mrs. Watson's classroom for our scheduled meeting.

Her classroom is set up in a traditional format: all the desks are lined up in rows facing the white board, and her desk is at the front. Windows line the outside wall, and bulletin boards featuring different historical time periods line the opposite wall. There are shelves of books at the back, but it is obvious there isn't a lot of non-traditional instruction going down in here. She's a lecturer, and the kids take notes, pop quizzes and tests for their grade. As I sit down, I take a second to look around the room. "Which one is Mia's desk?" I try to make it sound cool and casual, like *hey, I'm just curious what it's like for my daughter in here*, but it's actually all part of my master plan to bring home the message that Hainslee was trying to cheat.

Mrs. Watson cracks a small smile, and points to me. "Actually, that one. Like mother, like daughter. She says she focuses the best when no one is in front of her."

"Yes, she and I both can get a bit distracted by all manner of things. Who sits around her?" I ask, trying to still sound casual, and she hesitates, biting her lip. "Oh, I don't know if you're allowed to tell me that or not. I'm just curious if she has more willpower than I do and can sit by friends and stay focused, or if she's removed herself from that temptation, you know?" I let out a small chuckle that sounds a little more strangled than I would have preferred, and I cringe inwardly that I am messing this up.

"No, I can tell you. Emily Scott sits to her left, and Hainslee Lane sits behind her. Finn Hayden sits on her right." Bingo.

"That sounds about right. She and Emily have been friends since they were three, and I've heard a lot of giggles about Finn. Hainslee is kind of a new friend since they both made cheerleader for next year," I venture, hoping she will just take this bait, and admit that she knows all about this already, and we'll get Mia's grade taken care of ASAP.

"Yes, that's been a bit of a different relationship to watch develop," she says drily, and I can't tell if she approves or disapproves, and if so, what exactly she disapproves about it.

"Well, I'll just come right out with it. This is very uncharacteristic of Mia. Is there anything we can do about this, or will she have the ability to bring it up with other assignments? I'm just trying to get to the bottom of things since it is so uncharacteristic, you know?" I give her a genuine smile, and even though she's younger than me, and probably smaller than me, I'm suddenly terrified of her.

She first nods in agreement. "Yes, this is highly unusual for Mia. She has been my curve buster all year. If I'm honest, she doesn't have the most popularity in this class because she typically does significantly better than her peers testing, and I don't give curves for fun. Curves are meant to adjust what the class as a whole failed to understand, so if one person gets it, the entire class had the opportunity to get it."

"I see. I think I'm proud of her? Hard to hear other kids don't like your kid, but it sounds like it's for a good reason."

"Yes, I would be proud. Do you have any reason to suspect something is wrong or different with this test? Do you have a theory on why she did so poorly?"

I pause, trying to decide the most diplomatic way to share this. I absolutely don't want to come off as accusatory with basically no proof other than Mia's word, and I know it will also be awkward that Mrs. Watson works with Becki Lane and knows her as well as Hainslee. I seriously considered chickening out on this meeting before the funeral yesterday afternoon and just letting it all ride, but after the debacle with Asa's stroke, I want Becki nailed to the wall now more than ever.

"Mrs. Watson, how well do you know Becki Lane?" She pauses, and I can tell she is thinking about how to answer my question diplomatically. "I'm not asking for any salacious intermediate school gossip; I just need to know if I can trust you with something Mia told home."

She instantly softens and nods silently. I take a deep breath and choose my words carefully to try to sound decently non-biased. "Mia shared with her dad and me that Hainslee is not doing well in this class," I pause, and Mrs. Watson gives me the slightest flinch of confirmation. "She said that she was told by

Coach Lane in the computer lab before the test to allow Hainslee to cheat off of her test, or she'd arrange for her to be kicked off the cheerleading squad for next year. I have no idea if she has that kind of power or not, but Mia was terrified. Her solution was to throw the test so that Hainslee wasn't given a grade she didn't earn."

Mrs. Watson exhales slowly, and I feel just nauseous and unsettled. Why is it that we're made to want to defend our kids to the death, but also want everything to be peaceful and not rock the boat? "Do you have any proof?" She asks after a long minute of silence, looking defeated and disappointed. Her question takes me a bit aback, and I try to find an answer out of thin air because I was not expecting that question at all.

"Uh, well, not like concrete, would pass in court evidence. Just Mia's word for it. Which is exactly what she told Shep and me, that Coach Lane told her if she tried to tell that no one would believe her."

Mrs. Watson sighs and nods. "I've suspected Hainslee has been trying to cheat for the last few tests, but I can't prove it. The principal is great, but he's a very no-nonsense, objective evidence kind of man, and I don't know how to take this to him without any proof or evidence. If I tell him I suspect and just have a feeling, he'll dismiss it right away. I believe Mia, but I don't know how to get any justice for her without being able to prove it. I've seen other instances that involved the Lanes and nothing happened because there was no proof."

I nod in agreement, and try to rack my brain for an answer. "I'll try to think of something, but I appreciate that you at least believe her. She said this wouldn't tank her grading period average. Is she right?"

Mrs. Watson opens her school-issued iPad and pulls up her online grade book. After some flicks and swipes, she enters numbers into a few different boxes and lets it all calculate and average. "Yes, if she gets at least a 90 on the remaining

3 exams, she should still pull an A overall in the class. And if we can prove her story, I'll be allowed to let her retake that test."

I gather up my things and get ready to leave. "I appreciate you meeting with me. It's nice to hear nice things about your kid, you know?" I smile and give her a brief handshake as we walk to the door.

"She's one of the good ones. It takes creativity and courage to do what she did, you know?"

"She's got moxie, that one," I say, glancing up at the bulletin board to the right of the doorway. There are projects describing each of the founding fathers featuring photos and paragraphs of texts condensed onto one-page reports. After a few seconds of searching, I find Mia's page featuring each paragraph and photo backed with embellished paper and cut with decorative edged scissors, detailing the life and times of Alexander Hamilton. "Not Throwing Away His Shot" is the title of her project and I laugh to myself a little that the hours and hours of listening to *Hamilton* together paid off given the "A+" written in dark red marker at the top. I take a few steps down the inside wall looking at the different projects stapled across the bulletin boards until I make it to the corner. Something catches my eye up on the wall in the corner and I peer up at it to get a better look. "Mrs. Watson, what is that up in the corner?"

She follows me down the aisle and looks up into the corner with me. "Um, I think that's actually a camera. The school board decided to put them in last summer to cut down on bullying and in case there is ever an active shooter situation. It's a closed-circuit system that all feeds to the main office. It mainly monitors classrooms, hallways, and the bathroom sinks, so it's not an invasion of privacy."

"Do they have sound?"

"I'm not sure, maybe?"

I quickly walk around her and head for the door. "You coming?" I ask, looking back to see she hasn't moved.

"Um, where?"

"The main office. We're going to get our evidence."

"Mrs. Jones, it is against school and district wide policy to just release our closed-circuit footage when parents request." After waiting for thirty minutes in the front office, the principal finally has a few free minutes to meet with me. I've explained the bare-bones points of the story, and am hoping we can just pull the footage, and I don't have to turn into the super obnoxious "my baby is always right, how dare you" mom. Mrs. Watson had to go back to teach her second period class, so I am flying solo, and hoping I can pull this off.

"I understand that, sir, but it's not just for fun or being nosy. My child has told me that a member of your faculty has put her in an egregious situation, and I need to know if it's true, and if so, what can be done about it. Quite frankly, what is the point of having surveillance footage if it can't be used to solve problems?" Mr. Pine stares at me skeptically, and I can see what Mrs. Watson means when she says he's no-nonsense and doesn't work off conjecture.

"What is Mrs. Watson's opinion of this? Does she support your theory? These are serious accusations," he replies, leaning back in his desk chair and looking at me like he's essentially calling my bluff.

"Mr. Pine, have we ever met in here before?"

He looks a little confused, and stammers, like I'm trying to catch him in a gotcha moment. "I don't believe so, Mrs. Jones. If we have, I'm afraid I don't remember."

"Exactly. My girl doesn't cause problems. She told me she

was threatened, and I have no reason not to believe her, and neither do you or Mrs. Watson. Just check the tapes. If it never happened, then it never happened, and I'll gladly move on and apologize to Mrs. Watson and Coach Lane. But if it did happen, we need to deal with it." I give him my sternest look, and clasp my hands together in my lap so it's not so obvious my hands are shaking beyond my control. "I appreciate your desire to protect your staff, but if you really believe she's innocent, then this will exonerate her anyway. This age is hard enough to deal with peer pressure, standing out, being embarrassed, etcetera, etcetera. There is no way I would be in here potentially making life harder for my girl if I didn't think this was true."

We have a staring contest for what feels like the longest minute of my life. As the large industrial clock up on the wall between us ticks by, he finally sighs with his entire body, like he is mentally and physically relenting. "What day did this supposedly happen?"

"Mia said it was the day before the test, and the test was on Tuesday, so... this past Monday? I think she said their computer lab time is in the afternoon." I scoot to the edge of my seat as he turns away from me to his double computer screens on his built-in desk behind him. He clicks around on his screens until he pulls up a grid of black and white camera feeds. After running through a list, he clicks on one string of numbers and the picture shows a U of computers and students milling around. It feels like Mr. Pine is intentionally trying to block as much of the view as he can so I lean to the right as much as I can without being super obvious. I finally spot Mia sitting at a computer working intently on something. There are maybe three other kids in the room, and no one is near Mia. She finishes up whatever she is typing, and sends her project to the printer, standing up and walking over to the printer bay near Becki's desk to retrieve it. It feels like an out-of-body experience to watch my child on camera in a setting that I have no frame of reference for, and I have to keep reminding myself that this is really my child, and not some really weird show we're watching.

As Mia walks to the printer bay, Becki slowly stands from her desk, and walks around to stand near the printers, opening the paper drawers in the first few acting like they might need paper. Mia grabs her project and turns to walk back to log out of her computer as she is reading through the top page. She runs right into Becki as Becki steps directly in front of her. Becki says something to her and Mia frowns slightly, her little eyebrows knitting together. I feel heat up the back of my neck, and I clasp my hands back together because I have started to ball them into fists, knowing that I wasn't wrong. I can't hear what they're saying, but their body language is saying all I need to know.

On screen, Becki turns to check the other handful of kids in the lab, and then bends down slightly to make herself eye-to-eye with Mia, and Mia's sweet eyes look as big as saucers. I work to keep my backside planted in my seat as my emotions start to rise. Mia nods without saying anything as Becki talks to her, then walks around Becki back to her computer as Becki smiles to herself and returns to her desk. A minute or two later, Mia leaves the computer lab as quickly as she can, hurriedly shoving her papers in her backpack.

Mr. Pine pauses the footage and I take a deep breath to keep from immediately screaming at him. I know it's not his fault, but seeing that with my own eyes makes me want to run through a brick wall from my pure rage. He doesn't turn to look at me right away, and I wait to see if we're going to listen to this nonsense, or just watch it like a silent horror film again.

Instead, he just turns away from his computer and looks

to me silently. We have another seemingly endless staring contest until I finally can't stand it any longer. "Sir, respectfully, tell me what else you need to see?" I say, gesturing to the screens.

"Again, Mrs. Jones, innocent until proven guilty. It does appear there is some validity to your claim, but I'd like to speak to Mia and Coach Lane before we proceed any further. As soon as you leave, we will pull them both in here and get to the bottom of this."

"You absolutely will not speak to my daughter without me present."

"Your presence won't be necessary, Mrs. Jones."

"Have you ever heard of coercion, Mr. Pine?" I snap back, sitting up straighter in my chair. "Becki said this exact thing to Mia: there wasn't anything she could do about it because no one would believe her word over an adult's. Play the audio."

"Coercion works both ways, Mrs. Jones. We wouldn't want Mia feeling led to uphold your story since you seem very convinced of this. I would prefer to check the audio myself before it is made public out of privacy for my employees." He gives me a condescending look, and I clutch the sides of my chair as I try not to black out from anger. He is trying to maintain a cool façade, but I can see a little bit of squirm breaking through.

"With all due respect, sir, if you don't have anything to hide, there's no reason not to play that audio for me. I don't know exactly what's going on, but if I didn't know any better, I'd say you are in on whatever it is."

▭

"Mom, what is going on? Are we in trouble?" Hayes asks as he and Mia load up in the back of Billie's Bronco twenty minutes later. Mr. Pine refused to show me anything further, and I refused to allow him to talk to Mia without me, so I checked both kids out after reaching an impasse. This has very suddenly turned into quite the scene that I promised Shep I would not be making.

"No, you're not in trouble, guys. Mr. Pine and I are just not seeing eye-to-eye about Mia's situation in history, and I don't want y'all here right now. Who wants something from Delilah's?" I was planning to get myself a "good job for dealing with an adult situation" coffee after I finished at the school anyway, so now it looks like treats all around. Shep and the boys are spraying for flies and checking on our herd this morning, with plans to saddle up and move herds out in the far pastures this afternoon, so I decide to catch them up on everything the next time we see each other instead of bothering them with a phone call.

I pull into the parking lot at Delilah's a few minutes later and take orders from the backseat for raspberry lemonades and German chocolate cake cookies. When I run inside, there are a few people in line ahead of me, despite the fact that it's mid-morning. I glance around to the tables to see them mainly empty, except for the small square one in the back right corner. Sitting right there in front of God and Buffalo Creek are Wendy Foster and Thomas Hodges. Thomas looks just bewildered, as there are stacks and stacks of papers spread across their table, along with remnants of an early chicken salad croissant lunch stacked in one corner. I hesitate for a minute, knowing I need to stay out of it, especially considering all the monkeys I have in my circus right now, but I just can't help myself.

"Hey, Wendy," I say quietly, tentatively walking up to their table. A slow smile spreads across Wendy's face.

"Molly, hi! How are you?"

"I'm fine, how about you? Looks like you've still got your

boy in town," I say, gesturing to Thomas and smiling back. He looks a little surprised, looking from me to his mom, and I laugh a little to myself how unfamiliar he is with small town life despite having grown up in one. Everyone knows everyone, man.

"Yes, ma'am, it's always a good day when your favorite guy is in town, right?" She beams, patting his arm proudly. Thomas gives me a slightly queasy smile and I have to think whatever is going down in the documents all over the table has something to do with the birthday surprise he was discussing at Silver Spring a few nights ago.

"Y'all look like you're working hard over here! I thought you'd be headed back to the north by now, Thomas," I say, trying to sound upbeat and not nosy.

"My grandmother and dad headed home early this morning. I have some... things to take care of down here now," he says, gathering up a few of the papers and looking overwhelmed.

"Well, we're glad to still have you around! This looks like quite the project. You're in the right place, though, they have the best snacks and coffee here," I say with a wink, hoping they will divulge something, anything, about what they are working on.

"That actually sounds good. Mother, I'll get us some coffees," Thomas blurts, jumping up from the table and jumping in line.

Wendy hesitates, checking to make sure Thomas is out of earshot in line, and then looks like she can't help herself from just bubbling over. "We are working on some paperwork here. It wasn't completely the fortieth birthday gift I planned, and it's a few months late since he never comes home, but I felt like it was time to tell Thomas who his real dad is, and give him his piece of a legacy. I wasn't completely honest with you before. Charlie MacDougal is Thomas's biological father. And because of that, he's inherited the McDougal property outright since the trust belongs to heirs of Richard and Charlie. We're going through the trust paperwork now so our attorney can get the will and everything moved through probate." She looks downright giddy, and I honestly don't even know where to start. I mean, part of me felt like he was the likely heir anyway being that it seemed no one survived the original line. I mean, wouldn't family get the property even if they were disinherited over the state if no one is left? Plus, I had already found his birth certificate so his paternity wasn't new information. But it seems like it was very much new information to Thomas and he is unsure how to handle it all.

"Wow, that's big news! Can I ask if Peter knew, or is this a surprise to him, also?" I say tentatively, hoping it doesn't sound too forward or nosy.

"He didn't know for sure, but he always suspected. Which is maybe part of why I subconsciously pushed them to have a close relationship. It was the early eighties, so he wasn't really at the hospital when Thomas was born or that present in the process. They don't really question paternity when the father isn't there to argue, so one questioned when I put Charlie on the birth certificate. I knew Peter would raise him, and I wanted that to happen, but I just wanted him to have one connection to his real father. It looks like that worked out for him better than I imagined."

"Uh, definitely. Does Thomas have plans for the place, or is he still figuring all that out?"

Wendy pauses, and glances over to Thomas standing at the counter ordering their coffees and desserts. "He hasn't really decided yet. Obviously, this is big information, especially considering how close he and Peter are. I loved Charlie. I mean, I've always loved him and always will, but I really loved him back then. But I knew he could never provide a real life for me like Peter could. I got the greatest gift from Charlie, and now I always have a little piece of him. Thomas will catch up, but I've got a 40-year head start knowing this, so he just needs some time. I'm hopeful this gives us a chance to have more of a relationship, and this gives him a reason to spend a lot more time down here."

"That's... great, Wendy. I hope it works out how you are wanting. I was just curious from an across-the-road neighbor standpoint," I laugh, now also secretly wondering if this might be our chance to lease some of this land and push toward a big expansion.

"Here you are, Mother. One vanilla cappuccino," Thomas says, sliding a large mug on a saucer over to Wendy as he returns to the table. He sets his own mug and saucer on the table in front of him and picks up a stack of papers. As he starts to read them, it seems like his eyes are glazing over, and he is losing interest.

"Molly, how long have you lived across from the MacDougal estate?" He asks me abruptly, slapping the papers back on the table. His formal conversational style throws me off every time I speak with him because it seems so foreign to our everyday norm.

"Uh, five years? Six years? It's been several years now. Why do you ask?" I stammer, wondering what that has to do with anything.

"I'm just curious how manageable you think the property is. Will I need a full-time caretaker?" I give him a bit of a puzzled look, and he shakes his head quickly. "I'm so sorry, I just assumed Mother told you the news while I was gone. She's been so happy to share thus far."

"Oh, right, yes, she did share. Well, Richard didn't have anyone leasing it before he passed, and he was very adamant that he wouldn't. We approached him a handful of times over the years and he continuously said that he didn't want anyone else's- and I quote- "mangy sale barn trash" on his family's land. I mean, adamantly would not lease it, despite the fact that it's more than enough to support an entire ranching operation. I think if you had someone leasing the land, you would be fine. They would look after it and upkeep your fences and all that. If you keep it unleased like he did, you'll have to check it more often for fence damage and stray cattle, and make sure the fire breaks are taken care of, especially in the summer."

Thomas frowns, then starts digging through his stacks of papers. "No, no, there is a tenant. I meant do I need a caretaker in addition to the tenant... Wait, so if he was adamantly against leasing it, why is there a current lease in this paperwork? These are Richard's records we found in the office at the ranch house." He pulls out a thin, stapled stack of papers and hands it over to me. I'll admit, legalese makes my eyes glaze over, too, but I try to stay focused and glean the high points off this document.

Truman J. Walker, dba Shoemaker Cattle Company, LLC, leasing 18 sections of grazable acreage, starting April 1, 2024 and ending at the cessation of lifetime of Mr. Walker, or the cessation of Shoemaker Cattle Company, LLC, whichever comes second. The paperwork continues discussing a very miniscule payment into the family trust until the cessation of the lease (True's death or SCC's dissolution), or the cessation of the family line, at which point there is the option to buy the property at an embarrassingly low sum, like 1880s going market rate. This is ironic considering no one else really knew there was a continuation of a family line, and it would effectively cease with Richard. Pretty sweet deal to make given those circumstances considered. Could True and Thomas be in this together? True pays Thomas for the lease and they push Richard out completely so they both get what they want and he's not in their way to stop it?

"Have you looked into this at all, Thomas? Wendy?" I say, my eyes bugging out of my head a little. There is no way

Richard would have signed this lucidly. NO way he would have agreed to this whatsoever. I knew it sounded like True's new lease was a little too good to be true when he reluctantly shared those few details, but this is wilder than I imagined.

"No, is there something wrong? It seems like decent terms to me," he replies, shrugging. I can tell Wendy has no clue what's going on, and won't really care unless it starts to threaten Thomas being around more often.

"This is a clearly one-sided deal, and not really in your favor. I really don't think Richard would have signed this in his right mind." True's signature at the end looks legit, but Richard's looks like a wobbly scribble that is completely illegible. Like this probably wouldn't even hold up in court kind of illegible. The date is less than a week ahead of him passing away, feeling like it was maybe finalized under the gun, so to speak. It looks like it was thrown haphazardly in the back of the file, to be there if needed, but hopefully no one would notice it if they didn't have to.

Thomas and Wendy exchange looks, and I slide it back across the table to them. As I lean over the table, I can't help but notice the paper sitting on the top of the file now is a single sheet that looks exactly like the letter we received from the development company expressing interest around the time Richard starting really going downhill. The only difference between the letter we received and this one is a signature at the bottom. A signature that looks suspiciously familiar to one I've seen at the bottom of other notes recently.

"Thomas, what do you know about Digitron?"

He gives me a confused look like I've caught him completely off guard. "The heart failure medication? It was widely prescribed in the nineties. I don't believe it's in production anymore, at least not with our company. Too many side effects for too little benefit. The drugs we have in production and in development have far less side effects and much more forgiving dosing regimens. Some niche specialty pharmacies can maybe get it, but it's hard to come by. I'm not even sure where you'd get it anymore."

I'm not either, but someone did. And I have a feeling now that I know exactly who, just not how.

chapter
seventeen

"DEAD."

"For sure?"

"Yep. Donny says new transmission." Later that afternoon, Donny has called to say my car is officially dead as we once knew it. I mean, it still works other than the stutter, but apparently that stutter means it needs a new transmission, which is as good as dead to us. As soon as I get off the phone with Donny, I call Shep even though he's just down at the pens. They are getting horses ready to move cattle from one pasture to another, so it's faster for me to just call him than to go walk down there.

Shep sighs in the phone. "Well, that's basically what we were expecting, right?"

"Yeah, this isn't a total surprise. You still good with the Suburban?" I hear Cooter and Roy in the background playing rock, paper, scissors for who is going to open gates as they ride through and the phone muffles for a second.

"Sorry, I was throwing my saddle up," Shep says when the audio returns. "Yes, I'm good with the Suburban. If you'll call Donny back and get it set up, Mom can take you to pick it up, and I'll go sign my part when we finish up here. You can tell him I'll be there about 5:30 if that's good?"

"Yes, that sounds good. I'll call him now."

After I hang up with Shep, I get everything lined up with Donny, and arrange for Billie to pick us up in about an hour.

I'm still reeling from my run-in with Wendy and Thomas and what this means about True. We've known him for so long, it's hard to think he'd do anything he shouldn't have in the name of keeping a ranch alive, but desperation does weird things to people. I have typically not been one to jump to conclusions; I'm more likely to fly into them headfirst without looking back, so I'm trying to refrain from any thoughts or assumptions until I have a chance to really talk through all of it with Shep, my voice of reason.

In addition to the chaos of new vehicles and the possibility of a longtime friend being a murderer, the kids are home until I can figure out what the heck is going on at the school, preferably before a truancy officer hunts us down. I can tell Mia is not thrilled with me as she sits in the corner of the den reading a book by lamplight only, with all the shutters and curtains closed like it's a dungeon. Hayes ran off to help the guys get horses ready, so it's just me and her in the house. I meant what I said that my last intention was to make her life harder, but sometimes—oftentimes-- the right road is the hard road. And I am at least 85% sure this is the right road.

"Hey, babe? Do you want a snack?" I call, hoping to break the awkward silence. She maintains eye contact with her book and shakes her head silently. Boy, am I looking forward to the teen years at this rate.

I slowly head into the den and take a seat quietly in the armchair next to Mia's with only the small side table holding the lamp in between us. She still doesn't look up, and I briefly debate if I want to be cool, calm, and breezy mom, or the "look here, missy, I'm in charge" mom. "Mia, you understand what's going on, right?"

She plops her book into her lap, and stares at me with quite the look of defiance. "I was asking for you to answer me without a side of contempt and attitude, actually," I say with a large sarcastic smile, obviously leaning more "listen, missy".

"Mom, why did I have to leave school today? I'm going to be so behind," she whines, sitting up, tucking her bookmark in her place, and setting her book on the side table.

"Mia, something is going on at school. Definitely with Coach Lane, and maybe with Mr. Pine. They want to talk to you, and they don't want me or Daddy there, which tells me they are not going to be truthful or do the right thing," I take her hand and pull her over to my chair to sit her on my lap. She rolls her eyes like she's too big and grown to sit with me but still snuggles up anyway. "Have you heard of Coach Lane being mean to anyone else? Mrs. Watson thought she might have been doing the same thing to other students, but there wasn't any proof and Mr. Pine wouldn't believe them."

"Oh, Coach Lane is mean to students all the time. But she never gets in trouble. And she won't."

"What do you mean?" I ask, sitting up a little while trying to keep her balanced in my lap.

"Mom, if I tell you something, you have to promise not to tell anyone."

I pause, trying to decide how to handle that type of information. "Mia... I can't make that kind of promise. But I do promise to be very careful with whatever you tell me, and I won't use it to embarrass you or tell anyone who doesn't need to know. I can't promise not to tell anyone because if people are going to get hurt, we can't keep secrets, love bug."

"Mom..." She groans, rolling her eyes again and trying to roll off my lap. I wrap both arms around her and hang on so she can't get up.

"Mia, I'm serious. You can trust me, but I'll be honest that whatever you tell me might not be able to stay between just us."

She turns back to me and stares for a long minute. "Okay... here's the deal. Hainslee told us that her mom and stepdad are getting divorced because Coach Lane has a thing going with Mr. Pine."

My jaw drops and Mia gives me a look indicating she still expects me to uphold my end of our agreement and only use this for discreet good. Darn these kids and their morals and expectations.

"Okay, what kind of thing?" I ask, praying she's talking about a bowling team or something else equally harmless, even though I know this is grasping at straws. She gives me another look, this one of frustration and annoyance, and I wince to think she can be so casual about knowing that her cheer coach and principal, who are supposed to be trusted adults, are so seedy, and well, gross.

"I see. How does she know this?"

"She's seen them together several times, once at their house. And Hainslee said one time that she asked her mom about getting in trouble for cheating in her classes and she said she's got Mr. Pine right where she wants him so nothing will happen."

Oh, Lord. Shawn Pine is clearly not my favorite person right now, maybe ever, but this was not anywhere on my Bingo card. I don't know him super well, as my kids (thankfully) are not frequent flyers in the principal's office, but I've obviously seen him around town and know some about him. He and his wife, Lauren, moved here a few years ago after she finished residency and fellowship. She's a pulmonary/ critical care attending at the hospital where Shep used to work, but they had no overlap. I've seen her at Delilah's and other places around town, and she seems pretty humorless and not overly friendly, but I could have caught her on a bad day. Or days, I guess, as she's basically been the same every time I've interacted with her. She seems pretty dominant in their relationship, but I think maybe it's harder for women in medicine to turn down being in charge when they get home, even with their families. They have no children despite being in their late thirties', and he is typically at all the school functions by himself. Just from my little observations, and what I know about medical marriages, I could see where the demands of her schedule would leave space to allow Becki Lane to slither in and cause all kinds of problems, which is what sounds like has happened.

"Well, that seems like quite the mess, huh," I say, still a little speechless. I mean, kids are supposed to think adults never mess up, and have it all together, right? I'm sure that's the stuff therapy dreams are made of, but I hate that they lose all their innocence these days because stuff like this is a part of their everyday life. I absolutely want my kids to have a grasp on the real world as they grow up and not be too sheltered, but murder, affairs, secret illegitimate children, and blackmail have been all too prominent on the menu lately and aren't really what I had in mind, if I'm honest.

"It's their business, so I don't really care. I just want Hainslee to leave me alone in history so I can make the grades I want to make. Did Mrs. Watson say I could retake the test?"

I nod in agreement, wishing I could have that kind of laissez-faire attitude because it is indeed their business, and I want to not have to care. "She said you could if we can prove that Hainslee was told to cheat off you. If not, she agreed with you; you can still pull an A overall. I watched the surveillance camera footage from the computer lab with Mr. Pine, and it's clear that Coach Lane talks to you alone, but he wouldn't let me hear the audio. He said he needed to talk to you and Coach Lane before making it 'public', but I would not be surprised at all if something "happens" to the audio recording before anyone else has a chance to hear it."

Mia sits quietly, like she is deep in thought processing everything I've just said. This is some next level soap-opera garbage for a pre-teen to deal with; they don't even have a remotely developed frontal lobe, but somehow, they are expected to roll and cope with adults' elevated high-stakes drama. "I think I might be able to help, actually," she says finally, climbing off my lap and returning with her phone. "I didn't want to say anything at first because if we get caught with our phones at school, they get locked up in the office, and I didn't want to get in trouble after the fact."

Shep and I agonized over getting her a smart phone for way too long, rationalizing that anything she would need a phone for could be accomplished with a flip phone, but we eventually relented, embarrassingly bowing to the peer pressure of our friends and her friends. As predicted, there are days I want to chunk that thing in the trash and give her nothing but a walkie-talkie or two solo cups with a string tying them together because it can be so distracting and cause so many unnecessary problems, even with parental controls. But wouldn't you know, here it is, potentially saving the day.

<hr>

"Well, this is an exciting day! I've always loved getting a new car. I haven't had that many, but it's still always a fun day," Billie bubbles as we pull up to the lot less than an hour later. I smile absently at her, gathering up my purse and water before jumping out and pulling my seat forward to let the kids out of the backseat. After our little heart-to-heart, I feel like Mia has given us an ace up our sleeve, and I'm trying to be very thoughtful and discerning about when and with who to use it so it isn't wasted. In the meantime, I have to get all this vehicle stuff sorted out so I can get the show back on the road. Literally.

The 2024 black Suburban is sitting in front of the office building, shiny and gleaming in the spring afternoon sun, just waiting for us to take her home. I mentally add this to the long list of things I didn't have on my 2024 Bingo card, but that seems to be the theme of the year, and it's not even half over. After holding open the glass door to Donny's office to let Mia, Hayes, and Billie file in ahead of me, I bring up the rear, and take a seat in one of the cushioned chairs in front of Donny's desk.

"Alright, Molly, all you need to do is sign on the dotted line," he says absently, shuffling different stacks of papers around his desk. He stops searching suddenly and looks to have a light bulb moment. "These are yours," he spins around in his desk chair to the table behind his desk, and pulls out a stack of papers from under an open bright yellow bag of tortilla chips with a large orange logo declaring them $2! a bag.

For the next fifteen minutes, he flips through each page and tells me where to sign, and then makes notes for where Shep needs to sign later on. We wrap up the paperwork and he hands me a flat key fob with a smile. "She's all yours," he says, and I try to smile back, but suddenly feel a little sentimental.

"What's going on, Molly? Is there something we need to do to the Suburban before you take it?" Donny asks gingerly, looking a little bit like he's not equipped to deal with whatever emotional breakdown I look like I'm about to have.

"It's nothing, Donny, just a little sentimentality. I just get a little too emotionally attached to stuff, you know? Even to things that cause me problems that I need to move on from," I say, tearing up a little. I hold up the fob like I'm making a toast and give him a wink. "Here's to a brand-new transmission with a warranty!"

"Yes, ma'am. Well, y'all enjoy it, and send Shep over whenever he gets a chance. No rush," he nods and pats me on the shoulder as he walks by to open the door for us to leave. I give him a hug on the way out, and Billie stops to chat with him for a few minutes. I walk out of the office into the bright sunshine and stop in front of my new mom-mobile to give it a good survey before we load up.

"Molly, it's really pretty. Proud for you, babe," Billie says as she comes out the office door and gives me a hug.

"Thanks," I say quietly, giving her a hug back, and opening the back driver's side door for everyone to load up. "And thanks for letting us roll in the Bronco for a while." Billie smiles and gives me a thumbs up before she jumps back in her Bronco and heads out of the parking lot. I have the kids get in the backseat, and I climb in the driver's seat to get ready to head out.

After chucking my purse in the passenger's seat, and familiarizing myself with some of the different features, I depress the brake and push the start button. Nothing happens. I try again, trying to do both at the same time, thinking that might help. Still nothing. I take the fob and hit a few of the buttons, and nothing seems to happen.

"Hang on guys, I'll be right back. Y'all can open a door if you get too hot," I say, hopping out and running back into Donny's office. As I am running in, Donny is walking across the foyer with another set of fobs and a sheepish grin.

"Sorry, Molly, that would have worked for the red Tahoe out there, but not yours!" he laughs, tossing me the fobs in his hands. I stop and catch them before tossing my set back to him.

"Thanks, Donny! We'll see you later!"

As I head back out the office door, a white flat-bed ranch truck pulls up next to the Suburban and rumbles to a stop. I walk over to the driver's side of my car and True rolls down the window of the truck and a look of recognition, with maybe a slight hint of nervousness, washes over his face.

"Hey, Molly, how's it going?" He says cautiously, resting on the open window. "Did you get you a new ride?"

"Pretty good. Yeah, we were having issues with my transmission so it was time to move on. What are you up to?" I say, gesturing to his truck.

"I'm having some engine trouble, so I wanted to talk to Donny about what a trade-in could look like."

"Oh, that's exciting. How's Asa doing?"

True pauses, and shrugs a little. "He is doing a little better. They've got him in a medical coma right now, so no one has been able to talk to him or anything. It was pretty lucky y'all were at the funeral, huh?" he says, a little more pointedly than I find necessary.

"That's good, the coma will give his brain time to heal without excess stress. Is he still at BCMC?"

"Yes, on the third floor."

There are a few seconds of silence between us, and my stomach turns over a little. There is something going on, and I hate that I suspect him so much. When I look at him, all I can picture is fourteen-year-old True with gangly limbs and coke-bottle glasses. He's definitely grown up, and I'm scared to think that he might be on a road he shouldn't be on.

"Well, I gotta get these kids home and check on Shep out in the pasture. He's moving northside groups from east to west this afternoon. He needs to get cleaned up to come in and buy me this car," I joke, winking at him. He cracks a small smile and opens his door to jump out.

As the door opens, the wind kicks up for a second and a handful of trash blows out of the door and floorboards toward me. He grabs a few feed store receipts that are making a getaway as I snag an empty Whataburger cup and a crumpled napkin as they fly by. A small, empty, green plastic bottle rolls into my sneaker and I bend down to grab it just as a look of terror crosses True's face. He lunges toward me tentatively and I dodge him as I read the faded label. The date says September 30, 2014, and is a prescription for 30 pills of Digitron for Asa James Shoemaker.

True stands frozen next to me on the pavement and I immediately jump in my car and take off for home, leaving him speechless and fumbling for what to do in my rearview mirror. I was trying not to leap to conclusions before talking to Shep, but now I know I need to talk to him as soon as possible because I've already leapt.

eighteen

ONCE WE ARRIVE HOME, I lock my new car in the garage, and lock my children in the house with Crabcake and Beignet with strict instructions not to answer the door for anyone, and to only answer the phone for me or Shep. I try to explain all of this as calmly as possible without really any details, but I can tell they are already on edge a bit from our *Fast and Furious* exit from the dealership. They are handling it well, without arguing or asking too many questions, and I kiss them both on the top of the head and say a little prayer before grabbing my boots and running out to the barn.

Years ago, when we were first getting into ranching, Shep and I took horseback riding lessons and fell in love with horses. Our cattle have always been gentle, but there are times and places you just need help gathering them, and a feed bucket and a UTV just can't get the job done, so we decided to start getting horses of our own. It took a while to find the right horses for each one of us because calm, gentle horses are sometimes hard to come by, especially because it typically takes a while to invest the time and energy needed to make them calm. Our first horse, Penelope, was Shep's for a while, until he found one that was equally as calm, but more game to lope and work cattle, which is what he was ultimately after. Penelope became mine, and since she is now in her late twenties', she doesn't mind that I'm the one that rides the least around here. She spends most of her time grazing the pasture in front of our house and getting apple treats from the kids.

I bust into the tack room in the barn as quickly as I can and grab my saddle and bit off the wall. Luckily, Shep haltered Penelope to the fence when he was saddling Jalapeno, his horse, because she will come stand ridiculously close to him in an effort to get treats. He started tying her to the opposite side of the pens every time they get saddled up to keep her in her own space and out of their way and usually leaves her until they get back and unsaddled for the same reason. I've never been so thankful she's a treat hound than this moment.

"Hey, girl. We've got some major business to attend to. You up for a little ride?" I ask her quietly, cinching up the saddle as she exhales, and threading the bit into her mouth. After untying her from the fence, I hoist myself up, and start out of the barn pens to head north to the pasture to find Shep.

Even though it is just mid-spring, it is the time of year we like to call Texas's pre-heating season, and I kick myself for not grabbing a hat before I took off. The high afternoon sun feels like a heat lamp as I wind my way through the different pastures. I keep my eyes peeled for any sign of Shep, Cooter, or Roy, or even a black cow, as cattle of any size means the boys are likely to be nearby. Cell phone service is somewhat iffy through parts of these pastures, so it's not surprising that all of my calls to him have rolled directly to voicemail.

After what feels like an eternity of zigzagging through the pasture, I finally spot Shep's Stetson hat high on the top of a hill. "Shep!" I call out, pushing Penelope to get up the hill a little faster.

"Molly? What's wrong? Why are you out here?" He turns back to see me riding up the hill to meet him, and he instantly looks alarmed. He turns Jalapeno around to face me, and he moves to climb down from the saddle.

"It's okay, stay up there. I came up here because we have an emergency," I say, trying to catch my breath. Penelope did all the work to get up the hill, but I'm somehow winded along with her. "True did it, babe. True killed MacDougal."

Shep looks speechless, and I dig around in the pocket of my army green three-quarter sleeve utility jacket to pull out the empty pill bottle. I toss it over to him as the horses shuffle their feet and we dance around one another a little. He turns it over in his hand and squints to read the faded label. "Where did you get this?"

"True pulled up as we were leaving Donny's and this rolled out of his truck. He absolutely did not want me to see it. He tried to grab it back but I jumped in the car and drove off. We need to figure out what to do with him before he tries to retaliate."

"Okay, the answer is to call law enforcement, Molls. You make it sound like we need to dispose of him before he disposes of us. This isn't the Sopranos."

"But what if he has some kind of excuse about it and they don't take us seriously? I don't want to turn this over and they do nothing with it and then he just gets away with it! Or worse, he comes after us next," I say, the panic starting to rise in my voice. "Shep, he has a lifetime lease with MacDougal. It was in the paperwork Wendy and Thomas had from Richard's files. Thomas is the rightful heir because he's biologically Charles's son."

Shep looks at me with sheer confusion. "What? Who are they? What do they have to do with this? Start over from the beginning."

I take a deep breath, feeling simultaneously like I want to laugh and cry. "Okay, are you ready?" He nods, and I launch into the culmination of all my investigating. "The MacDougal estate is in a trust meant to be inherited by the heirs of Richard and Charles only. Their father had a sister, Nancy. She chose to marry a man from Massachusetts and move there, so she and her family were removed from the trust. Even though they were cut out, they still came to visit in the summers, and Richard, Charles, and Peter, Nancy's son, all grew up together. Wendy Foster was really good friends with Charles, and also friends with your mom, growing up. She met Peter when he came to visit in the summers through Charles. When they were older, Charles died of complications from pneumonia, just a few months after he got Wendy pregnant. She made Peter think it was his baby, and they married before Thomas was born in December 1983. She never told Peter that Thomas wasn't his, and she put Charles on the birth certificate without him ever knowing. And apparently no one questioned it because they didn't question anything in the eighties, according to her." Shep raises his eyebrows at me, and I just shrug in reply. I honestly don't have an answer for that other than her explanation. "So, he's the legit, undisputed heir of that place now because he's a direct descendant of Charles. At some point like a week before Richard died, True convinced him to sign a lifetime lease with him. Like he pays basically nothing to the "family estate" for his or Shoemaker CC's lifetime, and if there is no longer an heir to pay, they have the option to buy out for pennies on the dollar. So, he wins either way. He can lease this super cheap and not have to worry about upkeep if there is an heir, or buy it outright for super cheap and just exponentially multiply the assets of the operation."

"Okay, do you think True knew there was an heir?"

"I don't, just because why would you put in a buyout clause if you thought you could just lease for basically nothing and were contractually protected to with the estate? He needed a safety net in case it reverted to the state or someone bought it and he didn't have first dibs. You've been over there recently; don't you think the whole Shoemaker operation is drowning? They are out of grass and it would bankrupt them to supplemental feed all those cattle."

Shep hesitates, and then nods in agreement. "It's pretty bad over there. They were getting pretty skinny, and they're overgrazed for sure."

"So, I think True came up with this whole plan to take over that land to keep them from going under. It's his first ranch manager position, and he wanted to be successful, but he just made some bad decisions and got them in a bad situation. He knew Richard had a decent amount of land that was primed and ready for grazing, but he had no idea until he started researching the area that Richard had 18 sections. I think True initially just tried to get him to sell it to them, but he wouldn't bite. That letter from a 'developer' recently was a scam trying to scare him into selling it so it could stay as "ranch land", signed by who I think is his partner in crime. When that didn't work, he started slowly poisoning him to get him weak enough to sign the lease paperwork. He might have started the process just to get him weak enough to sign and then let him live, but like we saw when we took those cows back, it was just making him more agitated and hostile, so he had to go. He probably googled how to give someone an untraceable heart attack and ran across the threads on Digitron that still circulate. It was the perfect plan since Asa was prescribed that a while ago and then probably taken off it before he finished it so it was just hanging around the ranch house. It's pharmaceutical and causes a natural health consequence so it's much harder to trace or look purposeful."

"So, is Asa involved in this?" Shep's eyes look worried, and my heart sinks even more. It's hard enough for him to hear this about True, a kid we felt like we took under our wing and watched grow up, but Shep has looked up to and respected Asa for years now. That's a little too much to take all together.

"I really don't think so. I think that's why he's in the shape he's in. I think he somehow stumbled across some evidence, or figured something out, and they tried to take him out too, but it didn't work. I wouldn't be shocked if his stroke wasn't a coincidence either."

"They? Who do you think is 'they'?"

"Okay, hear me out... I think Becki Lane is involved in this, too."

"Molly," Shep groans, giving me a skeptical look.

"Seriously, Shep! This isn't about how much I dislike her or some personal vendetta. Who has something to gain long-term with Shoemaker continuing to be successful? Becki, if she's Asa's heir. I think she and True are in on this together. Richard identified Becki at the bake sale as having seen her recently. The developer interest letter that came from Richard's house has a signature on the bottom that looks suspiciously like the one at the bottom of all the cheer squad notes we've gotten home recently. It was the perfect partner-ship- they get MacDougal out of the way to get all of his ranch land, and they get Asa out of the way and Becki can have a working business to support her now that she's getting divorced and needs to support herself. Honestly, supporting herself is probably the motivation behind her making that scene at the Little League field, too. She's grasping at straws for possibilities to be taken care of. But I think she had to be the one to go in and talk to him like a developer because he would have known True. She might have planted the Digitron too, because she could have made the fake label in the computer lab at school with their design software. He had to have been just completely out of it to sign that though, because you know True didn't interact with Richard well."

"Very good, Molly. You've been following along really

well. And you're right that we didn't interact well. I hated that son of a bitch." Shep and I both turn in surprise to see True riding up on his long-time beloved palomino mare out of the brush. He looks slightly manic, like he clearly knows this is likely not going to end well, but he is trying not to panic and lose any more control over the situation. "Rule number one of being in the middle of everything, Molly? Don't tell your main suspect where you're headed with the main evidence." I look at Shep to try to control my panic, and he holds up a steady hand to silently tell me to keep calm.

"True, what can we do for you?" He says evenly, discreetly slipping the pill bottle in the bag of his saddle.

"Cut the bullshit, Shep. Give me the bottle and I'll be on my way," True says, dismounting his horse and squaring up in front of Shep and Jalapeno.

"I could have sworn we had plenty of discussions in middle school youth group about foul language, but it seems that wasn't the only point that you missed," he replies, making no move to give him anything.

True momentarily flushes, like a child who's been scolded for having his hand in the cookie jar, then he pulls a hard exterior back on. "I'm not kidding, Shep. I don't want to hurt you or Molly but this doesn't concern you. Give me what's mine, and we can call it even."

When Shep doesn't budge or say anything, True reaches into the back of his waistband and returns with a Colt .45 pointed straight at Shep. "I don't want to do this, Shep, but I will. I've gone this far," he says pointedly, the slightest shake in his voice like he isn't completely confident, and I strangle a scream in my throat trying to stay calm.

"Truman Joseph Walker, how dare you! You were raised better than this; what would your mama say?" I shout, sounding completely unhinged and unable to contain myself anymore. I reach deep into the recesses of my brain and recall a segment from some morning talk show ages ago that advised talking about personal matters with a potential kidnapper or murderer to help humanize yourself and convince them not to go through whatever they are planning. It's probably dirty to bring up his mother, but we're clearly not playing by the rules here.

"Don't you bring up my mother! This is about you not just keeping your mouth shut and staying out of something for once!" He shouts back, waving the gun over to me. I can't help but flinch and I try to keep Penelope from backing up in case that scares him into firing. "Everyone hated him and no one was going to miss him! It was supposed to just be a heart attack and we all move on. We get the land because we need it and we deserve it. He was a selfish, mean old bastard, and we're all better off without him. You should have just let it go!" True keeps the gun trained back and forth between the two of us, and I have no idea what we're supposed to do now. All I can think of is Mia and Hayes and if our will is updated, and where the updated will would be, and if they'll be okay without us. At this point, I'm agreeing with True that I indeed should have stayed out of it. The kids will only remember that their mom being a busy-body got both of their parents killed.

"True, put the gun down and let's figure this out. There's no situation too far gone that we can't find a good solution. Shooting us is not going to make your situation better. You could have gotten away with the heart attack, but you can't get away with shooting us," Shep says, still no waver in his voice. I imagine this is the Shepherd Jones that ran the endoscopy room flawlessly and calmly for years. There really aren't unexpected pharmacy emergencies, so I am truly unprepared to be held at gunpoint like this.

"It's too late. I can't have y'all going around running your mouths now," he bites back, starting to shake a little.

"True, think about Mia and Hayes. You can't take their

parents away. They don't deserve that. Don't make them orphans," I choke out, trying not to cry in front of him so he won't feel like he has that much power over me, even though my insides are crumbling like he has all the power.

"Don't try to give me a sob story-- this is your fault! You just had to go along with the heart attack and no one had to be the bad guy!"

"Okay, True, we're at an impasse then. It's clear that you think the only way out of here is to get rid of us, so go ahead and shoot us. There's no sense in wasting time. Just get it over with," Shep tells him, stepping down off Jalapeno and remaining perfectly still. I gasp in fear and disbelief and watch as True shakily lines up the gun to Shep's head and moves to pull the trigger.

"NOOOOOOOOOOOOO!" I scream as loud as my lungs allow, squeezing my eyes closed with tears streaming down. The deafening sound of the bullet makes everything silent but a high-pitched ring, and Penelope rears back a little at the boom of the pistol.

"That's for saying we sucked ass at the Cavalcade!" I hear Roy yell a second later, and I open my eyes to see Cooter and Roy on their horses on either side of True lying on the ground, with Cooter's rope holding True's arms to his abdomen, and Roy's wrapped tightly around True's ankles. They have literally ridden up and roped True like a calf at the perfect moment, apparently partly in revenge for True smack-talking them about losing the team roping at the Cavalcade. I take a second to process what I'm seeing before I snap out of it and look to my right to Shep.

"Thank God you're okay!" I scream, flying as quickly as I can off Penelope and running to hug Shep. He's standing casually and completely unscathed next to Jalapeno, like he wasn't just shot at, and I've never been so mad at him and so thankful to see him at the same time. "Why on God's green earth would you tell that psychopath to shoot you?" I yell, smacking his bicep as hard as I can. He lets out a laugh like he's been holding his breath, and that makes me a little angry for him to laugh at something so serious, but also a little relieved that it turns out he's human like the rest of us and was maybe holding his breath a little through all of that.

"I saw Cooter and Roy riding up behind him getting their ropes ready. I was trying to maintain the element of surprise for them," he explains, wrapping his arms around me and squeezing me. My heart rate attempts to slow down, and I hug him back equally as tight. There is absolutely no competition that we just lived through the scariest moment of our lives.

"Clue a sister in next time! I was scared to death!" I shriek into his chest, and he lets out another laugh.

"Molly Mason Jones, there better not be a next time. I hope you just retired from being a detective, full stop."

I pull back and look up at his ocean blue eyes, the ones I fell in love with twenty years ago, giving me that serious, sincere look I see so rarely. "Agreed. I did my duty, and I am now officially retired."

As I refuse to let go of this squeeze chute of a hug, we hear a blood curdling whelp from True and turn to see what is going on. Cooter and Roy have dismounted to deal with getting him back to the barn.

"Really, Coot? A titty twister?" Roy shakes his head as he picks up True's feet and Cooter lifts him up by the ropes around his middle, letting his head dangle a little.

"I mean, he deserves way more than that, but that's a good start," He shrugs as they heave True over his saddle to ride back to the barn basically folded in half, his head hanging off one side and his feet off the other.

"What are we going to do with him when we get him back to the house?" I ask Shep quietly, and he shrugs.

"I guess call Sheriff Cooper," He replies, stepping in his

stirrup to get back on Jalapeno. I nod in agreement, and jump up on Penelope to follow him back to the barn.

When we arrive back at the house, we are shocked to see several Crawford County Sheriff's Department trucks lining our driveway, and Sheriff Cooper standing by the side door to our house with Mia and Hayes. Crabcake and Beignet are laying at their feet on the smooth concrete with giant grins and drool strings dripping down. I know in my heart that they would protect the kids, and I've seen them be defensive, but they don't exactly look like the pinnacle of protection at this point. If there's a vacuum involved, those fools act like they could tear down a wall.

"What is going on?" I ask, dismounting Penelope and passing off my reins to Shep as I head for the kids. "I told y'all to stay inside. What did you do?" I look between them and the sheriff, waiting for one of these yoo-hoos to answer my dang questions.

"We called the sheriff, Mom," Hayes says simply, gesturing to the mustached man standing between him and his sister. Sheriff Cooper looks like he's been standing on our driveway for longer than he'd prefer, as a few streams of sweat are rolling down his forehead. He's in full tactical gear, complete with his signature flak vest struggling to cover his generous torso.

"I see that, babe. Why?"

"Well, we just felt like there might be an emergency, so we thought we'd save you some time. Plus, we saw True ride from across the road through our pasture like it was on fire and it seemed suspicious, so we went ahead and called," Mia explained, looking a little sheepish.

I pull both of them in and give them the longest hug I might have ever given them. "Thank you for looking out for me and Daddy. That was brave and responsible for you to do. We're really proud of you both."

Sheriff Cooper gently pulls me away from the kids, and we

walk over to Cooter, Roy, and Shep gathered around the horses and True. "What do we have going on here, gentlemen?"

"I believe what we have here is the man that murdered Richard MacDougal, sir," Cooter says proudly, waving his arms like Vanna White to True hanging upside down off the side of his horse like Sheriff Cooper has just won Final Spin.

"You can't prove that; untie me! I'm suing all of you for assault!" He hollers, wiggling back and forth like an inchworm across his saddle.

"Just out of curiosity, is there any reason or proof to suspect him of this?" Sheriff Cooper asks, stifling a laugh.

Shep reaches in his saddle bag and retrieves the pill bottle. "Molly says this rolled out of True's truck at Donny's. I think Donny's probably got security cameras on the parking lot to confirm this," he says, handing the bottle to Cooper. He turns it over and reads the label.

"Digitron, huh? Remind me, retired pharmacist, isn't that the drug MacDougal essentially overdosed on?" Cooper muses, walking over to stand next to True's horse, as I nod affirmatively. "Quite the coincidence, isn't it?" He lifts True's head by grabbing him by the hair on the back of his head like a dog and holds him upright. "Do you have an explanation for this coincidence?"

"That was Asa Shoemaker's prescribed medication, and I live and work with Asa. You can't prove that I, or that, killed Dick," He spits viciously, wriggling under Cooper's grip, and a fresh wave of sadness washes over me for what he has become. This is not the True we know and love, and it hurts my heart for him, and also for his mom. Cooper shakes his head with a little sadness in his eyes like he's disappointed it's turning out this way.

"No, that's not proof that you killed Asa," I say, stepping over to him. "But this confession, and your attempt at murdering me and my husband that I recorded ought to be enough to at least detain you," I pull my phone out of my back pocket and bring up the video I recorded the entire time we were in the pasture. The visual is just the inside of the little pouch on the side of my saddle meant to hold my phone, but the audio is clear, and that's the more important part. It's incredibly long, as I started it when I first started explaining everything to Shep, and didn't end it until we were riding back to the barn. It's likely going to take up all the space in my phone storage until I can off-load it to the cloud, but it should be worth it. Something about the look on True's face as we left told me that he was going to find us as soon as possible. I, like Mia earlier this week in the computer lab, wanted to protect myself from ill-intentioned people, so I employed her tactic of filming everything as extra insurance.

I fast forward the video to the part where True joins us, and play it for Sheriff Cooper as we all listen. "Yep, I think that'll about do it. Molly, forward that to me, please," he says as he reaches into the pocket of his flak vest to pull out zip ties. He hauls True off the horse onto his feet and secures his hands behind him before having Cooter and Roy remove their ropes. "Truman Walker, you have the right to remain silent," he begins as he walks True to the back seat of a department truck. After he gets True situated in the truck, he turns back to us, and gives me a very solemn nod and tip of his hat, probably the closest thing to a 'thank you' or acknowledgement that I was in fact right this entire time I'll get, which is fine. I didn't do it for the acknowledgement or the glory, just for the feeling of solving something that didn't feel right. But, I mean, if he wanted to give me more of an acknowledgment, I probably wouldn't turn it down, you know?

The kids join us out on the driveway and Shep and I pull them into a family hug. I stand still in the group hug for several long minutes, working to get my heart rate down. I know all of this will hit me probably sooner than later when my adrenaline runs out, but for now, I'm just going to be thankful in this moment that we are all safe. "Way to go, guys. Looks like y'all can listen after all," Shep teases, patting them both on the back. "Do we need to go to Dairy Queen to celebrate?"

"Hell yeah, let's go!" I hear Cooter whoop behind us. I whirl around to shoot him a disapproving look just as Roy elbows him. "I mean, heck yeah, Dairy Queen sounds great," he corrects nonchalantly, continuing to wind up his rope and tying it back on his saddle strings, looking appropriately apologetic.

"Alright, Dairy Queen it is. Right after I go sign the papers for Mom's new car. We gotta make it before Donny closes."

"Mom, did True really kill someone?" Hayes asks quietly, leaning into me as we walk back toward the house. I put my arm around him and squeeze his shoulders as we walk.

"Well, we think True got himself into a bit of trouble managing his herd, and he needed a way out, and that ended up being Mr. MacDougal's land. Y'all know Mr. MacDougal wasn't the nicest, so he didn't really work with True, and that all ended badly for both of them. So, what do we learn from all of that?" I ask pointedly, trying to make this a teachable moment as we head inside. Everyone else files around the kitchen island and takes a seat on the stools as I stand across from them at the sink like we've all done a thousand times.

"Don't mess with Mom," Hayes jokes, and Shep, Cooter, and Roy all stifle laughter.

"Haha, very funny. But remember how all of you thought I was crazy when this started? Who's laughing now?" I say, raising my eyebrows and pointing at all of them sitting around the island staring at me.

"Mom, did you use my trick to catch True?" Mia asks a

moment later, gesturing to my phone. I smile to myself and nod.

"Yeah, babe, I did. That's a pretty smart trick," I say, winking at her.

"You think so?"

"I do. And on Monday, we're going to use that trick to finish catching all the bad guys."

FIRST THING MONDAY MORNING, I drop the kids off at the intermediate school, and make my way to the central office for our meeting in their conference room. The central office is on the main street in town and houses the district superintendent and her staff. Nadine Everett has been the superintendent over Buffalo Creek ISD for close to ten years, and has been overall respected and successful, although she does have a bit of a reputation for being pretty strict and not overly warm and fuzzy. This is our second meeting, and the culmination of everything we planned over the weekend.

Once all the dust settled Friday night, I made a call to Jacquie Welch, longtime friend of Nadine Everett, to explain our situation with Mia, Coach Lane, and Mr. Pine, and to ask advice for how to go about it. After calling Mr. Pine every G rated church lady insult she could think of, she suggested we meet with Dr. Everett on Saturday morning to explain every-thing and make a plan to bust our remaining culprits.

I wish I could say that Dr. Everett was shocked to hear these allegations, but she admitted these weren't the first she'd caught wind of. But, like Mrs. Watson, she had no proof so she hadn't been able to do anything. Just as I'd suspected, when she pulled the closed-circuit footage from the intermediate school's video cloud storage, there was a suspicious static over the audio, and Becki and Mia's conversation is inaudible.

Mia admitted later that she wasn't the first of their group to be targeted. Apparently, Becki cornered sweet Emily Scott first, and got a few good grades out of her before Hainslee reported back that Mia had the best grade in the class and they changed their target. Becki had given Emily the same garbage about her not being believed if she came forward, so Mia was the only one she told. Mia said the day she was working in the computer lab, she didn't feel super comfortable being essentially alone with Becki, and propped her phone up on her computer monitor and turned on her camera with her phone flipped over to just record. Because she had it flipped over, it wasn't obvious she was filming, but it caught everything: the action and the audio. After Dr. Everett played the essentially silent version, I played Mia's version, and let her fill in the blanks. She slowly removed her reading glasses when the video cut off, and looked up at Jacquie and me with no emotion on her face.

I wish I could say I had a lot of gumption at that point to say, "There's your proof! Justice for my daughter, posthaste!", but I felt nothing more than slight terror in that moment. I can see why people find her incredibly intimidating: the lack of discernable emotions or thought can definitely be daunting and make you second guess yourself. If I didn't know better, I would have thought I was in trouble in that moment.

"Molly, thank you for sharing this. We will definitely take the appropriate steps to rectify the situation." She looks at me, still stone-faced, and I feel the slightest amount of relief, but also still some measure of nerves and disappointment. Obviously she has to remain professional, but this wasn't really what I was expecting after my chat with Jacquie the night before.

"Thank you, Dr. Everett. I just felt like it needed some attention. I appreciate your time. Let me know if I can help in any other way," I say quietly, not sure if we're finished, or if I am allowed to get up and go home. I'm missing Shep's Saturday morning breakfast spread-- eggs over easy, bacon, pancakes, and hashbrowns-- for this meeting, and if that's all that's going to be said, I'd just as soon get home to breakfast.

Dr. Everett and Jacquie exchange silent, emotionless nods with one another, and then after another few beats of silence, die laughing at one another.

"Molly, we're just teasing you!" Jacquie gasps out between laughs, clutching the heavy polished oak table with both perfectly manicured hands. She reaches over and pats me on the arm as Dr. Everett dabs her eyes with a tissue because she's laughing so hard she's now crying. I feel like I'm being punked by two ladies old enough to be my mother.

"Oh, honey, we're going to nail them to the wall, don't you worry," Dr. Everett says, reaching over and patting me from across the table, too.

After their good little laugh, we worked out details for the meeting today, first thing on Monday morning at the administration central office. Even though I know I have the right people on my side and in the know on the truth, I still feel really nervous as I get out of my car and walk inside the office. The assistant secretary takes me back to the small conference room adjacent to the larger one. Typically, it is used for the public to watch school board meetings without interrupting the meeting. They share a large glass window and I take a seat in the back corner where I can see all the action happening in the large room without being visible. Then, I wait.

I was a little nervous dropping the kids off, hoping Dr. Everett is right that she can get Mr. Pine and Becki Lane here before they have a chance to talk to Mia. After a few minutes, the door cracks open, and I immediately tense up to prepare for whoever is about to join me.

"Oh good, I'm not late," Mandy flips her long blonde ponytail over her shoulder in relief, and slides through the sliver of open door, hurrying over to sit beside me. We felt since Emily was targeted too, Mandy deserves to be present at whatever is about to go down. I give her a quick hug, and we sit in nervous silence for another five to ten minutes until, through the window, we see Dr. Everett, her secretary Phyllis, and the district's human resources department head file into the larger conference room. Dr. Everett takes a seat at the head of the table, directly opposite of where we are sitting so we can see her fully. Phyllis sits to her left, and Robert Payne, HR specialist, sits next to Phyllis. Finally, at just before 8:30, Shawn Pine arrives in the room.

"Dr. Everett, nice to see you. How was your weekend?" He strolls in the room and walks straight to Dr. Everett to shake her hand. "How are you, Phyllis? Robert?" He says, seeming more puzzled with each greeting about what he is doing there. "Is everything alright? You didn't tell me if I needed to bring anything, so I don't have this month's attendance records, or state reporting numbers." He takes a seat to Dr. Everett's right, looking confused about why his presence was needed so early first thing in the week.

"No need, Mr. Pine, that's not why we're here. We need to discuss a situation with you. To begin, I'd like you to watch something," Dr. Everett says, powering on the wall mounted TV with the remote next to her, and hitting a few buttons on her iPad. The scene in the computer lab fills the screen with the annoying static noise over the conversation and the video plays in its entirety. Shawn Pine looks slightly dumbfounded, and we can tell panic is starting to rise a little, but he's trying to maintain his cool. I'm sure he's thinking that he's covered his tracks with this doctored version of the video, and if he can just remain calm, this will all blow over.

"Mr. Pine, this video has been brought to our attention recently, and I need to know what you know about the situation," Dr. Everett says flatly when the video is over. She leaves the TV on and turns to face him. He stammers slightly before attempting to answer.

"Well, uh, that is a video that has also recently been brought to my attention by a disgruntled parent. You know the type: upset her daughter got a bad grade and wanted some excuse to blame it on instead of acknowledging that her kid isn't perfect and just got a bad grade. I handled it internally because, as you can see, there isn't any proof of misconduct by Coach Lane. I work really hard to protect my staff and make sure they are not harassed by ill-intentioned or ill-informed parents," He gives her a smarmy smile and my stomach turns. I know he's just spewing that slop to CYA for himself, but I have a sudden rising burn of resentment and anger at him for insinuating that I'm causing all this trouble because I wouldn't accept that Mia got one poor grade on a test. Dr. Everett maintains her emotionless look with unforgiving constant eye contact as she replaces her reading glasses and picks up her iPad again. "I see. Well, there's another version I'd like you to review as well." She hits a few buttons on her screen and the same video pops up, this time with sound.

And once again, I hear the whole heartbreaking conversation, this time from the unbiased view of the school surveillance system. I don't know how she did it, but Dr. Everett tracked down the un-doctored surveillance footage to corroborate Mia's video.

"Don't even think about saying a word. You're just a kid, and no one will believe you over me. Mr. Pine does whatever I say," Becki snarls on the screen, and I tear up a little bit. Mandy puts her arm around me to squeeze my shoulder, and I work hard not to break down to a full-blown cry. I've never been good at managing my emotions- anything on any extreme- too hot or too cold, too sad or too happy has me crying, and this feels like a combination of everything hitting me suddenly-- everything happening here, and everything that has happened in the last few days.

"Mr. Pine, what is your opinion now?" Dr. Everett says, a little more irritation in her voice, but still calm and relatively emotionless.

"Well, uh, obviously, if I had known that, I would have taken action, but as you can see, I didn't have the original audio. Trust me, when I get back to campus, I will take care of this immediately." He tries to sound confident, but he seems shaken up. He squirms in his seat a little, and Robert from HR starts shuffling papers out of file folders in front of him.

"Forgive me for finding that unacceptable. I don't believe you have any intention of handling the situation. Mr. Pine, save your pathetic excuses for someone gullible enough to believe you. Do you know where I got the second video?" He wordlessly shakes his head, his eyes growing by the second. "From the district hard drive here in the main office. Every-thing is saved down here first, and then additionally saved in each campus's cloud storage. You edited the copy in the local storage, not main storage. We also have the time stamps where you edited the video and uploaded it back to the cloud. Or, I should say, someone using your computer did. So you are either guilty directly, or you are guilty of allowing someone onto your password-protected computer and the password-protected storage system to alter state property," She gives him a stare down as she removes her glasses, setting them quietly on her iPad.

Shawn Pine says nothing, maintaining a stunned silence like he wants to speak, but has no idea what to say. "Can I be honest with you, Shawn? I wouldn't say anything if I were you. Better to keep your mouth closed and let people wonder if you are not smart than to open your mouth and confirm it." Shawn's jaw gapes open for second, and then he quickly pulls it back up as she leans forward to go in for the kill.

"Do you want to know what I consider the worst part? The parent you tried to blame for this? She brought in a video the student in question made because she felt uncomfortable being in that setting with your employee and wanted proof of anything that might potentially happen to protect herself. What sort of educational environment are you breeding that your own students don't feel safe with their teachers?" She raises her eyebrows to silently punctuate her statements, and Mr. Pine only keeps eye contact with the table. "Full transparency, there are further allegations against you, Ms. Lane and your relationship that will be investigated in the coming weeks. For now, Mr. Payne will be sharing this paperwork with you detailing your upcoming administrative leave during the investigation." Robert Payne slides a stack of legal looking papers from human resources across the table to him, and Pine looks dumbstruck.

"We will need your signature on the last page, but please take your time to read through all the fine print of what you are and are not allowed to do during the leave and investigation periods before signing it," Mr. Payne says quietly, also sliding him a pen.

Mr. Pine picks up the pen and flips to the last page to scribble a signature on the line over his typed name and credentials without reading a word on any page. He straightens the stack of papers, sets the pen on top, and slides it all back to Mr. Payne. "Am I free to go?" he asks, sliding his chair back a little on the thin industrial carpet, looking completely defeated.

Dr. Everett nods, and gestures to the door without saying anything. "A word of advice, Mr. Pine?" She says, as he moves to the door. Mr. Pine turns back to her with one hand on the doorknob with a look on his face like someone just ran over his dog and is about to insult his mama, too. "Perhaps next time, make decisions with your brain and your extensive training and not your pants."

Both mine and Mandy's jaws drop to the floor as he exits the room and shuts the door behind him. After he leaves, Mandy elbows me with a big smile. "You did it!" She whispers, as Dr. Everett and her staff prepare for the next meeting. I give a timid smile back, feeling just sick to my stomach in that moment. I never meant to get multiple people fired, or to break up multiple families. All I wanted was justice and accountability for a select few who think the rules don't apply to them.

"Are you okay? You look pretty pale," Mandy whispers again, putting an arm around my shoulder.

"I'll be fine. This vigilante thing seems more fun in theory than in actuality. I just feel kinda bad right now," I say, my voice wavering a little. I take a deep breath and shuffle my legs to cross them the opposite way just to get some nervous energy out.

"Oh, Molly, you have no reason to feel bad. The people being held accountable right now are the ones that made the decisions that call for these actions. Don't feel bad for bringing darkness to light." She gives me a little squeeze and we both freeze as the door to the conference room opens again and through the window, we see Becki Lane walk in and take a seat.

"Good morning, Ms. Lane. Thank you for joining us," Dr. Everett begins, looking down her nose over her readers at Becki sitting to her right. Becki has a nervous smile, and I wonder if she and Pine had a chance to speak to one another before this, or if she is going into this conversation completely blind. If she did get a heads up, she seems calmer than I would have predicted, which makes me think she has no idea what kind of hammer is about to come down.

"Ms. Lane, we need you to watch a video from the school's closed circuit surveillance system, and then provide us with commentary or an explanation, please," Dr. Everett skips straight to the video with sound and we watch Becki's smile drop right off her face the moment she realizes what she's watching.

"Dr. Everett, I can explain. You see, my husband and I are getting divorced and my uncle has been terribly ill the last few months, and that's really taken a toll on my sweet Hainslee, to the point that she's fallen behind in her classes. Mrs. Watson is so strict that she wouldn't allow her to come in for any kind of tutoring or make-up work. Cheerleading is the only bright spot she has right now, and if she wasn't able to keep that going, I just knew she'd be set down a path of depression and other terrible outcomes. I was trying to protect her mental health," Dr. Everett holds up a hand sternly and silently to stop Becki, and her blubbering sob story abruptly comes to a halt. Hearing her explanation again begs the question in my mind of why cheerleading is this important? All this trouble so your daughter can be and stay a cheerleader? And then I remember that in Texas, women have literally had other women murdered so their daughters can be cheerleaders. So maybe I should just be thankful we're all alive and it is only academic fraud we're caught up in.

"Ms. Lane, have you ever heard the expression that you either overcome your circumstances or your circumstances overcome you?" Becki stares at her without saying anything, like all the lights are on in the house but no one is home. After a few moments of awkward silence, Dr. Everett continues, trying to regain her composure. "What I'm saying is that all of those things may be true, but they are no excuse for this conduct. Ever. Quite frankly, your threats could be considered assault in the state of Texas."

"Those weren't threats, it was all a big joke, and like a little team-building exercise! You know, like how far would you go to help a teammate in need! Mia knew I was kidding and that I didn't really want them to cheat!"

Dr. Everett gives her a disbelieving smirk and continues. "Aside from this situation, there is the separate but related matter of your inappropriate relationship with Mr. Pine. I believe the legal term for it is extortion."

Becki looks completely stunned, like she was not expecting multiple allegations, and a slow look of understanding crosses her face, like we're seeing her think in real time. "Yes... that's actually right; he has been taking advantage of me since I started at the first of the school year!"

Phyllis literally chokes down a laugh, and Dr. Everett shakes her head as she picks up her iPad again. After a few swipes, a video of the back parking lot of the intermediate school appears on the screen. We have a bird's eye view of Becki's Yukon parked next to Pine's Land Rover, like the camera is placed up on one of the parking lot light poles. They are standing between the vehicles, casually having a flirtatious conversation, and before we know it, Becki grabs Shawn by the tie and starts aggressively kissing him. Mandy and I both watch, jaws dropped again, as the two of them carry on in the parking lot for several minutes before breaking apart and hurriedly getting into Becki's car and careening out of the parking lot.

"No way," Mandy whispers, and I feel stunned myself. We knew the girls had said this was the case, but we had no idea anyone had any proof of it, or that we'd all get to see it with our own eyes. Dr. Everett must have done her own research after our meeting on Saturday.

"This is an invasion of privacy! You cannot record me or

my personal relationships without my consent!" Becki cries, jumping up in her chair a little bit. Mr. Payne starts shuffling through his files again, and comes up with a few stapled pages to slide over to her.

"Oh, but we have your consent. You signed an acknowledgement of the closed-circuit surveillance system at your employee onboarding. That may be your "personal relationship" as you call it, but this is state property. You also signed an acknowledgment of the system in your parent paperwork pertaining to your daughter. In addition, you signed a no fraternization with administration policy in onboarding. This is typically meant to protect employees on the lower power end of a relationship from being taken advantage of by those in higher authority, but it seems you managed to work the unequal power distribution to your advantage." As Dr. Everett explains all the ways in which Becki is indeed busted, Mr. Payne continues to slide stacks of paper trail evidence over to her in the form of every consent and policy she signed at the beginning of the school year. She gawks silently at all the legalese in front of her, looking dumbfounded as Dr. Everett finishes. "Suffice it to say, Ms. Lane, you are suspended indefinitely pending an investigation into the allegations made against you and your interactions with students, and with your alleged inappropriate relationship with your superior." Payne leans over the table and slaps down her suspension paperwork on top of all the other papers. He sits back down and slides a pen across the table to her like he's playing sugar packet hockey and has just aggressively scored a goal.

Becki looks around the table at the three of them with tears welling in her eyes, and I get that pang in my gut again. I know it's not my fault she has been the absolute worst, and I should feel so happy that she's getting such a full-circle comeuppance, but I just have a bit of a hard time watching someone's life go up in flames before my eyes. She signs her suspension paperwork and gets up to leave.

"Ms. Lane? One more piece of advice. Off the record?" Dr. Everett says, gathering up her things, and standing from her seat to move toward her. She stands directly next to her and speaks quietly and discreetly. "Lauren knows. And they have a prenup with an infidelity clause. He won't get a dime of her money in that divorce. Next time, check your sources before you try to hit an easy jackpot. When you get in bed with dogs, you get up with fleas." Dr. Everett pats her on the shoulder, a bit condescendingly, and exits the conference room ahead of her. Phyllis and Mr. Payne leave behind her, and we watch as Becki slowly leaves the conference room, looking dazed. Mandy and I count to ten, and then check the hallway to see if the coast is clear. We're not scared to run into either of them, but we'd prefer not to have any more confrontations until some of this is a little less fresh and new.

There is no one in the hallway, so we consider it safe to slip out the side door to head out to the parking lot. I told Dr. Everett I'd catch up with her later that afternoon if I had any questions, so Mandy and I decide to take the rest of the morning to have brunch at Delilah's and decompress after the morning. We walk around the side of the building to our cars parked on the street, talking about what a crazy morning it has been when we stop short at the sight of multiple sheriff's department vehicles with whirling lights and quieted sirens, and a small crowd outside the main doors to the admin office.

"What is going on?" Mandy asks quietly, linking arms with me as we slowly walk over to our cars, trying to decide if we are allowed to be there or not.

Sheriff Cooper spots us, and starts extricating himself from his serious looking discussion to come over to us on the sidewalk. As we get a little closer, we see a few deputies handcuffing none other than Becki Lane and walking her to the backseat of a department vehicle. I have a sudden feeling of déjà vu wash over me thinking of True a few days prior, and I shudder a little. This has literally been a picture-perfect small Texas town for as long as anyone can remember, and now that boring persona has been all shot to hell.

"What's happening, Coop?" I ask when the sheriff finally makes it to us. He shakes his head, and takes off his hat to wipe the sweat from his brow.

"Picking up the last piece of the puzzle in the MacDougal case. Asa Shoemaker woke up this morning and immediately called us to pick her up. She's been messing with his medication to try to knock him off, too. Trying to cash in on her inheritance from him as early as she can. He's filing charges for elder abuse. We also leaned on True a little and he folded like a cheap lawn chair. She wanted to take over Asa's operation, and he wanted to expand, so they put together their whole sham to knock Richard out and take his place over. She was the legs: she pretended to be a developer to try to get Richard to sign a lease with True, and then she started slipping him Asa's old pills. We have a full written confession from True, and he's getting a potentially lighter sentence for cooperating and selling her out. Your video with the explanation also ties a lot of things together, so... thank you, Molly." Mandy and I stand dumbfounded on the sidewalk as the department vehicles start to disperse. "Well, we need to get to the station and get her booked into interrogation. Let me know if you hear anything I need to know," Sheriff Cooper says, patting me on the shoulder and giving me a wink.

"Are we living in an alternate universe? This has been the wildest morning," Mandy breathes, shaking her head. She elbows me playfully, as we walk to get in our cars to head to Delilah's. "How does it feel to be right all along?"

"I've said it once, and I'll say it until I'm blue in the face. You learn all you need to know about someone by watching them go through kindergarten pick-up line."

chapter
twenty

LATER THAT AFTERNOON, I pull up at Buffalo Creek Medical Center, and park at the back of their main parking lot under a large oak tree. After consulting the main information desk, I find my way to room C311, and quietly knock on the partially closed door. I hear a weak "come in", so I slowly push the door open and head inside.

Asa Shoemaker is propped up in his bed with wires and tubing coming out of various places and looking run down, but in good spirits. His sweet, well-worn face lights up a little when he sees me, and I'm thankful because I was a little worried it would be too overwhelming to have visitors.

"Girl, who let you in here?" he jokes, his voice quiet and scratchy as a large smile spreads across his face. He's not even twenty-four hours from being extubated, so talking probably isn't super comfortable, but he's trying anyway. I take a seat in the chair next to his bed and pull a small foam food container out of my oversized purse.

"I bribed my way in with sweets, of course. Luckily, there's just enough left for you," I say, setting the box of strawberry lemonade cookies on his rolling table after flashing the contents to him. He chuckles and reaches out a wavering hand to pat me on the shoulder.

"That's mighty kind of you, Molly. Especially after all the trouble my family's been causing around town," he rasps, punctuating each sentence with a weak cough.

"Don't you worry about that. It doesn't look to me like any of that was your fault. But I did hear you saved the day this morning when you woke up."

"Oh, I didn't save anything, just tried to clean up some of the mess. You know my sister was always a wild child. She did whatever she wanted whenever she wanted, everyone else be damned. I hoped she wouldn't pass that on to her daughter, or at least Becki would see how unstable and selfish she was and not want to be like her. Turns out that's exactly how she's turned out. Her mother all over again."

I honestly hadn't ever thought about the fact that Asa would have to be a sibling to one of Becki's parents, and how that all connected. It just goes to show that you can't always judge a book by its cover, or a family by one member. There are some parts of families that have such a strong through line that it makes complete sense that they are all related, whether that is through good traits, or not good ones. But there are some families that seem to be such a random grouping of individuals that you wonder if heritability is real at all. We've spent all our years in ranching studying and putting into practical practice breeding heritability in our cattle to produce some of the strongest genetics in various traits. Each year the different target traits are continually improved upon until they reach an optimal level, and then bred to stay in the optimal range. If only people could be that predictable, to know that if you interact with a certain family, there will be honesty, integrity, and kindness, or the flip side, so you know where to steer clear. I pray in this moment that our family is one that shows clear desirable heritable traits.

"Asa, that's not your fault. You were kind and generous to her, and to True. What they did with that is on them."

"I suppose so. Well, given everything that's going on, with them, and with me, I've decided it's time to stop storing up earthly treasures."

"Wait, what do you mean? Are you going to sell?"

"It's already done. Hank Douglas told me years ago that if I ever decided to sell, to let him know since he's just north of the road from me. That's a pretty easy jump for him. I had the nurses call him this afternoon, and he left right before you got here. Shoemaker Cattle Company and the ranch is now his."

My breath catches in my throat a little, and I hold back tears. Hank has wanted to expand for as long as we've known him, but the opportunity has just never presented itself until now. This is a game changer for him: to really hit the big leagues of ranching and make a big name for himself.

"That's wonderful, Asa. The Douglases are the best people, and I know they will honor your legacy well. So, are you going to be a full-timer at your townhouse now?"

"Oh, with the state I'm in now, I think that's still too much for me. I think I'm going to take your advice and see if I can get me a place down at Cinnamon Court. If Jeannie Miller likes it, I bet I can, too."

"I think that's a wise choice. You better let me come eat lunch with you every so often. They make a pretty good steak finger basket, you know."

"I didn't know that, but that seems like a bad idea for a bunch of old fogies with heart disease and the like. But you know I'd be plum thrilled to see your pretty face anytime."

I reach over and squeeze his wrinkled hand, still webbed with purple veins and large bruises, along with a few IVs jabbed in and trailing out. He's got that old man paper-thin skin that shows just about every touch in some way, and it makes me tear up to think that these tried-and-true cowboys spend all their good years being tough as leather just to wear down like this. They are tough as nails on the inside, but I guess they're human after all.

"Well, it sounds like you've got it all figured out. Can I help you with anything else? I'd be glad to help move your townhouse when you're ready."

"There is one thing I think I need your help with, actually."

"Name it."

▭

FOUR WEEKS LATER

"It should be illegal to be up at this hour," I whine as Shep and I get in the truck. It's 4:45 AM and Shep has convinced me to join them for a Saturday meeting of the Dad Bod Squad. I've done this at various times over the years, but for some reason, I'm especially tired today and crankier than usual about it. The last few weeks have been a rollercoaster, to say the least, and I don't like being awake to see the 4:00 hour really ever, much less on a Saturday, especially after several of the craziest weeks of my life. Shep maintains that working out puts you in a better mood, particularly to start the day, and I agree. It's just usually that better mood for me happens at 9:00 AM Pilates.

We pull out of our driveway and head down the gravel road to Hank's. Just before Hank's, we pass the new signage on the Shoemaker gate declaring it Douglas Land and Cattle South now. No one would have ever predicted that turn of events, especially considering the rest of the story.

Asa sold his ranch and ranch entity to Hank for a song- he wanted to be rid of it, and didn't need the money anyway. Selling his townhouse and his savings, plus those proceeds, more than paid for a nice one-bedroom apartment at Cinnamon Court for more than enough time. Also, with no heirs at this point, he didn't want to accumulate any more wealth that would be difficult to distribute when the time comes. He said he mainly just wanted it to be used and loved by a fellow rancher, so he let it go at a shockingly low price on the condition that Hank keep on the three hands that still worked there, provided they had no knowledge or participation in the whole MacDougal situation. The rumor around town is that despite his adamant complaints that he would not participate in Hainslee's raising whatsoever, her biological dad supposedly took custody of her after Becki was arrested, and that she lives with his family now. I'm honestly hopeful a more stable, consistent environment will be good for her, and she can thrive without the negative influences she had. Shawn Pine left town a few days after his meeting with Dr. Everett, putting in his resignation, and preemptively serving his wife with divorce papers. Supposedly, Lauren is planning to head to a larger hospital system to be closer to her family, and with that, we really have no remaining reminders of the whole school situation at this point. We're nearing the end of the school year, and I'm thankful we've all been able to move on fairly seamlessly with a summer ahead of us to put everything really in the rearview mirror.

In the middle of this transition of ownership, a property attorney reviewed the validity of the lease between Shoemaker Cattle Co and the MacDougal trust, and found it to be completely legally binding. So in addition to purchasing the land and entity, Hank also gained lease rights to all 18 sections of the MacDougal estate. Thomas Hodges was more than happy to hold up the lease as is, provided he was allowed to keep the ranch house to use whenever he wants to check on the property and visit his mother, which has thrilled Wendy. He plans to continue living in Massachusetts full time because he loves his job, but he does want to learn more about this side of his family and heritage, and that makes it much easier to visit. To no one's surprise, he admitted that he's pretty confrontation averse, so not having to interview or negotiate a lease with someone else was music to his ears. The one tweak that Hank asked for was the option to sub-lease sections he wasn't using. Thomas agreed, and now Red Rock Cattle Company leases half, while Douglas L&C/ Shoemaker leases the other half.

As Shep pulls through Hank's gate, we head up the long gravel driveway and stop in front of their barn gym near their ranch house. Lights are on inside and I can hear the clang of weight plates and the thump of workout music. Shep gets out and heads inside with me dragging behind, still sipping my coffee from a travel Yeti tumbler. Hank is setting up barbells on mats while his wife Tiffani is sorting through resistance bands. I stop to give Tiff a hug before setting my coffee down on the side of the pool table and turning to the white board where Hank writes out the day's workout to see what I'm in for. And right there, in black and white on the board is my least favorite word in the world: the B word.

"Hank, does that say what I think it says?"

Hank drops the weight plate he's holding and peers at the white board. "Not sure what you think it says, but it says ten sets of ten burpees after the dead lifts." Then he casually picks the plate back up to slide it on the barbell in front of him.

"Hank Douglas, I thought we were friends! Are you trying to piss me off this early in the morning?" I start to walk out the door and Shep catches my arm laughing.

"Where are you going?" he asks with a chuckle.

"I hate burpees and y'all know it. I'm going to take a nap in the truck. Wake me up when that nightmare is over."

epilogue

"ALRIGHT, BABE, WHAT DO YOU THINK?" I say later that morning as I unlock the front door and walk inside. We finished up the morning workout and had our normal Shep Saturday morning breakfast special, and are now checking out our newest adventure. Stepping inside, there are cobwebs galore, and dust thick on the hardwood floors, but the mid-morning sun is streaming through the large windows on the east side of the building giving the whole room a beautiful glow. About halfway through the room, there is a large straight staircase with dark, heavily waxed stairs and an ornate banister running alongside. The main floor runs back to a large counter with an old marble countertop and big built-in shelves behind it. After I walk through the first floor, I turn around and realize Shep never came in with me. I walk back to the front door and see him standing on the large covered porch outside, hesitating to come in. I join him back outside and stand next to him, looking through the open front door trying to figure out why he hasn't walked in.

"What's going on?"

"It looks haunted as hell in there," Shep says with all seriousness, and I struggle to hold in a laugh. For whatever reason, this is one of Shep's few 'icks', as the kids say. He doesn't do potlucks, and he doesn't do places that look like they could be ghost infested.

"I had someone come do a ghost inspection and exorcism in here before we closed yesterday. We're supposed to be good." I pat him on the back and encourage him to walk inside.

Hank and Tiff got the Shoemaker ranch property, but Asa's one thing he wanted me to take care of was this: the Russell building, a gorgeous turn of the century red brick two-story building with a huge, wrap-around porch on the bottom and a wraparound balcony on the second story. It had apparently been in his late wife's family for more than a century, and, like the ranch, he wanted it to go to someone who would take good care of it and love it like they had. He knew I'd had eyes for it since we moved to Buffalo Creek, but I'd never really had a reason to need or use it. In his dispersal of assets, he wanted us to have first dibs on it, and it is now about to become the Red Rock Shoppe, home of Buffalo Creek's finest fresh beef, other culinary delights, and a little eclectic mix of homewares and clothing. Shep and I have been discussing opening some type of storefront for this purpose for the past year or so, saying we'd move forward when the right opportunity came along, and here we are.

I am able to convince Shep to go ahead and come inside, and we start looking together through the different spaces on the first floor, while brainstorming different layouts and options. Most of the space is open, and will be perfect for racks of unique clothing pieces, and big round tables to put up displays of housewares and other trinkets and chotchkes. There is a perfect amount of room under the staircase to fit the row of standing freezers that will hold the beef and other perishable food items. The back counter will be great for ringing customers up, and I can rig part of the shelves to hold large rolls of luxury wrapping paper to send people out with beautiful gifts. There is another smaller counter and alcove on the other side of where the freezers will go, and I excitedly note that mine and Mandy's plan of opening a flower shop section could go perfectly there. It's all perfect. It is the absolute perfect space for our vision.

"Have you been upstairs at all?" Shep asks cautiously, putting one foot on the bottom stair, but not moving up any further.

"I ran up there briefly when I met the inspector last week but didn't really look around too much. I'll go up there with you." I meet him at the bottom of the stairs and we slowly start to head up. I'm making mental notes that a funky wallpaper would look amazing on the top part of the wall above the wainscoting running up the staircase, and I would love to find some vintage pictures of Buffalo Creek to frame and hang there as well.

"What is your plan for this part?" Shep asks when we reach the landing as we both stop and look around. We open the old stained-glass door separating the landing and the first floor from the hallway of the second floor. There are three rooms up here and two bathrooms, one in the hallway and one en suite. The story is that the Russells, Asa's wife's grandparents, built this building in the late 1800s to have a general store downstairs and living quarters upstairs. I love that we're going to bring back some of the same vibes, only with a modern twist, but it does leave the entire upstairs a bit murky on how to best use it. Asa used it as offices for his cattle and oil businesses up until about five years ago when True took over ranch operations, and it's been vacant ever since.

"Well, I have a few ideas. The obvious one is just to use it like Asa: it can be offices for the cattle business and for the shoppe. Or..." I start, knowing the next idea will probably be a hard sell, but I'm going to pitch it anyway. Shep turns from inspecting a piece of peeling wallpaper in the hall and raises an eyebrow to me. "We could make this an Airbnb!" I give him a big smile and throw my hands up to gesture at all the potential.

"I've never had any part of me interested in being a landlord, much less a landlord to a revolving wheel of strangers that we have to clean up after."

"I'm just saying, it's already set up to be the perfect little charming getaway for guests to stay. It could be a nice little additional income to help cover shoppe costs. Just think about it," I pat him on the arm, and pass by him to peek into each bedroom to see what we're working with.

"Based off everything you're seeing here, when are you shooting to open all of this?" Shep peeks around a doorframe after me, and tries to hide the disgust on his face. He's always supportive of my endeavors, but at the end of the day, he is who he is, and who he is finds none of this appealing. He doesn't do clutter or antiques, and prefers things that are new with warranties that he can break in and wear out himself. I know he'll help me any way he can, but I'm going to have to make it a little less haunted mansion before he actually feels comfortable here.

"I think the downstairs will come together pretty quickly, and that's the main part that matters. It just needs a good deep cleaning, and some aesthetic touches before we get the shoppe items set up and get going. It seems fine structurally. I think that it could be ready to go in a month? Six weeks? Whatever we decide to do with this part will take longer obviously."

"That's not too bad. Hopefully we won't need to do any big renovations right off the bat, but I'd like John Walter to take a look through everything just to make sure there isn't anything that needs attention right away," he says, referring to a longtime friend at church that has been a builder and handyman for longer than anyone can remember, as he kicks a piece of floor trim that has pulled loose. "Is there space downstairs for inventory? What will that look like? If you plan to keep a decent amount of inventory on hand, we could use one of these rooms as a storeroom."

"That's not a bad idea. I don't think there are any additional rooms downstairs that would be big enough for that, so that may be my only option. And I appreciate that it conveniently gets you out of the Airbnb thing," I laugh, hitting the end of the hallway. "Oh, look, there's an attic. That might be an option! I could put inventory in the attic!" I see a door in the ceiling for a set of pull-down stairs with a worn and yellowed string hanging down. I'm not generally the biggest fan of attics; I think I have residual PTSD from hauling our Christmas décor down from the attic every year when we were in residency and fellowship and that was our only place to store all of it. I convinced Shep to get me a ground-level shed to store everything in when we moved to the ranch, and I've never looked back. So, if I'm honest with myself, I really don't think I'd want to store anything in this probably dank and animal-infested lair anyway. But, I want to keep the Airbnb idea alive for just a little longer.

I reach up and yank the pull string to bring down the stairs just to take a little peek at what we're working with. It seems a little heavier than I anticipated to pull down, but I keep pulling just to keep it from pulling me back up with it. Shep rushes over and helps me get it pulled down, and when it finally opens all the way, we hear a very loud whoosh accompanied by a small breeze, and then a loud thud and crash on the dusty hardwood floor of the hallway. From under the pull-down door, we can see a large pile of something on the floor, but it is unidentifiable at first. We both step out from under the door and approach the large pile with a slow recognition coming over both of us.

"Shep... is that a... a dead body?" I back away toward the

open attic door, not believing this is really happening... again. He starts shaking his head and backing away as well, letting out a high-pitched scream I didn't know he was capable of as he runs out the stained glass door for the stairs.

"I knew this place was freakin' haunted!"

acknowledgments

Writing this book has been the culmination of a lifelong dream. Building these characters and this world has been one of the best things I've ever had the privilege to do, and someone taking the time to read it truly means the world to me. Thank you!

And a very special thank you to...

... our wonderful circle- from first readers to cheerleaders, y'all have blown me away time and time again with your kindness, supportiveness, expertise, and genuine love for our family and this project. I couldn't have done this without y'all. And a very special shout out to Kay Whitton for her editing and beta reading. You are the real MVP!

... my amazing kids. You two are the best gift I've ever been given, and raising you is the privilege and blessing of a lifetime. I love you chocolate chip cookies, dinosaurs, and Angus cows.

... Steven- words cannot express how supportive and amazing you have been through all of this— biggest supporter doesn't even begin to cover it. What a joy and honor it is to live this life with you, and I pray we have more years than we can count together raising kids and cattle, and glorifying the Lord in it all.

about the author

Morie Smith lives in west Texas with her husband, and two children. As a family, they own and operate Red Bank Cattle Company, a registered Angus seed stock operation. Morie graduated from Texas Tech University with a BS in Speech, Language, and Hearing Sciences, and a Doctorate of Audiology (AuD), but is currently focused on ranching, writing, and raising kids.

instagram.com/morie_smith

goodreads.com/morie_smith

bookbub.com/authors/moriesmith

amazon.com/author/moriesmith

facebook.com/moriemsmith